Hidden In Time

Shadows of a Past Life

By

Jan French

Copyright © 2025 Jan French. All Rights Reserved.

No part of this publication may be reproduced, distributed, or transmitted in any form or by any means, including photocopying, recording, or other electronic or mechanical methods, without the prior written permission of the author, except in the case of brief quotations embodied in critical reviews and certain other non-commercial uses permitted by copyright law.

For permission requests, please contact the author at: janfrenchauthor@yahoo.com

This book is a work of fiction. Names, characters, businesses, places, events, and incidents are either the product of the author's imagination or used in a fictitious manner. Any resemblance to actual persons, living or dead, or actual events is purely coincidental.

Published by Amazon Kindle Direct Publishing (KDP)

ISBN: 9798313633350

Printed in the United Kingdom

First Edition: 2025

All rights reserved under UK and international copyright laws. This book may not be resold, shared, or distributed in any format without the express written permission of the author or publisher, except where permitted by law.

'The soul is neither born, and nor does it die... it is eternal, indestructible, and continues its journey through many lifetimes.'
Bhagavad Gita

Prologue
Caroline Manning

When you ponder your mortality, do you think of it as the end, or do you think of it as the beginning? One thing for certain is, it is a journey into the unknown. Some people see it as the end, that we switch off, never to think or feel again. Others view it as a continuous cycle of birth, death, and rebirth. The concept of reincarnation asserts that death is merely a transition from one incarnation to the next. Each transition giving us the opportunity to learn and grow. A kind of spiritual evolution.

    This subject fascinates me and is fuelled by the many stories from people who claim to have lived before. Working as a psychotherapist during the year 2000 gave me the opportunity to indulge my curiosity about the subject. The therapy centre was the perfect setting to test a theory that could be neither proven nor disproven. I offered both the setting and the skills by which to experiment.

    Regression therapy is the name given to the process of taking clients back through their birth to an earlier forgotten time. Unlike standard therapy, there was no therapeutically motivated outcome for my clients. No healing, growing in self-esteem, or letting go of the past in mind. I distributed leaflets advertising the trials through existing clients only. Calling it a trial made it sound professional without promising an outcome. Ideal for my needs and ideal for the willing participant because there was no charge. Not charging meant the client had nothing to lose, so they couldn't be disgruntled if it didn't work. My first five clients were varied and all quite disappointing. A couple couldn't get past birth, and the others couldn't get a clear picture or verbalise what they were seeing. And then along came Jess, a person with a good reason to believe she had lived before. Jess brought the breakthrough I was looking for. The failures were no longer important; this success was all that mattered.

The events that followed that first meeting with Jess created an ethical and moral dilemma. It uncovered family secrets that crossed three generations. My father had more than his fair share of skeletons in his cupboard, and a story to tell from beyond the grave. Jess held the key to uncovering the truth, and only through her could I access it. At the risk of my professional career, I broke every rule. I was on the brink of something monumental, a way to access a realm that exists parallel to our own. Like an echo that never dies. This story belonged to me as much as it did to her. I was driven beyond morality, in a quest to transcend the boundaries of human understanding. Past lives do exist. If I could perfect the process, then the accolade would bring phenomenal personal and professional rewards. It was enough to drive me forward, to convince myself that this could be the breakthrough that would launch my career.

Chapter 1 Jane 1946

The blazing sun of June 1946 was a rare and welcome visitor for the folks of Yorkshire. It was the kind of day, that not only warmed the skin, but also warmed the soul. A day sorely needed to brighten the grey hearts of the post-war people still grieving for their dead. The red check picnic blanket laid out on the grass like a bright flag of celebration, a white parasol discarded by her side. Jane closed her eyes and tilted her head back feeling the warmth, a smile of contentment on her face. She kicked off her shoes letting her toes curl into the cool grass. Reaching up she untied her golden hair letting it fall loose around her shoulders, her wavy locks floating freely on the gentle breeze. She listened to the hum of the bees collecting pollen from the poppy field beyond. Her eyes opening briefly to take in the perfectness of the endless blue sky. She wanted to saver every moment before the dependable rainclouds and grey sky, returned. This was not a day for running, it was a day for picnics and ice-cold lemonade.

If only that moment could last, but it was not to be. There was no time for frivolity. She could see his body laid prostrate on the railway line, his arms and legs bent in impossible positions. All she could think was she must get to him; she must save him. Running and stumbling trying to put her shoes on at the same time, there was no time to lose. She could hear the train slowing down as it neared the bend in the track, after which, she knew it would speed up once more. She ran as fast as her nimble eleven-year-old legs would go, the train advancing, blowing it's horn as it came into the straight. Panting through tears she reached the side of the track. He was there, right in front of her, one small step forward, a grab and a step back would do it, but the train was almost upon her, too close for Jane to make her move. With anguish stinging her eyes, she folded her arms in front of them, not baring to see the carnage that was about to unfold.

Suddenly she felt hands on her back, the unexpected making her body go ridged with fear. 'Who...? What...? Would it be quick...? Would it hurt...? The rumble beneath her feet grew louder, her thoughts turning to what she was leaving behind. Her mother sat in her favourite window seat, sipping her tea with her little finger pointed. Her father lifting her in the air and spinning her round as she giggled with joy. Jojo telling her one of his corny jokes. Did they know she loved them? She shouted it out, hoping somehow her message would reach then over the sound of the mighty train. She felt the rush of hot air before the shove propelled her forward. Time slowed down, 'this shouldn't be happening... not today... not to me.' She could feel herself falling but the action seemed to last an eternity. 'When will my body touch the ground...?' 'When will the train hit me...? Then everything went black.

As consciousness slowly returned, she had no shape or form, yet she felt more whole than she had ever felt before. For a while she remained still, acclimatising to the transformation. Her new environment felt familiar and safe, a realisation that she had been here before. Her thoughts were coming fast, like she had been plugged into a computer programme.

She became aware that she knew everything. She had the answers to questions that would baffle the most renowned scientists, and to questions that had never been asked, questions beyond the realm of human understanding.

She knew she had to go, but she longed to take him with her. The answer was instant, she could imagine but she could not touch. In the past she would have felt sad at the loss, but what she felt now was inevitability, everything was as it should be. Leaving the noise and confusion behind, Jane went home, the place her soul always returns to.

Chapter 2 Caroline 10th March 2000 – session 1.

They say that every journey begins with a single step. Mine began with a decision. A decision to conduct trials into Past Life. The idea of running the past-life trials came to me after I had worked with one client, a man who held the belief that he had been killed in the trenches during WW1. He was convinced that this experience was responsible for the anxiety attacks he was currently experiencing. He had been having a recurring dream for many years of being chased by soldiers with guns and bayonets. His fear of loud noises was making it increasingly difficult for him to leave the house. He said he sat on the floor of his lounge because he didn't like to be seen through the window. If anyone knocked on the door he would hide. This man was convinced he had been killed charging out of the trenches during the Great War. Now, as a therapist, this isn't a problem. I worked with his belief system in the same way I would with any past traumatic experience; in other words, I treated his belief as real.

His belief fascinated me and made me stop and think, I mean really think. 'Have we lived before, and will we return to live again?' I know the question of past lives and spirits is one that has been pondered by most of us. If you're like me, it would be nice to think that we have lived before, and that the awareness of 'self' lives on in some form or another. I also had my own reasons for believing in a past life. For many years I had been having a recurring dream, vivid, haunting visions of places I had never been and people I had never met. The clarity of these dreams felt more like memories rather than a figment of my imagination. The big question for me was 'how do we know if we have lived before?' 'Is it possible to find out?' So, I thought of offering free sessions to clients who were interested in exploring the possibility. I didn't advertise; instead, I printed some small information leaflets and gave them to my existing clients. I wasn't willing to do the trials with anyone who hadn't had previous experience of hypnotherapy.

The journey started off slow and almost came to a halt. I'm impatient, I always have been. When I want something, I want it now. So, when my first five clients for 'past life regression' produced zero results, I was ready to give up. March 2000, trial number 6 was booked in for 4,30pm, a session that would take two hours at the end, of an already, long, and exhausting day. Maybe she wouldn't turn up and I could go home early, put my feet up, open a bottle of wine and order a take-away for me and the kids. No such luck, the buzzer sounded in the therapy room telling me my client had arrived. Exhausted as I was, I knew that once I opened that door the adrenalin would kick in and I would be ready to perform to the best of my ability.

Jessica Barker looked younger than her 30 years. Her short blonde hair was cut in a stylish bob, and her clothes were modern and appropriate for the early spring nip that was still lingering in the air. Her heavy parka coat, over knee-high boots, was removed to reveal a knitted beige skirt with thick burgundy tights and a tight ribbed cream polo-neck. Her trendy, youthful appearance made me feel frumpy and old, and I wondered if she thought that too. Yes, I have a pretty face, but the rest of me is short and dumpy. I am often told I look like Dawn French, the comedian and actress. I'd like to think it's because Dawn is so relatable and approachable with a warmth that people connect with. But maybe not!

'Hi Jessica, come in, please take a seat, make yourself comfortable. I'm Caroline.'

'Thanks,' but please call me Jess; Jessica always sounds like I'm in trouble.'

She giggles as she removes her coat and settles into the chair. There's something familiar about her. I wonder if we have met before.

'No problem, Jess. Have you brought your pre-session questionnaire?

I checked her name, date of birth and address at the top of the page. She lives in Low Dean, the same village I lived as a child. Her detailed questionnaire confirming she was born there. Maybe that's why she seems familiar, a shared history of treading the same pavements, attending the same schools, buying sweets from the same corner shop, albeit thirteen years apart. Jess was bubbly with one of those squeaky, childish voices that are popular in the ever-increasing number of American soaps on TV. But her accent was unmistakably Yorkshire; sharp, witty, and down to earth. As we made small talk, she reminded me of my younger self, before working in education had smoothed out my accent.

'I believe you have had hypnosis before,' I inquired.

'Yes, once when I was trying to stop smoking,' she opened her handbag to reveal a packet of cigarettes.

'It lasted about six months and then I started again. 'But' she hurried to say, I don't smoke as many now. I used to be on twenty to thirty a day, but now I only smoke about ten.'

She sounded pleased with herself, and she obviously wanted to reassure me that she wasn't trying to say that the hypnosis had failed.

'So, tell me, Jess, what brought you here today?'

'My friend, Tracy, gave me your leaflet, and I have always been interested in reincarnation. I've been to lots of Spiritualist meetings, so I believe in spirits and that they try to communicate with us. Reincarnation seems like the next step. Maybe they move from being spirits to being re-born. I would love to know if I have lived before.'

Her response surprised me. She didn't look the kind of girl who would go in for deep spiritual thinking. More like the deep partying and spirits from a bottle type. Please don't judge; even therapists make assumptions based on first impressions. We all do; it's human nature. The key is to keep assumptions fluid, allowing new information to wash them away.

'Do you think you have lived before?' I probed.

'Possibly, I once had a very strong sense of déjà vu; I mention it on the sheet,' she says, pointing to the questionnaire I had pushed to one side.

I turned the page of the sheet to see she has indeed written two full pages of her experience. I knew these would be useful to look back on later, but for now I wanted to focus on my new client. You can learn a lot from observing a client as they speak; where they move their eyes to access information, how they use their senses in speech, and their body language. 'The body does not lie!'

Jess described her experience of déjà vu when visiting somewhere she knew she had never been before. She said she had been dating a young man who lived in a small village near Brighouse. As she drove into the village, she became aware that she recognised the area.

'It made me feel uneasy and a little light-headed, so much so that I pulled the car over. I knew that if I took the next left, there would be a church on the left and some playing fields opposite.'

Jess moved to the edge of her chair as if she were taking me into her confidence.

'I was right...' she paused to add a sense of dramatization to what she was about to tell me. 'There was the church, and there, straight opposite, was a playground with swings and a roundabout. I knew, with absolute certainty, that I had played on those swings.'

Jess described her talks with her parents. They couldn't explain it, other than that she had dreamt it. They couldn't drive back then, and didn't know the area or anyone there.

'From that day on, I became convinced that I had experienced a memory from a past life.' She smiles and shrugs her shoulders in a 'but who knows' gesture. 'Well, hopefully we will find out. I can't promise you a definitive answer; we can only explore the possibility, and then it will be up to you to decide.'

'I must tell you there are lots of theories about whether there is such a thing as a past life. Let me try to simplify some of these. You may have heard the term 'repressed memory.' This is something you suddenly remember that you had forgotten. You had put the memory to the back of your mind and some experience has made you remember it. Taking your déjà vu experience. Some critics would say you had been there before, but you had forgotten. This is often the process of hypnosis; we are unlocking the unconscious mind to bring these forgotten memories to the surface.'

Jess interrupted. Insisting she had never been there before. So, she couldn't have forgotten playing on the swings. I nodded and continued with my explanation of the possibilities.

'The second possibility is that your experience or memory is something called 'genetic memory. This is the idea that memory is passed through our genetic make-up from one generation to the next. But this only tends to apply to physiological responses. For example, the fear of something, or the dislike of a taste or smell, or being drawn to a specific occupation or hobby. So, your déjà vu experience doesn't quite fit this theory.'

'I have a fear of trains,' Jess interrupted once more.

'Thank you for that; I'll certainly come back to it. The last explanation I want to give you for a past life memory is that it is 'a past life memory.' This is what we are looking for; this is the reason for these trials and the reason you are here. Together we will explore this possibility. You and I are both curious, and we are exploring this subject because of our curiosity. I'm not offering you any therapeutic intervention to deal with a symptom, and this is why I do not charge for this work.

You are helping me indulge my curiosity as much as I'm helping you indulge yours. But before we begin, I want to know more about your fear of trains and any other fears.'

Jess sighed. 'I have had a fear of trains for as long as I can remember. My mum said that when I was about 3 years old, she was taking me to Leeds on the train. She said my crying and shouting caused such a fuss that we had to get off at the next stop and walk home. They always make me feel cold and shivery.' Jess gave a shiver for dramatic effect. 'I don't have any other fears that I'm aware of. I'm okay with lifts, heights, and insects and all that stuff.'

'Brilliant, now before we start, would you like a drink, tea, coffee or a glass of water?'

Over tea, I ran through the case history questionnaire with Jess. I wanted to learn more about her family and relationships. I could see that she lived with her mother, her father was dead, and she was divorced from Craig.

'How long were you married?'

'You will laugh; we were together for seven years before we got married, and then three months later, I left him.'

'Why do you think that was?' I questioned.

'Well, I had been really overweight,' she gestured a big round ball with her hands and puffed up her cheeks with air. 'Then I joined a slimming club and lost six stone in two years. I went from a size twenty-two to a size ten. It changed me; I started buying new clothes, going out with the girls, and generally having a good time. All the things I had wanted to do for years but felt too fat. Craig was jealous and we started having a lot of rows. I started to resent him, and I know I shouldn't have married him; I knew then it was over, but it felt too late to pull out. The wedding and honeymoon were booked and paid for, and our parents were excited for our union. I did love him once and I will always remain fond of him.'

She looked down as she connected with her emotions for a few seconds, and then she continued.

'Craig was the only man I had ever been with. You know, the only man I'd had sex with.' She spoke in a whisper, as if someone might overhear her and sex wasn't something you discussed.

'I wanted to try other men.' She had a quick look around in case that disapproving parent was watching. Then she looked up to her left and giggled as she remembered some sexual encounter. She brushed the air with her hands to waft away the naughty memory. I drew a face with VR above the left eye for visual remember.

'Is that when you moved in with your mum?'

'No, I rented a small bedsit to start with. I was there for about four months, but when my dad died of a heart attack, I moved in with my mum so she wouldn't be alone. I never intended to stay so long; it's been two years now. I have recently been looking at a couple of houses to rent, and I've seen one in Bingley which is near my hairdressing salon.'

'Can you imagine yourself living there?'

'Yes,' she mused, looking up to her right. 'It's cosy, with a lovely fireplace in the lounge. It will be perfect to get in from work, switch on my music, open a bottle of wine, and chill in front of the fire.'

She was painting a picture in her head; I wrote on the scribbled face above the right eye, VC for 'visual construct.'

I now had all the information I needed. I knew she processed information predominantly kinaesthetically and visually, and I knew where she moved her eyes to access remembered information and to construct information. I find this extremely useful and a good gauge as to whether a person is telling me something they remember, or something they are making up.

'Is it your own salon?'

'Yes, Mum helped me to set up after Dad died. She used some of the insurance money; otherwise, I would still be renting a chair and working for peanuts.'

I was about to say something crass like 'lucky girl' but then I thought better of it, so I smiled. If it hadn't been for my family, I wouldn't have my cosy cottage. Parents handing down and shoring up the next generation has become the norm.

'Now, Jess. The process could take about an hour, maybe longer. So, I need to check if you're okay for time and you don't have to be anywhere.'

'No, I'm all yours, and I'm excited about starting,' she said, rubbing her hands with glee.

I explained the process and technique I would be using. I could use different techniques in past life regression therapy. But, after failing with a few, I chose a 'timeline'. I explained to her that she would be travelling along a timeline to the past, through her birth and further back into a time before she was born. I explained how we would communicate while she was in trance; presupposing that she would be able to hear everything I said and would be able to verbally respond to my questions. I also set up finger responses as a back-up in case her voice wasn't clear, or the trance was too deep. We practised her raising a finger on her right hand for yes, and her left hand for no.

'Now Jess, I would like to invite you to relax and close your eyes, and with your eyes closed you can become more aware of your body inside…. and outside…. Now scan your body, noticing any tension and let it go… Your legs… thighs… abdomen… chest… arms… head… Letting go… fully relaxed… Now turn your attention to your breathing… Take a deep breath in… and let it go… One more time, deep breath in… and let it go… Continue to breathe naturally and notice that the air you breathe in is colder than the air you breathe out… Turn your attention to the part of your body that feels the most comfortable… Let that comfort spread to every part of your body… and take comfort in knowing you are perfectly safe…'

After the basic induction, I deepened the trance using the countdown from ten to zero method. All the time reassuring her that she was safe and could come out of the trance at any time if she chose to do so. When I knew she was sufficiently induced, I instructed her to allow her awareness to float above her body to a distance where she could look down and see herself sitting in the chair.

'Notice how relaxed you look and notice that you are perfectly safe… I want you to imagine a timeline stretched out in both directions, towards the future and back into the past... Now stand on this timeline in a position that represents the present... I want you to turn to the past and travel back in time to when you started your first job... Look at what you are wearing and notice any emotions you are having and let me know when you have done that.'

I got a right finger response as well as a faint yes. Great, all was working well.

'Let's now travel back to an earlier time when you were at school; how old are you?'

I got a verbal reply, 'Ten'.

'Again, notice what you are wearing and any emotions associated with this event, and let me know when you have done that...?'

We continued like this back to her birth and the people around her when she was born. We travelled back to when she was inside the womb and how nurtured and safe she was. Then came the moment I was nervously anticipating as I asked her to travel back even further, before her birth to an earlier time, and to let me know when she had done that. I paused and held my breath, waiting for a response.

She said, 'Yes.'

I released my breath. 'Jess, have a look around you and take in your surroundings. Tell me, are you on your own?'

'No.'

'Are there other people there?'

'Yes.'

'Is there more than one person there?'

'Yes, a few... I see a child.'

'Does the child see you?'
'Yes.'

Her verbal responses were exceptionally good, so I decided to ask more open questions.

'Tell me what else do see?'

'There are men working, and a woman and a man close by; they are looking at the child. It's some kind of wood yard... There are lots of planks of wood, a tall wooden structure behind a stone building..., and some other tall wooden barns.'

'Where are you, Jess, in relation to what you see?'

'I'm behind a fence... there's a railway line and the wood yard is on the other side.' I sensed a quiver in her voice that indicated anxiety.

'Jess, float a little higher above this event until you feel comfortable, and be assured that from this observation point, you are perfectly safe.' I waited until I saw her body physically relax.

'Do you know this child?'

'No,' she hesitated, 'Maybe... I'm not sure.'

'Take as much time as you need to observe your surroundings and make a mental note of what people are wearing and what the area looks like. Their clothes will give you a sense of the period and also a sense of their social standing or cultural background.'

I paused to give her time to do this. I watched as her eyes twitched, waiting for her to stop processing and relax.

'Soon it will be time to come back to the present, so if there is anything you want to say to the child, go ahead and say it now.' I paused.

'Now say your goodbyes and turn to face the future and travel back along your timeline, all the way to the present, so that once again you can see yourself relaxed in the chair.'

I then brought her back counting from one to ten, finishing with, 'Feeling fully awake and refreshed'.

She was back. I instructed her to have a good stretch and a shake and to stretch her legs before debriefing. I let her pace the room while I swiped a highlighter pen over a few of the notes I had made whilst she was under,

'Now while it's still fresh in your mind, let's go over what you experienced. How was the travelling on the timeline for you?'

'Yes, it was fine. I kept remembering snippets of things I had done and places I had been it was a really nice experience.'

'And going back through your birth, what was that like?'

'Nothing to start with, only blackness, and then suddenly there was a bright, blinding light, like when someone switches the light on when you're asleep and it takes a while for your eyes to adjust. When my eyes adjusted, I was outside looking through metal railings to some kind of wood yard on the other side.'

'Describe the child to me.'

Jess went on to describe the child and the entirety of her experience.

'The child was a girl of about 9 to 11 years old and was wearing an old-fashioned school uniform in a pinafore style. It was all grey with knee-length white socks. The girl had shoulder-length blonde curly hair and was wearing an Alice band... with a red stripe on it. The workers were all men, and they were wearing bib and brace overalls with jackets open over the top, and they wore flat caps... They were all a bit shabby... but they looked strong and healthy. The adults..., I think, might have been the girl's parents..., but I can't be sure. It was the way they kept looking over at her..., like they were checking she was safe. There wasn't a barrier between where she was standing and the railway line, so I got the impression they were checking that she didn't get too close. There was a young man..., probably early twenties. The little girl was shouting his name to get his attention... 'Jojo,' she kept saying. Jojo looked like he was trying to impress her by balancing a ball on his head... I got the feeling they were close.'

    Her recall was far better than I could have hoped or dreamed for, and I could tell by her eye accessing cues that she was genuinely recalling what she had experienced. I pressed her further. I wanted to get as much information out of her as I could while it was still fresh in her mind.

    'What about the parents' clothes? Could you describe what they were wearing?'

    'Um, smart, but so drab, the woman was wearing brown from head to toe... The man was wearing a dark suit..., possibly black, and a tie..., and dark-rimmed glasses; it's hard to say how old either of them are.'

    I pressed her on this because first impressions are often right. Although I was starting to think my first impression of her had been way off the mark. Despite her childlike voice and constant giggling, she had come across as quite level-headed and had the most infectious smile. I felt warm and protective towards her.

'If you knew, how old would they be?'

'40ish or maybe older; I'm not sure.'

'What about your surroundings? Did you recognise anything?'

'I got that same sense of déjà vu that I told you about before. It could be the same area..., but I don't know of a railway line in Bradbury. I will have to check it out. It was definitely some kind of wood yard. The large barns looked to be made out of wood with corrugated sheet roofs. The fronts were open, so they were more like a canopy than a building, but they were very tall. I think it was where they stored the wood... I got a strong feeling that I had been there before, and I had climbed on the wood to the very top. It was very untidy; there were old broken-down carts and bits of machinery. There were some cars or small trucks... but I'm not sure; my memory is feeling exhausted.'

She slumped forward, releasing a deep sigh that told me she'd reached her limit. Sensing her fatigue, I said, 'That's okay, we can stop. Where would you like to go from here?'

Her eyes brightened as she replied, 'I'd love to come back, but I insist on paying you; I can't ask you to do this for free.'

'That's very generous, Jess. I'd be happy to continue at a reduced rate. How about £20 an hour instead of my usual £40? I'm just as curious as you to see what else we can uncover.'

We chatted a bit longer and arranged to meet at the same time next week. I no longer felt drained; in fact I felt energised. Jess has brought the breakthrough for which I had hoped. Today I really had taken that first step on a journey full of possibilities.

Chapter 3 Jess March 2000

March 2000. I sat in my car for a while taking it all in. 'What did it mean – did I imagine it all?' I felt excited and exhausted at the same time. I hope Mum's home; I can't wait to tell her what happened, I thought to myself. My mind was racing over the events and for a while I felt unable to drive. I wasn't sure if I would be able to concentrate on the road. 'Oh, I wish I had got a taxi.' I started the engine and put the heater on. It was cold outside, only 10°C according to my car's thermometer. 'Come on, 'I can do this.' I slapped the car steering wheel and said out loud, 'Take me home, girl; let's get back and see what Mum thinks.'

    My relationship with my mum is good and comfortable, too comfortable. At the age of thirty, I can't help feeling I should have a place of my own, but I guess I'm too busy with the salon to find the time to look at properties, and if I'm honest I love living with my mum. She does my washing and cooks the meals, and it's nice to have someone to come home to. The house is full of warmth, with the smell of her cooking and the sound of her singing along to tunes from the seventies. It's also probably true that mum is my best friend, and as much as it pains me to admit it, it was true. Friends I had in my teens had married and moved away, and friends I had made with my ex, Craig, had all turned their backs on me when I left him. 'Poor Craig,' they would say, but they didn't have to live with him. Sometimes the lack of close friendships stung. I knew lots of people through work, but most were married or had their own lives to get on with. If it weren't for mum,

I would have no one to go out with. I really must join some groups, I thought, but then again, when I get home from work, I'm too tired to go out. I like the simple comforts of opening a bottle of wine, changing into my pyjamas, and curling up to watch TV.

Home had always been a safe and loving place for me. I was born on the 6th of July 1970. My mother said I was an unexpected surprise. My parents, Christine, and Frank Dale had been trying for years and had finally given up on the idea of having a child. Then one year later, along I came, 'a beautiful bouncing baby girl,' according to my mother. It was fair to say that Mum and Dad had spoiled me rotten. I always had the best clothes and shoes. Every weekend, they'd find something for us to do, like trips to the seaside or weekends at Flamingoland in a caravan. Although sometimes it was lonely being an only child, and I envied my friends who had siblings to play with. My best friend at school told me she hated her little brother and said I was lucky being the only one, so I guess it's all about perspective.

I will always be grateful to Mum for helping me set up my hairdressing business. I had always wanted to be a hairdresser but couldn't find an apprenticeship when I left school at seventeen. I ended up working in an office. Twelve years I had worked in that office and had hated every minute with a passion. But it was a job, and I needed to earn a living. It was only when Dad died, and Mum got the insurance payout that I was given the financial opportunity to change my career. I had taken a one-year, full-time course that qualified me as a hairdresser. The course was intensive; there was so much to learn and the competition from other students was fierce, but I kept my eye on the end goal. Mum and I had found a little salon in a busy village, and with Mum's help I had set about modernising it and turning it into a trendy little salon. We went for the luxurious look. Silver damask wallpaper and deep purple velvet seating.

There's something special about being your own boss, that turning of the key in the door on the first day of opening, the space waiting to come alive with laughter, conversation, and the soft hum of dryers. I wasn't just walking into a salon; I was stepping into a new life, one that relied on me to make it work. I remember breathing in every detail, the sleek chairs, the targeted lighting I'd spent hours deciding on, the display cabinet promoting high end hair products. It was all so perfect. I had spent years deferring to bosses, following orders. Now, I was the one who would make the decisions, set the rules. The weight of that responsibility filling me with both pride and purpose.

Mum helped daily during that first year of opening, her bubbly personality adding to the ambience. Within a couple of weeks, I had taken on an apprentice as well as another girl willing to rent a chair. Mum still comes along to the salon to help on busy days; not that she needs to, but she likes the buzz of the salon, and it makes her feel important. Mum loves to be the centre of attention; chatting away to the customers and telling funny stories. Customers sometimes sound quite disappointed when I tell them that Mum isn't coming in today.

I was almost home but decided to stop off at the Co-op to buy some Prosecco and nachos for later. I also threw in a few bars of chocolate to satisfy my sweet tooth. Mum would try to resist the chocolate because she was always on a diet, but she would inevitably give in and then scorn me for putting temptation in her way. Mum had no need to be conscious of her weight. She's always been petite and slim, but for some reason, she doesn't believe it. On a Saturday night, we would both curl up on the settee and watch a movie. I like horror films, but I have seen so many, I'm running out of choices. Mum likes Murder Mystery and would happily wade through an entire box set of Morse in one weekend. Tonight, I doubt I will want to watch any TV, well at least not until Mum and I have mulled over my past life experience. 'Better make those two bottles of Prosecco,' I said out loud, absentmindedly forgetting I was in a busy supermarket. Blushing, I paid for my shopping and hurried home.

When I arrived home at 6 pm, my mother was in the kitchen preparing a smorgasbord of savoury delights. I unpacked my shopping and opened one of the bottles of prosecco. I poured two long-stemmed glasses full to the brim and handed one to Mum. Sitting at the kitchen island, I watched Mum decoratively arranging the food she had prepared onto a wooden platter. Dinner tonight would be hummus, olives, carrot sticks, crusty bread, pâté, and samosas. Mum refused to cook on a Saturday. She said it was her day off, so dinner was either a takeaway or snacks, and, of course, a glass or two of white wine or prosecco. It had become a comfortable habit, so I waited until we were both sitting down before relating my experience.

To the best of my memory, I retold what I had seen during the regression therapy. Mum had listened intently and threw in the occasional 'wow' every so often.

'Do you think that you were the child you saw?' Mum asked, her eyes shining with hope.

'I don't know, but it all felt remarkably familiar, like I had been there and knew everyone there. It was odd because I could smell the wood even though I was quite a distance away and wasn't really there.'

'As it happens, your grandfather, my father, worked with wood; he was a Master Carpenter. I wonder if there's a connection?'

'Probably a coincidence.' I sounded dismissive, but I know how Mum can get carried away, leaping to conclusions before the facts.

'You know,' Mum said, 'there's a new group started in the WI looking at building a family tree. We had a woman come to our meeting on Wednesday who told us all about it. It's amazing the amount of information you can get from various sites on the internet as well as old newspapers. Most of the local newspapers for West Yorkshire have made their content available on the internet. And I guess you can search for almost anything using Google.'

'Yes, Mum, I know,' I muttered with a sarcastic tone, 'my generation invented the internet.'

'Well, I was thinking, there's a lot of what you have told me that we could investigate, for example, railway lines and timber merchants nearby. The woman at the WI also told us about the author Harold Turner. He lives in Todmorden and holds weekly meetings there. He's written many books on the history of the local area. She gave us a leaflet on information for the Historical Society. I'll fish it out later and maybe he could help you.'

'Worth trying,' I pondered, taking another sip of my fizz. 'Do you remember that time I went to Bradbury? I was sure I'd been there before because I knew where everything was.' The question was rhetorical, so I didn't pause for an answer. 'Well, this felt like that, so our search could start in Bradbury.'

'Sounds like a plan, shall we look now?' Mum was eager as she reached for her laptop.

'I'm not in the mood for doing it tonight; my brain already hurts, but definitely tomorrow.'

I stretched out, resting my feet on Mum's lap, feeling the weight of the day settle over me. I was fatigued, bone tired. It had been a long day, and now, all I wanted to do was close my eyes and let everything go.

The next morning, I woke up refreshed and ready to go. Over breakfast, I could hardly wait to dive back into our conversation, my mind already buzzing with new thoughts and questions.

'Mum, do you think that when we're reborn we come back into the same family? I read something once about Spirit Circles. That people we love and connect with stay with us forever. For example, someone who was your mother in one life could be your son, daughter, or lover in the next.'

'That reminds me of a programme I watched on TV.' She scratched her head trying to remember. 'It was a little boy in India or Pakistan or somewhere like that, who from a young child talked about another family. He said that he had another mother and father and a wife and children. When he got older, he met this family, and they were convinced that he was in fact who he said he was. He had run a family store, and his past family were still there running it. He told them things that only the dead man could have known. So, who knows? If there is a family connection, then it might be worth looking through some old photographs. I tell you what, I have a box of old photos under the bed; would you like to look at them?'

'I will have seen them before,' I said, sounding bored and disinterested. I didn't fancy the idea of Mum taking me on a trip down memory lane. She has tons of photos of me growing up, birthdays and holidays, and school photos.

'Not these,' she pursed her lips, I only found them recently. They were amongst all those old boxes in the cellar that belong to your Grandma Ivy. She stored them here when she moved to her new bungalow because she said she didn't have the space to store them there. They are not of you; they're old relatives of my mum and a few of me when I was a child, and there are a few of my dad. And maybe you are amongst them,' she said, making 'Ooo ooo ooo' spooky noises.

As Mum had said, the photos were old, their edges frayed and discoloured with a brownish hue. They had the look of something that had been stored away for decades, with flecks of dust and a faint musty smell clinging to them. I didn't recognize any of the people in them except for my grandma, Ivy. Even then, she looked so much younger in these pictures, I might not have known it was her if Mum hadn't told me.

'Grandma Ivy looks very glamorous in these photos; how old would she be?

'In all likelihood, she is in her early twenties. She always was a looker.'

Mum looked nothing like her, so I assumed she must have taken after her dad. I didn't remember my grandad, and Mum had rarely spoken about him.

'Your grandad, Joseph, passed away when you were five,' Mum murmured, 'so I don't expect you to remember him.' He was only fifty-six years old when he died of lung cancer. He was a lovely man, and you would have liked him. He adored you and even made you your crib.

'Oh, I remember that crib vividly; it was adorned with intricate carvings of fairies and flowers. I have fond memories of tracing the gentle curves of each decoration with my fingertips. It was like being in a fantasy world. Do you still have it?' I said excitedly.

'Yes, of course I do. It's still in the loft. It's waiting for you to give me a grandchild,' she said, laughing and poking me in the stomach.

'Mum, do you think Joseph could be Jojo? Could I be a reincarnation of Grandad?' I stopped to think. 'How silly of me, of course I can't be him because he was still alive when I was born. When I went through my birth to my past life, I should have seen myself just before I died, so I must be one of the other people there. I wonder if I was the little girl?'

My mum tucked her feet under her and took a sip of her prosecco; she looked lost in thought.

'I have fond memories of my dad,' she said, smiling, 'but he had always been a bit of an enigma to me. I called him Uncle Joe until I was fifteen; that was when my mum told me he was really my dad. He came, went, and showered both mum and me with presents, but to tell you the truth, I never knew much about him. If I ever asked where he lived or who his family was, she would say, 'he has his own life and that's private.'

'There was something going on between my mum and Joe; he was there to see her as much as he was there to see me. Sometimes I would come home from school, and I could smell his aftershave lingering in the air. If I asked if he had been, she would say no. I knew of course that he had. The only reason she would lie to me was if they were having an affair. When I asked what he did for a job, she was always vague. I could never get her to tell me anything other than that he was a carpenter. I knew he must work locally because he would often come straight from work. But I never found out where he worked. I only recently discovered his full name because it was written on the back of one of those photographs of him.'

My mind was racing with possibilities, but nothing made much sense at the moment. Grandad was a carpenter so that could be a connection, he could possibly be Jojo. But who was the little girl? What was her connection to the wood yard? I knew the only way I was going to uncover more of this story was through another session with Caroline Manning.

Chapter 4 Caroline March 2000

When I returned home after my Saturday therapy session, a sense of satisfaction settled over me, and I couldn't help but feel a little smug. The regression therapy with Jess had gone exceptionally well, better than I had even hoped. I felt as though we had broken through the barriers to unlocked pieces of the past, which had previously eluded me. The Timeline had worked well so this would be my go-to process in the future. It was a small but significant victory, and I couldn't wait to review what we had uncovered.

After kicking off my shoes and shrugging off my coat, I made my way to the kitchen, craving something warm and soothing. I prepared a steaming cup of rich hot chocolate. With the mug in hand, I settled at the breakfast bar, letting the heat from the mug warm my icy cold fingers. Eagerly I reached for the folder that held Jess's case notes. I opened it and spread the notes across the counter. With a deep breath, I began to pore over every detail, recalling the emotions and memories Jess had shared.

There was something bothering me. I looked at some of the words I had highlighted: wood yard, railway, little girl, parents, Jojo. It was the name Jojo that was bothering me. My father, Joseph, was a Master Carpenter. He had worked all his life for Stevensons Joinery. I had not revealed any personal information to Jess so it couldn't be a form of transference, but the similarity or coincidence was taxing my brain. Could it be some form of telepathy, not that telepathy has ever been proven to exist outside of science fiction? It all felt too close, like there was a crossover between her life and mine. I needed advice. When I first set myself up as a psychotherapist, I needed a mentor, someone who was experienced and could give me advice and guidance when required. After my experience with Jess this afternoon, now was the right time to call on that guidance.

My mentor, Malgorzata, Malgo, for short, has been practising for many years and is brilliant at her job. Malgo comes across larger than life. I always thought she should have been one of those celebrity hypnotherapists, like Paul McKenna. She has a stage presence even in everyday life. Her clothes are flamboyant, multi-coloured, and flowing. Her long red hair is untamed, and her high prescription lenses make her eyes look larger than humanly possible. Malgo moved to England from Poland in the 1970s, and has largely lost her Polish accent, except for when she is working with clients or giving interviews; then she likes to 'turn it up'! She says it makes her sound more exotic. It's impossible not to love this woman; she is the most hypnotic person I have ever met. I gave Malgo a call, explaining briefly what was on my mind. She listened thoughtfully, and after a pause, suggested we meet for coffee the next day to discuss it in detail. I agreed, feeling a sense of relief at the prospect of getting her perspective, knowing her advice would help me see the situation more clearly.

I heard a stirring from upstairs, Gail and Simon were on their way down. They would be hungry and eager for food. Saturdays are always take-away; I don't have the energy to cook after a long day at the clinic. As usual, an almighty row erupts between Simon and Gail over what they want. I tell them to fight it out and let me know when they have made their minds up, and if they can't make their minds up, then it will be beans on toast. The threat is usually enough to get them to compromise. They're not bad kids, but as they have got older, I see little of them. Gail spends all her time in her bedroom, listening to music and chatting to friends on her phone. If I ask her how she is, I generally get a grunted 'fine' and then she's too busy to talk because she's on a call. At the age of seventeen, she towers above me. She's a leggy brunette with an amazing figure that she hides under baggy clothes. I wish she would dress more femininely. I dream of the day when we can go on shopping trips together, picking out stylish outfits, experimenting with new looks, and swapping makeup tips like close friends. But sadly, that vision feels far off. For now, her shopping excursions, rare as they are, usually involve rummaging through the racks at charity shops, with her mosher friends. I hope that when she is a little older, she will ditch the black and wear some colour. I imagine her blossoming like a flower.

Simon plays golf twice a week, but other than that, he's on his computer playing video games. Simon is also going to be tall; at thirteen he's already taller than me, which doesn't take much doing seeing I'm only five foot one. Simon is more affectionate than Gail; at least he will give me a kiss and say, 'love you mum' before going back to his room. I shouldn't complain. Their absence lets get on with my work. It's just sometimes, I'm lonely. Yes, they're in the house, but the lack of communication gets to me.

Their father Phillip used to see the kids every weekend when we first split up. After his new baby came along it was down to once a month. Phillip always has an excuse, like the baby isn't well or the car has broken down. Neither Gail nor Simon have taken to his new wife. So, they have followed Phillip's lead and now make excuses of their own. He isn't a bad man, but he is lazy. Being available for the kids requires planning and that's not something he does well. He's more of a spur-of-the-moment type of guy. I'm careful not to bad-mouth Phillip, but I also don't try to fight his corner. If he wants a better relationship with them, then he will have to try harder. I have enough on my plate with my career and teenage tantrums. I don't miss Phillip, well not anymore, but I do miss having a man in my life. Gail thinks I should join one of those dating apps, but I'm too busy plus I don't think I could stand the rejection. I'm an intelligent woman with a lot to give, so to be swiped past because of my figure would be degrading.

Time for a relationship would be nice, but as it is, I work long hours. Tuesday to Thursday I lecture in psychology, Friday, and Saturday I put what I preach into practice at the Therapy Centre. Choosing the psychology route wasn't an easy choice for a working-class girl. I didn't come from a family of forward thinkers. And when I started my hypnotherapy training, well, let's just say, I came in for a lot of stick. I always found that my so-called nearest and dearest were too quick to poo-poo the subject. Jokingly they would demand that I clicked my fingers, put them under a spell, and have them behave like a frog or something equally as ridiculous. Which of course I couldn't do, nor would I ever want to. I hate not being able to discuss this aspect of my life with my family but it's easier to keep quiet.

After I graduated, I secured a full-time post at Bradford College, lecturing in psychology. As my interest grew in the application of psychology, I cut my hours at college and set-up my own psychotherapy practice. I put a small advertisement in the Yellow Pages, and to separate the me that is a Lecturer from the me that is a Psychotherapist, I used my middle name, Caroline. I rented a room near Bradford town centre. The room is in a large Victorian terrace. These houses would once have been owned by the wealthy businesspeople who had made their money out of the growing textile trade in Bradford. This area would have been considered affluent in late Victorian times, but now the area was a little shabby, to say the least. Most of these beautiful properties had been divided up into student apartments. You could see dirty rags of curtains half-hung in windows that looked like they hadn't been cleaned for some considerable years. But the student properties were behind the main row. The main row was for business use, including a dentist, a solicitor, and a sex shop.

The 'Therapy Centre,' as the converted house was now called, was one of the front row properties. My room being at the front of the building on the ground floor close to the main entrance. There's a row of seating outside the door and a poster saying, 'Quiet Please (Therapy Session in Progress)'. The décor inside is bland, with walls in magnolia and a plain beige carpet. Someone had tried to add some colour to the room. They had used scatter cushions and chair throws in shades of orange and yellow. The room is of good proportions with a soft seating area in the large bay window. A grand fireplace stands in the centre, but an out-of-character three-bar electric fire spoils it. To one side, there is a treatment bed that belongs to the aroma therapist who uses the room earlier in the week. All the oils and candles in the room make it smell floral, like a mixture of rosemary and ylang-ylang. A dream catcher hangs in the window and a Buddha sits in front of the electric fire. Despite the odd additions, the room's Victorian splendour still manages to shine through in its lofty ceilings and ornate cornicing.

All my clients, so far, had experienced positive outcomes after a therapy session, and word-of-mouth referrals were growing fast. Very soon, I started having to turn clients away or book them weeks in advance. It was tempting to work less at college and take on another day doing therapy, but I earned more at college. My parents had inherited a large estate back in 1970, so my family now had money, but I was determined to make my own way. Being a single mum, I had to pay the bills and to put food on the table, so for now college would have to remain my main source of income.

After tucking into a takeaway of samosas and rogan Josh, Gail and Simon retired, once more, to their virtual lives. I poured myself a large glass of red wine and curled up on the settee with my case notes. Jess had mentioned Bradbury more than once. Bradbury is a small rural hamlet about three miles from Low Dean, it was where the Stevenson Joinery company used to be, the company my father had worked for. It was also home to the Stevenson residence, Bradbury Hall, a place my family now owned.

That night I retired to bed with mixed feelings. Excitement that I had broken through to a past life, and unease that the similarities were too much of a coincidence.

When I arrived at Jill's café in Bradford the next morning, Malgo wasn't there but I knew she wouldn't be long, because she can't stand unpunctuality. I sat in a booth that was furthest away from other customers and would afford us a modicum of privacy. I ordered two cappuccinos as she came walking through the door. She was dressed as flamboyantly as usual, with a brightly patterned cape over a flowing floral skirt. Malgo knew how to make an entrance, and every head turned as she waved and bounced across the room to greet me. Once seated, she got straight down to business.

'Now tell me, my angel, what is troubling you?' Her Polish accent sounded stronger than ever.

I related my concerns about the similarities and asked if she thought it was wise to continue.

'Well, it does sound unusual, but I'm inclined to think it may be a coincidence. Other than that, is it possible you could be related?'

'That's an interesting question because I do know my father had another child. None of us knew about it until after his death. When I was going through my divorce, I told my mum about Philip's infidelity, and that he was leaving me to be with his mistress who was now pregnant. My mother then confided in me that my father had been unfaithful to her, and he had a child, a little girl, to another woman. Mum said he always denied that the child was his, but she believed he was guilty; otherwise, he wouldn't have been so quick to support them. He had supported the child financially but had stayed with my mother and us. But this child would be in her sixties now. I know it was long before I was born.'

'So, my angel, it's possible, is it not, there could be a connection?' Malgo pondered while staring at the ceiling. 'Could Jess be related to you, could it not be, that your father's child went on to have a family of her own?'

'I have no idea. None of my siblings knew anything about her. It had remained a family secret. None of us dared to ask Mum about it for fear of upsetting her. Mum had taken me into her confidence, and I had betrayed her. I begged my brothers and sister not to say anything to her and, as far as I know, they kept their promise. My sister Sheila researched our family history and made a family tree. But she found nothing about an illegitimate child on my father's side. I guess it didn't help not having a name or even a date of birth. We only knew it was sometime after they had got wed and after my eldest brother was born. What do you think, Malgo, should I tell Jess about the similarities? I don't know what to do.'

'I think it's too soon to make a judgment. Like I said before, it could be a coincidence. I believe at this stage there is no reason for you not to continue. If, after your next session, you still see a connection, we will need to rethink things. But for now, I tell you, say nothing to Jess, do not reveal your concerns and continue, my angel, as normal.'

It was reassuring to hear Malgo's take on the matter, and I promised to keep her informed of any developments. For the time being, I would try to put it to the back of my mind and concentrate on all the work I had to do for college. I had to mark a pile of student assignments. I also had to prepare for the external examiners' visit. More than enough to keep my mind busy.

Chapter 5 Joe April 1935 age 16

April 1935. The Gaffa and his wife are coming into the yard today with their new baby. Mrs. Stevenson's been nervous since the birth. This will be her first time out of the house since the baby was born three months ago. My mum says it will be the 'baby blues' and she'll soon get over it. Mum has baked a cake and a batch of scones, and my dad has made a paper banner for the office which says, 'Welcome Miss Jane.' I've been busy all morning scrubbing the office to get it as clean and as dust-free as possible. This isn't easy when us carpenters constantly trail it through from the workshop, but overall, it's cleaner than I've ever seen it.

I hear the sound of a car pulling up in the yard, so I shout to the others to let them know they're here before we all run out to greet them. My dad Jim 'the foreman,' old Mike who we call 'the expert' because he is the most skilled carpenter amongst us, or so he says, and our two labourers Fred and Arthur. Then there's Harry. He retired over ten years ago, so he no longer works for us. But he says he's addicted to the smell of the wood. So, he shows up every day for the love of it. Lastly, there's Mrs Twopenny who manages the office. We are not allowed to call her by her first name; otherwise, we would get a clout round the ear. Come to think of it, I don't even know her first name, but I'm sure it would have to be something stern like Gertrude.

The Gaffa rolls up in his brand-new Rolls Royce Phantom, a present to himself and the wife to celebrate the birth of their first child. It was a handsome glossy black number with chrome trim and the all-important safety features, the new-fangled seat belts. 'You can't be too careful with a new bairn,' the Gaffa would say - 'Safety is paramount.' It was the pedestrians that needed safety features, with these new powerful cars bombing through the villages at 25 miles an hour. Mrs. Stevenson stayed in the car while the Gaffa lifted out the bairn, who was wrapped up snug in a Moses basket.

We all went over to greet the child. She was the bonniest of babies, with a mass of curly blonde hair.

'This is Jane, and Jane, this is the rabble, whom I forbid you to associate with.'

We all laugh and fuss around the baby saying the usual stuff like, what a bonny lass, and how proud you must both be. It's not until we have all stopped fussing that Mrs Stevenson steps out of the car. She looks very pale and fragile. Mrs Twopenny, being a very observant woman, takes her arm saying, 'come on lass, let's get you inside.'

It's a chilly April morning, so we all hurry for the warmth of the office. The office is large, with two chunky desks separated by a large coal fireplace in the middle. The building used to be an old railway cottage that had been knocked through to make one large room. Upstairs there is a kitchen and two toilets. The two toilets were Mrs Twopenny's idea. She thought it was inappropriate for ladies to use the same toilet as the men. She also refused to clean the men's toilet. So, Fred and Arthur had to take turns cleaning it each week. They were not incredibly pleased.

I lay a picnic blanket on the floor in front of the coal fire and the Gaffa places the Moses basket on top.

She's awake now and trying her best to climb out of the basket.

The Gaffa turns to me, 'keep an eye on her for me, Joe, I swear she'll be crawling before long; she's such a little fidget. Make sure she doesn't grab that fireguard; it'll be hot.'

'You don't need to fret, Gaffa, she's as safe as houses with me,' I say as I drop onto the blanket and lift her onto my knee.

She is so beautiful with her thick curly blonde hair and sparkling blue eyes. She looks like the baby on the 'Pears Soap' advert. Her skin is warm and soft beneath her little dress; she feels so fragile. Something is happening to me; I feel emotional and protective towards her. Her big eyes are looking at me, penetrating my soul. Is this love? Is this what babies do to a person? Little Jane giggles as I bounce her up and down. She seems fascinated by the buttons on my bib and brace overalls and is trying her best to eat them. I dip a piece of cake in milk and give it to her; she makes a terrible mess; it's in her hair and all over her clothes. Mrs Stevenson gives me a reproachful look, but the Gaffa quickly chips in,

'Look, she's fitting in already; she's almost as scruffy as you lot.'

After tea and cakes, and a chat about nappies and bottle feeding, the Gaffa asks me to watch Jane while he talks business with my dad. My dad does all the design work for the customers as well as helping Mrs Twopenny keep the accounts in order. Gaffa has been sourcing a lot of new business lately and there's talk of us expanding. When the Gaffa returned with my dad from the back office in the corner of the workshop, he said,

'Right Joe, I have an important job for you. I need you to take care of things here while Jim and I are in London. The job at St Paul's has come through and they want us there sharpish to go over the designs with them. I'll only be gone three days, but your father will have to stay a few weeks, maybe even months. But don't worry, he'll leave you a list of jobs to complete, but make sure you finish the pulpit for St James first. Mrs Twopenny will manage the paperwork. So, your job is to ensure our work meets our customers' exacting standards.'

I puff out my chest with pride. The Gaffa was putting me, Joe Metcalf, the youngest member of the team, in charge. This felt like a major turning point for me. I was no longer being seen as a child. I knew that I was good at my craft, but this responsibility was an acknowledgment that he and my dad thought so too.

As the months rolled on, Jane became a beloved fixture at the workshop. A honorary member of our lively crew. To keep her safely entertained, I'd initially built her a sturdy wooden playpen. But by the time she hit the age of two, she had figured out how to climb out of it. Once free, she would dart around the workshop, making a little nuisance of herself, causing chaos with her boundless energy. Not a single one of us minded, though; she was our little ray of sunshine, a bundle of joy we all looked forward to seeing each day. Jane had a special way of lighting up the room, charming everyone with her bright smile and cheerful little giggle. She quickly became a part of our extended family, and we thrived on the laughter and life she brought with her. Most days, she'd be covered in a fine layer of sawdust, her clothes perfumed with the scent of fresh wood. Jane was always enthusiast in offering her help. She could spot a mistake from the other side of the room. And she was like our little supervisor cracking the whip if we took too long over our tea break. She took her 'jobs' very seriously, especially when it came to assisting old Mike with sweeping up the workshop floor. For that, she even had her own miniature brush, handcrafted with care by yours truly. Watching her proudly push her little brush alongside Mike's big broom, her face scrunched up in concentration, was enough to melt the toughest among us. She had a way of making every corner of that dusty workshop feel warmer and more vibrant. So much so that even after her father had taken her home, the memories she left kept us cheerful until home time.

    Mrs Stevenson never got over the baby blues. So, she was happy for Mr. Stevenson to take Jane to the workshop at every opportunity. Mrs. Twopenny would sit her at her desk with a colouring book. When she got bored, she would come through to the workshop to see what the men were making. By the age of four, she was carving her own whip and tops from leftover pieces of oak. 'A master craftswoman in the making,' my dad would say. Even at such an early age, I could see the potential in her. So, I was eager to encourage her inquisitiveness. If I had my way, she would become the best master carpenter that ever existed.

Chapter 6 Jess April 2000

Mum and I decided we would be searching in the dark if we tried doing this alone. I opened my laptop and googled the address of the Historical Society branch in Todmorden and put it into the sat nav. The quickest route would take me 30 minutes, which is quite a long drive after a full day's work, so I hoped it would be worth it. I also hoped that Harold would be there and that my journey wasn't wasted. Deciding to see Harold Turner was one thing but knowing what I would say to him was another. If I talked about my past life experience, he would probably think I was demented.

I had done some research on Harold using the ever-reliable Google. I discovered that he was a renowned local historian with deep roots in Halifax. There was quite a lot written about Harold's life and career. He was described as a proud Yorkshireman. Born and bred in Halifax, with a career that started out as an Archiver for the Bradford Archives Department. So, he had dedicated much of his life to documenting and preserving the rich history of the area. His work included several well-regarded books: The Woollen Mills of Bradford, Low Dean: 1890 to 1940, and The Listers of Shibden Hall, among others. In his eighties, Harold had retired from giving talks and writing books. But he remained a key member of the Historical Society. He was a major contributor to the Historical Society National Newsletter. It keeps members updated on meetings, research, events, and lectures. It also shares articles on local history from members, mostly from Harold. It was Harold who had set up the group in

Todmorden. And he continued to lead a weekly meeting at the Todmorden Community Centre.

    I was feeling extremely nervous as I drove into the car park of the community centre on a Thursday evening. I checked my makeup in the mirror and re-applied my lipstick. I had gone for muted tones of eye shadow and lipstick; I didn't want to look like I was on a night out. I was wearing matching royal blue trousers and a jacket. As I checked my look in the wing mirror, I cringed. I looked like I was going for a job interview. Oh well, it was too late to change now; I would have to do. I entered the building and the woman at the desk asked me if I was looking for the Pilates class. She seemed a little taken aback when I said I was looking for the local Historical Society meeting.

    'Oh, that's in the annex,' she said, indicating with her hands. 'You should go out the door, then turn left down the side of the building. You'll see the annex on your left.' I thanked her and went where she'd directed. The side of the building wasn't flagged; it was a dirt path. My high heels were sinking into the dirt, and I was finding it difficult to walk. In my head, I was telling myself off for not dressing more casually. I should have put on a pair of trainers.

    The annex was a large porta-cabin. I sheepishly knocked on the door and heard a woman's voice say, 'come in, the door is open.' I took a deep breath and composed myself. I nervously peered around the door.

    'I've come to see Harold Turner if possible. I've heard that he runs these meetings. I hope I'm in the right place.'

A jolly woman, robustly built with a mass of curly ginger hair, said, 'yes, of course, my dear. Come on in; he'll be here shortly. Would you like a cup of tea?' Three more people arrived. A tall lanky bald man, a short but wiry, also bald man, and an elegant-looking woman with grey hair worn up in a bun. I was introduced to them by the first lady as 'a young lady here to see Harold.' I noticed she raised her eyebrows as she said it. I guess everybody else in the room was in their seventies or eighties, so I didn't exactly blend into the background. I could feel the cup of tea shaking in my hand, and I was too scared to take a sip in case I spilled it all down me. Everyone said hello and assured me that they were a friendly group, and it was always nice to get new members. To my surprise, everyone tried their best to make me feel welcome. They were all quite jolly and not at all stuffy, as I had expected. Harold arrived last; he looked me up and down and said, 'it's rare I get a pretty young lady asking after me; what can I do for you, lass?'

Harold was a sharp, astute man with a perfectly groomed handlebar Mustache that suited his commanding presence. It wasn't hard to imagine him as a formidable army general in his younger days, issuing orders with an air of quiet authority. His habit of twirling the ends of his Mustache hinted at his mischievous streak. I imagined he had an eye for the ladies. There was a twinkle in his eye and a sly smile as he harmlessly flirted with me.

'You are going to think I'm bonkers, but I would like to try to trace someone who might be related to me. I don't have a lot of information, so I'm not sure how easy that will be.'

'Interesting,' said Harold, with his head to one side. 'Tell us what you know, and we can work from there.'

Everyone was sat looking at me, which wasn't helping my nerves. I started to stutter out my words. 'I know there's a wood yard... It's next to a railway line... and there's someone possibly called Joe who works there and there's also a little girl.' My voice trailed off as I realised how little I was giving them to work on. I put my head in my hands and groaned. I looked up and blurted, 'It would be easier if I came clean and told you the whole story, if you don't mind and you aren't busy.'

There were sounds of 'no go ahead' and reassurances that they weren't busy, and they would love to help if possible. Yet, I could see a few raised eyebrows and intakes of breath when I said I'd been to a hypnotherapist for past life regression. But I rattled on. I told them everything I had seen and heard. I described, in detail, the buildings and the people's clothes. I even told them of my 'déjà vu' experience in Bradbury. The jolly lady who first greeted me, I learned, was called Beth, 'short for Elizabeth,' she told me. She was quite enthusiastic and said there was lots in my story they could work with. Frank, the tall bald guy, said, 'Well, this is a first! We have never had anyone who thinks they lived before wanting to trace their past.' He spun his chair around and started the computer. It was the only computer in the room, and it looked ancient. I guess funding isn't available for groups like this. I asked Frank if I needed to pay anything. 'It's only a pound for tea and coffee. The Community Centre gave us this space for free.' He looked around, dissatisfied with the meagre resources. Frank had to wait a while for the dated machine to boot up before he could start searching for any railway lines that ran through Bradbury. He couldn't find anything current. After a few more searches, he found an old map of the Halifax to Bradford line. It had indeed run through Bradbury and the nearby areas. He tapped a few more keys and discovered that the line had been discontinued in 1981. Next, he looked at the number of timber yards, joiners, and carpenters within these areas. He printed a list of companies that operated today. Some were in the right area. But, according to Harold, it would take more research to find those that had closed.

'It would help if we could get a sense of the period. You say the little girl was wearing a school uniform; could you describe that to me again?'

'It was dark, black, or grey. A pinafore dress with a long-sleeved white blouse underneath. She wore an Alice band with a red stripe. I think she had a red bow tied under her blouse collar. I don't think it was a standard school tie.'

'What about the lady you saw? Often women would follow fashion, so her clothes might give us a sense of the period. Are you able to remember what she was wearing in any more detail, other than drab?' he said with a laugh.

'Um... Also dark, black, or brown. It was a jacket and skirt suit, belted at the waist. I remember thinking the woman was so thin and she had a tiny waist.' Then I remembered a detail on her jacket. 'Oh, and yes, it had a leopard print fur collar. The skirt was below the knee, about calf length. She was wearing a hat with a small brim and the shoes I can only describe as sturdy-looking.'

The elegant lady, who I learned was called Caprice, suggested it could be the 1930s or 1940s, and Harold agreed. Frank tapped a few keys looking for 'women's fashion in the 1930s' and brought up some images. I hovered over his shoulder, looking at the various pictures. There were many conflicting images. They ranged from elegant, floaty evening wear to smart office wear. There was also a lot of fur: coats, collars, and embellishments.

'Um, I'm not sure. But that suit there, I would say, is remarkably similar.'

He then searched for images for the 1940s. The clothes had changed, especially the dresses that were more printed cotton rather than floaty chiffon. The ladies' suits didn't look much different except the hats appeared to have got larger.

'I'm leaning more towards the 30s than the 40s, but I could be wrong; after all, I only saw one woman.'

The room was booked for just an hour and a half, so before we knew it, our time was up. As we gathered our things, Harold leaned in with a warm smile and asked for my telephone number, his tone casual but his eyes flirtatious. He assured me, in his gentlemanly way, to 'just leave it with him.'

'I need to pinpoint the companies that were next to the Halifax to Bradford railway line in the 30s and 40s and see if anything significant pops up. And if it does, I'll give you a call. But if you don't hear from me, it doesn't mean I haven't found anything, so be sure to come back again next week, won't you?'

'There's one last thing,' I added. 'I should have mentioned it earlier. My grandad was called Joseph Metcalf, and he was a carpenter. Mum and I wondered if Jojo could be him.'

'Joseph Metcalf,' Harold said, rubbing his chin. 'That name rings a bell.' He paused, then said, 'Leave it with me.' He shook my hand briskly. Everyone else hugged me as we said goodbye.

Chapter 7 Joe 1938

January 1938, Molly came to work in the office with a view to taking over from Mrs Twopenny, who was itching to retire. She had a daughter in Devon and was keen to spend her last years living near her. Molly was the fastest typist I had ever seen, and her spelling was perfect. It was fair to say that Mrs Twopenny was more than pleased with her new charge. She was like a second Mrs Twopenny, with a stern manner and great efficiency. Within six months, she had that office shipshape. We were all banned from touching anything without her permission. Although it took me a long time to decide whether I liked Molly or not, I had to admire her pluck and the way she took no nonsense from anyone.

Outside of the office, Molly was a different person. She was very feminine and wore clothes that showed off her hour-glass figure. She had short curly auburn hair and large brown eyes, and a smile that captivated you. She certainly wasn't short of admirers. I would see her sometimes catching the bus on a Saturday night and jealously wonder if she was meeting a boy. Molly was stirring something in me, and it was pulling me closer to her. One month later, I plucked up courage to ask her out. Molly was alone in the office, so I took my mug of tea through and sat on the edge of her desk.

'So, what are you up to this weekend?' I said in a relaxed manner.

She told me she liked to go to dances with her friends. I asked her if she had tried the Gaumont in

Bradford, and she said she hadn't, so that was my cue to ask her out.

'I'll take you on Saturday if you fancy it?'
I was still trying to sound casual, like it was no big deal. I nearly fell off the desk when she said, 'okay then.' We arranged to meet at the bus stop in Low Dean. I was a nervous wreck all that day, which brought me out in pimples. I didn't imagine she would want to see a spotty twat like me again, but to my surprise, she did. We started going to the Gaumont every Saturday night. On Wednesdays, we would meet at the La Luna coffee bar in Bradford.

Molly was my first girlfriend. I was rather naive; I knew how to have sex, but I didn't know anything about foreplay, or the things women liked. Molly was a little older than me. I felt I wasn't her first. She would never admit it. But she knew what to do, and she was a good teacher.

There was no keeping anything a secret at Stevenson's, so as soon as Dad got wind of it, he invited her round for tea. Both Mum and Dad approved. They could see she was the sort of girl who would keep me on the straight and narrow. She was level-headed, intelligent and knew her own mind. No man was ever going to dominate Molly. We officially started courting and came in for some right stick at work. The men were always making carpentry related jibes. Such as, 'being good with my hands or polishing a piece of furniture like it was a woman's body.' I was working on a mural for the church that included scantily clad virgins. 'Looks like you had a model for that, Joe; I hope you are paying her overtime,' Fred teased.

Eight weeks later, the teasing got worse when they learned that Molly was pregnant. 'Old Mike loved to sing and to tease me. He would always be singing songs about love; 'I'm in the Mood for Love' was one of his favourites. And 'Let's Call the Whole Thing Off', which was constantly being played on the radio, would get everyone singing as loud as they could.

Molly's pregnancy hit us both like a tonne of bricks falling from a great height. Molly was worried about what her parents would say, and I was worried it was far too soon to be making a commitment this large. Yes, I wanted to be a father one day, but I had envisioned that to be something that would happen much later in life. It wasn't the most romantic of wedding proposals. We both discussed the pros and cons and decided we should do the right thing and get married. The following weeks were fraught with worry about what our parents would say. But to our relief, they were surprisingly supportive. Molly's parents insisted we got married before the baby was born, which made wedding preparations a bit of a rush, but of course I understood why. My dad was also of the same mind:

'If you get a girl pregnant then you must step up and take responsibility. You must do the right thing.'

When I told Jane I was getting married, she didn't wait to be asked; she blurted out that she would be our bridesmaid. I would have asked her anyway. I never quite knew if I loved Jane like a sister or a daughter. But she was the only little girl I wanted for a bridesmaid, and luckily, Molly agreed. I hoped that Molly would have a little girl, and I hoped she would be just like Jane. There was no time to waste if Molly was to hide her bump on the wedding day. So arrangements were hastily made for us to marry in the August.

Thanks to Mr and Mrs Stevenson, and Jane, we had a beautiful wedding reception in the Grand Hall in their home. There were elegantly arranged tables and a harpist playing in the corner. They even employed a team of staff to wait on everyone. As beautiful as the surroundings looked, we couldn't help but worry about the mix of guests we had coming. Our families weren't used to such grandeur. They were more used to the Old Crown on a Saturday night, which would usually end with someone getting a black eye. We had warned everyone to be on their best behaviour, but as the day progressed, we could see that a few of the guests were getting a little too inebriated. My mum and dad did an excellent job of keeping them in check, but I was more than relieved when I saw Mr and Mrs Stevenson making an early exit. Before they left, Mr Stevenson called me over and handed me a cheque for one thousand pounds. I protested that I couldn't accept it; he had already been generous in providing the reception.

'Now look, lad,' he said, putting his hand on my shoulder. 'You are the closest thing to a son that I have, and you know how I couldn't manage without your Molly. So, take it, use it as a deposit for a house; you will be mighty cramped at your parents' house when the baby arrives.'

Thanks to the Stevensons, we only had to live with Molly's parents for eight weeks before we moved into our own place. It was a two-bedroom mid-terrace in Low Dean, with a yard at the back. Molly hated it, but I promised her it wouldn't be for long.

'It had better not be because I want more kids while I am young enough to cope, and this will not do. You can't swing a cat around in here.' I wasn't asked how many children I wanted; I was told.

Molly was sparing with money. She made me tip my wage up each week; she would set some aside for bills and shopping, and the rest went into the bank. Whenever finances are involved, Molly treats me like a child. She says I have my head in the clouds and I'm not to be trusted. Who knew that getting married would still feel like I being a child? Molly had replaced my parents, except for the extra benefits.

'If we are careful, we can escape this shithole. With both of us working and earning good money, it shan't take long.'

Molly wanted to move to central Bradbury, which she said was much posher than Low Dean. I couldn't fault her ambition; we were both alike in that sense. She wanted the big house and nice neighbours, and I wanted recognition for my skill. Marrying Molly was the noble thing to do, but it wasn't the all-consuming love I had dreamt about. I wanted to feel a tingle down my spine when we kissed; I wanted to feel the ache when she wasn't there, but there was none of that. Molly was a good fit, like an old pair of shoes, but she didn't thrill me. Is that kind of love a dream with the reality being what I got? A good, intelligent woman, ambitious and hard-working. I knew with Molly beside me we could both achieve success. Love would come with time. Like the love you have for your parents or your children, but foregoing passion was the price I had to pay.

In the January of 1939 Mr Stevenson set-on a new lass, called Ivy. Molly would show her the ropes so she could have some time off when the baby arrived. It was clear that Molly took an instant dislike to Ivy. She said she was useless and only good for fluttering her eyelashes.

Ivy was what I would describe as a 'blonde bombshell', and all the men would fuss around her, including me. Fred and Arthur were always making excuses to go into the office, so they could see what Ivy was wearing that day. Ivy and I got on like a house on fire. We shared the same sense of humour. She was flirty and fun, and I know that at times the flirting went too far, but we were young and easily carried away in the moment. Mr Stevenson was the only man who seemed oblivious to Ivy's charm. He only ever had eyes for Molly, and I don't mean in a leering kind of way, but more as a fatherly figure admiring his protégé. Mr Stevenson showed his appreciation for Molly through her wage. She was earning as much as Fred and Arthur. Only Dad and I got paid more. He used to tell her the whole business would collapse without her, and she, of course, would always agree with him.

When the bairn was born, Molly couldn't work through the day, so she worked in the evening. As soon as I got home at 5pm, Molly was off to the office to work until 9pm. She kept the accounts in shape, which meant the new girl, Ivy, could focus on answering the telephone and taking messages. Molly insisted on calling Ivy her office junior. Molly liked to feel that she was in charge, and anytime she could get her mum to babysit, she would walk into the office and take over. I also think Molly's unexpected visits to the office were to keep an eye on Ivy to make sure she and I wasn't up to no good.

Chapter 8 Joe 1938

In the December of 1938, The Stevensons invited my father, Molly, and me to dinner. Jane didn't join us for dinner; she had hers in her nursery with the nanny. It was as well she couldn't join us because the talk was all about the impending war. Hitler had recently annexed Austria, and Neville Chamberlain had averted war with Germany by agreeing that Germany could occupy the Sudetenland, the German-speaking part of Czechoslovakia.

'It's an utter disgrace,' Mr Stevenson growled, throwing his napkin down in disgust. 'Chamberlain should be strung up. Churchill would never have bowed down to that megalomaniac.'

'I agree with you there, George,' offered my father, 'but the British people have no stomach for war. After those strenuous years of the last war, the people are not ready to do it all again. Twenty years, that's all it has been, and what did we achieve? Extraordinarily little from what I can see.'

'I've heard the government is bankrupt after spending so much on rebuilding the country,' I added. 'I doubt we have the money to finance a war.'

'Don't you believe it, lad,' said Mr Stevenson, 'we're not on our knees yet and there's still plenty of old money lying around. The gentry would shore up the finances if necessary.'

'Yes, but it won't be the gentry fighting the war, will it, George? It will be lads like Joe here that will have to do the dirty work.'

Mrs Stevenson shouted so loudly she made me jump.

'That's enough. If you men can't talk about anything else, then Molly and I will retire to the drawing room.'

'No, please don't do that; I'm sure we can save our talk for another, more appropriate time,' said Dad, looking at Mr Stevenson reproachfully.

Mrs Stevenson stood up and went over to ring the bell that would summon the cook.

'Martha, tell Nanny to bring Jane down.' She turned to us. 'She's been practising nursery rhymes on the piano. She's eager to show you.'

We all retired to the drawing room, and Jane came skipping in.

'Jojo,' she shouted, running over to give me a hug. 'I've learned to play Three Blind Mice, Jack and Jill, and Hickory, Dickory Dock. Can I play them for you?'

She was all smiles and full of enthusiasm; there was no way we could say no. After Jane had finished playing, with more than a few missed notes, we all applauded and shouted, 'Bravo.'

'How about a game of rummy?' said Mr Stevenson, getting up and walking over to a bureau.

'Mummy, can I play?' pleaded Jane.

Mrs Stevenson was about to object until I interjected.

'You can help me, Jane. You can be my lucky mascot.' She ran over and jumped onto my lap. She was almost squealing with delight.

We spent the next hour huddled over the table. The sound of laughter washing away the thoughts of war. Mrs Stevenson's voice brought an end to the fun. 'Time for bed now Jane.' Her words a gentle reminder that the evening was wearing on.

As she slid off my knee, I whispered to her, 'doesn't someone have a birthday coming up soon? I wonder who it could be.'

'It's me, it's me, she squealed.'

'And what would the birthday girl like for her birthday? I inquired.

'Pinocchio, Pinocchio. Please, Jojo, will you make me a Pinocchio puppet?' she said as pleadingly as she could muster.'

'Well, I'll try, but I might need you to help me.'

'Mummy, Mummy, can I help Jojo make a Pinocchio puppet, please?'

'Yes, but only if you go to bed right now. Not another word.' She covered her mouth to avoid speaking, then ran out of the room, chased by her nanny.

After Jane left, my father leaned over and whispered, 'I thought you made her a crib for her doll.' 'I did, but now I'll have to make a Pinocchio puppet as well.' We both laughed.

Mrs Stevenson announced that she was going to go and check on Jane, so to please excuse her. Mr Stevenson threw his head back. 'That's it, she won't come back now. 'How about a game of bridge, now that there are four of us?' Mr Stevenson put a decanter of brandy and one of sherry on the table. It was clear we were in for a long night.

On the way home, Molly asked, 'What did you think of Mrs Stevenson tonight? She seemed jittery. She was knocking back the wine quite a bit.'

'I know what you mean; I nearly jumped out of my skin when she shouted at us for talking about the war,' I replied.

Molly continued, 'When Jane came down to play for us, Mrs. Stevenson was at the back of the room, next to the cocktail cabinet. She was helping herself to glass after glass of sherry.'

Dad tilted his head back to look at Molly. 'Well, I know she has been struggling with her nerves for quite a few years now, ever since Jane was born. The drinking is probably to help calm her nerves.'

'That poor woman will drink herself into an early grave if she carries on like that. I can't help feeling sorry for Mr. Stevenson. He has a lot on his plate with her.' Molly sounded so indignant. I found it ironic since she'd had her fair share of sherry tonight despite her being heavily pregnant.

Chapter 9 Ivy 1939

In January 1939, I was just nineteen, fresh-faced and full of enthusiasm. I had landed a job at H. Stephenson's (Joinery) Ltd, to work in the office under the direction of Molly Metcalf, who was pregnant. They needed someone who would be able to take over during her absence. That January was particularly harsh, with snow up to the knees and a bitterly cold wind that could penetrate the heaviest of coats. Mum insisted I wore wool trousers and a pair of wellington boots. I folded a skirt into my bag and placed my high-heeled shoes on top. I might look like a tramp getting there, but I sure as hell wasn't wearing them all day. I was glad Mum had insisted on the warm clothes. By the time I'd got off the bus and walked up the steep hill to Stevenson's, the snow had gone over my boots and my legs were freezing wet.

As I opened the door to Stevenson's, the heat hit me. There was a blazing fire in the centre of the office welcoming you in from the cold. Molly looked me up and down with an icy glare.

'So, you're the new lass. I'm sorry I wasn't here when you came for your interview, but I had to see the nurse that day,' she said, tapping her enormous belly. 'That's your desk.' She pointed to a large desk facing the entrance. 'There will be no slacking because I have plenty of work for you to do.' I took that as a sign that she wanted me to get started straight away.

'Would you mind if I changed my clothes first,' I asked, lifting my coat to show her my wellies and wet trousers? She fixed me with a stern gaze.

'Well, don't take long; there's a lot to get through. The powder room is upstairs. The kitchen is also up there. You might as well make us two cups of tea while you're up there.' I couldn't help feeling that the tea-making was my first test, and it had better be perfect. I was right; when I handed Molly her tea, she took one sip and said 'urge – no sugar.'

'Sorry, should I go and get you some?'

'Yes, and mind you don't break your legs in those shoes. I suggest more suitable shoes in future. It might be nice in here, but there'll be times you will have to go into the workshop, and those will not do.'

Molly was married to Joe, a young senior carpenter at the company. His father, Jim, was the foreman. So, it was a family affair. Molly was older than Joe by four years and she was a right bossy mare. Anyone would have thought she owned the company; even Mr Stevenson would bow down to her. When Molly joined the company one year earlier, she and Joe had got together and had recently married. Now that Molly was pregnant, they had brought me in as her 'office junior.' Or at least that was what Molly called me, whereas I had been under the impression I was being trained up to take her place. Molly made it quite clear, from day one, that she was the boss. She said she would be taking as little time off work as possible because it was clear she would never be able to leave me in charge.

Despite her overbearing presence, I found comfort in Joe's company. Joe was tall and slim with unruly light brown hair. His fringe was always slightly too long, which meant he had to keep flicking it back out of his eyes. I rather liked that little flick he did; I found it sexy. Joe and I shared a similar sense of humour. We often sneaked off for quick fag breaks. He delighted in telling me the latest joke he had learned. Joe's easy-going nature was in stark contrast to Molly's strict, no-nonsense attitude. His charm and warmth drew me in. Before long, our innocent flirtations turned into a passionate affair. I wouldn't say that Joe was the best lover in the world because sex was always hurried, but still I fell deeply in love with him. Joe told me that his and Molly's marriage was one of convenience. Although he thought a lot about her, he said he wasn't in love with her. I couldn't understand why he would stay with someone he didn't love, but Joe said he felt stuck. He said Molly was a valued member of the Stevenson team and if he left her, it would be mighty awkward. Now that I could understand. No one said it, but I got the impression that the company came first, and anything else was secondary. Stevenson's was one big family, and a divorce would not be tolerated.

Molly didn't carry pregnancy gracefully. Her ankles were swollen like tree trunks. Her face was red and blotchy. Two of her teeth fell out, making her look like a vampire. But she had gaps instead of fangs. I felt sorry for Joe having to go to bed with that every night. As Molly's due date approached, she took time off to rest before the baby was born. This was a blessing for Joe and me because we could sneak off for sex at any time we chose. Once we even did it in the office, which was a risky move; anyone could have walked in at any moment. But when the urge took over, there was no stopping us. The day Molly gave birth to a healthy bouncing baby boy, I discovered I too was pregnant. The shock was overwhelming. I kept my condition hidden, knowing the scandal it would cause, especially since Joe was the father.

I waited until I was four months pregnant before telling my mum and seeking her support. Instead, she flew into a rage, telling me she couldn't believe how reckless I had been. She was shouting and screaming at me to get rid of it, but as she knew, it was already too late for that. Mum wrote to her brother in Manchester, explaining the situation, and he agreed to take me in until after the baby was born. Mum made me promise I wouldn't tell a soul who the baby belonged to and that we would sort something out to tell the neighbours before I returned. So, with little time to prepare, I was bundled off to stay with my uncle. Hiding my growing belly from the prying eyes of our small, judgmental village. It had been heart-breaking handing my notice in at Stevenson's and saying goodbye to everyone. Luckily, Joe was working away on a job, so at least I was spared the trauma of having to say goodbye to him. Molly, of course, gave me a load of stick. She said I was irresponsible to leave just as she was getting used to motherhood.

'I knew you would be a disappointment the moment I clapped eyes on you,' she said scornfully. 'Now I will have to bring the baby to work with me and that means we will have two kids cluttering up the place. We might as well call this the Stevenson nursery!'

I heard that Molly interviewed the next candidates. She chose a woman in her forties, as plain as day and as timid as a mouse.

My uncle John's house was small, and he wasn't particularly welcoming, but I was grateful to him for taking me in. My bedroom was a tiny space in the attic, and the wind blew through the gaps in the roof, making it constantly cold. In the small lounge, there was a coal fire, and I was always reluctant to leave it and go up to my cold room. I spent my days knitting baby cardigans in shades of yellow and white; either colour would do for a boy or a girl. I sometimes helped him on his smallholding. He kept chickens, rabbits, and a rather aggressive goat there. Until I got too big to move. The evenings were particularly lonely because Uncle John hardly spoke. He would sit there smoking his pipe, and if I tried to engage him in conversation, all I would get back was a grunt. As apprehensive as I was about giving birth, I couldn't wait for the day to come when I could get out of here and return home.

In December 1939, during a chilly winter, I gave birth to a beautiful baby girl. I named her Christine. I thought it was an apt name seeing that she was born so close to Christmas. The moment I held her in my arms, all the fear and loneliness melted away. She was my world, and despite the circumstances, I determined to provide the best life I could for her. I stayed in Manchester for three more agonising months until Mum decided it was okay for me to return.

After the snows had cleared away in late March, I returned to Low Dean with Christine in tow. I must have looked a right sight on the train journey back home. I had Christine in her Silver Cross pram, bought by my uncle. Two suitcases sat on top. There was me, back in my high heels and tight skirts, trying to manoeuvre the load I had in front of me. More than once, I had to flash my eyelashes at a passing gent to give me a hand.

It was wonderful to see Mum and Grandma again. Mum was instantly besotted with Christine, so my reckless actions were swiftly forgiven. My mother had concocted an elaborate story to explain my absence and the new baby. She told neighbours that my husband was in Ireland, shipbuilding. He would return soon to be with his family. I don't think Mum had thought very far ahead about what she would say when he never materialised. But Mum didn't have to wait long for a solution to present itself. In September 1939, the Government announced subscription for all men aged 18 to 41. Now Mum could tell everyone that my husband had been called up. Needless to say, my poor fictitious husband would never return from the war.

After Christine came along, it wasn't so easy to make ends meet. I was working in the local Co-op from 12 till 5 pm; I had a cleaning job two mornings a week, and I took in sewing in my spare time. I lived at home with my mum, which meant I had a built-in babysitter. Mum's health wasn't good due to years of heavy smoking, so I couldn't leave Christine with her for long periods. Which meant getting a full-time job an impossibility. As much as I loved Christine, I longed for love again, but my prospects of bagging a man with a small child were next to none. The local butcher had his eye on me and would always slip an extra sausage or two in my bag. He was old and bald, and if that were all that was on offer, I would rather do without.

Despite Mum's best storytelling efforts, I could tell that the other women in our local community didn't believe her. They looked down their noses at me; not so much for not having a husband, because many of the women's husbands had gone off to war, but because of the way I looked. I was a busty blonde with a great pair of legs and men's eyes would follow me wherever I went. I sometimes would hear the women calling me a tart, but I didn't care because it was obvious to me that they were jealous. I'd had a baby, but I had retained my figure and my looks. Whereas most of the women in the village had let themselves get fat and dowdy. Still, I didn't want to get on the wrong side of them. They were like a pack of fat wolves standing at their gates gossiping and pointing fingers. God forbid if they knew the truth about me being unmarried and having a child because of an affair. My life wouldn't be worth living. But as it was, I held my head up high, and I would deliberately dress provocatively to make them envious.

Chapter 10 Caroline, April 2000 - Session 2.

The college week had dragged. It got worse when the external examiners asked me to justify the marks I gave on the students' assignments. The bureaucracy of college was tiring. If we could just tutor the students, the job would be enjoyable. But there were always meetings to attend and reports to write. There were constant demands for retraining and so many bureaucratic boxes to tick. Next year, I thought to myself, I must take the risk and cut back my hours. It would be great if I could convince my family that psychotherapy was worth investing in, but somehow, I doubted it. My passion lay in therapy, and it was time I pursued it, even without their help.

I was looking forward to seeing Jess again. She had been a perfect hypnotic client and had fully engaged with the process. As a therapist, it is always preferable to work with a client who believes that the process will work. In fact, they're the only clients worth working with. If a client came to me and said, 'I'll give it a go, but I don't believe it will work,' I would tell them it will only work if they are willing to believe that it will. That would be like betting on a horse and hoping it will lose. They might as well keep their money in their purse. But Jess was perfect; I had a good feeling that today we would produce positive results once again.

4pm prompt: Jess knocked on the door. Once again, she was perfectly turned out in red ankle-grazer trousers, blue and white shoes, and a blue blazer. Jess and I chatted for a while, and she told me about finding a local historical group that had been extremely helpful.

She had thought about doing the research herself. But there were so many genealogy websites and records to check. So, she decided it was beyond her abilities. Jess had planned to see Harold and the others next week. She was excited about finding a company with a wood yard near the railway line in Bradbury.

'Do you think I'm doing the wrong thing focusing on Bradbury; do you think I should extend my search area?' she quizzed.

'Instinct is a powerful tool, Jess; you should follow it.'

'I've also learned a little about my grandfather. He was called Joseph Metcalf, and he was a carpenter, so there's a connection there with wood. Harold said he would investigate that, but it might be a coincidence.

For a moment I was taken aback. 'Jess, before we start, I'm going to pop to the loo; I won't be long, make yourself comfortable.' I hurried out of the room and let out a long, slow breath. Now I know for certain I will have to tell her, but if I told her we wouldn't be able to continue with the session. I was too curious to stop now; I needed to know more. I knew it was unprofessional. Malgo would be cross with me when I told her. But, for now, I needed to focus on Jess and put my feelings aside.

I used the same process as before to take Jess back in time. I didn't feel the need to change anything in any way. It had worked last time, and, with repetition, the journey should become easier. When Jess said she had arrived at the wood yard and was looking at it through the iron railings, I asked her to describe what she could see.

'There's the boy, Jojo, and the little girl. They are sitting on a blanket having a picnic. The girl is so pretty with beautiful long blonde hair. She's wearing her school uniform. I can't see anyone else. They are laughing. It's a lovely sunny day. It looks so perfect.'

'Have a look around at the surroundings; is there anything in particular that stands out?'

'They are sat on an embankment above the railway. There's a steep slope below them.' She pauses to visualise. Maybe ten feet above the railway line. There are a few small shrubs. No trees. The area in front of the stone building is cobbled…. There's a black car…. A large crane next to the wood stores…. Red poppies in a field….'

Her pauses between listing what she could see were becoming longer. I sensed she was struggling to recall details from the surroundings, so it was time to move on.

I asked Jess to connect with her feelings and to describe them to me. The colour in her cheeks, which had previously drained, came back, and she looked more relaxed.

'I feel intense love. It's all around me. I feel like I'm floating in a cloud of love.'

'What are your feelings towards Jojo?'

'Love, intense love.'

'And what are your feelings towards the little girl?'

'So much love.' I can see that there's a little tear running down her cheek as she speaks. I push my luck and say, 'Ask the girl her name?' The reply was soft and tearful, 'I'm Jane…. Stephen's son….'

'Ask Jane if there's anything she wishes to tell you?' There's a short pause and then a small voice. 'It wasn't his fault….' There's a longer pause, so I decide that it was time to bring Jess back. 'Say your goodbyes and float upwards, seeing the scene get smaller as it gets further away. Turn to face the future and come back to the here and now, back into this room, seated comfortably in the chair. 'On the count of five, I want you to open your eyes and stretch your arms.' I saw Jess's body process the info. Then, she opened her eyes and smiled through wet tears. Jess dries her eyes with her hands and takes a good stretch.

Leaving Jess sat in the chair, I hurry to the kitchen and make us two teas. I don't rush her to give me a de-brief; I let her sip her tea and take her time to come round. Watching her, I can almost see the gears turning in her head. The eyes accessing information from what she had seen and her head going up and down from sadness to delight. The room is silent except for the occasional little giggle from Jess as she connects with the memories. My teacup was now empty, and I could see that Jess had also finished hers.

'So,' I say, breaking the silence, 'are you ready to go over it?'

'Yes, I'm ready,' she replied, sitting more upright in her chair.

'I'd like you to walk me through the event step by step, starting from your journey into the past. What was that like?'

'It was a pleasant feeling of floating through the air. I could look down and see myself at different stages in my life. I think I saw my Grandad Joe. There was a man; he looked quite old and frail, and I was sitting on his knee. He's in a wheelchair. There was a warm glow all around him, and I could feel his love for me. That was a beautiful moment. You know, Caroline, I'm now convinced, more than ever, that Jojo is my grandad, Joseph. That feeling of love and connection to him must be a sign.'

'Tell me about what you saw at the wood yard?'

'It was a beautiful sunny day. The little girl and Jo Jo were having a picnic on a checked blanket looking out over the railway line. The scene was so idyllic, everything else seemed to fade away making it difficult to see beyond this. They kept gazing in my direction giving me the impression that they could see me.' She paused looking up to reconnect with the memory. 'Oh,' she said, 'I realise I was standing in a field of poppies so that could be what they were looking at. 'They were big red poppies as far as the eye could see. It was a magnificent sight.' She looked down connecting with her feelings. 'They looked so happy together and I could feel the love between them. The type of love that you get between a child and a parent. I felt sad that the moment had passed, and they would never get to experience that blissful time ever again.'

Jess looked like she was about to start crying, so I got her to look up at the ceiling for a minute until the emotion had passed. I continued, 'What else could you see?'

'It was difficult to avert my gaze from the two of them. Then they both turned around as if they were looking to see what I was looking at. Everything started to come into focus. I noticed the stone building was in fact a small house and not a barn. It was a small two-storey dwelling with a chimney. A very tall building stood out at the back of the house which looked like a large barn. The area in front of the house was cobbled, and a very handsome black car was parked there. It was the same car I saw last time so I think it belonged to the girl's parents. I could see the other barns, which were obviously for storing wood. It was all piled up in different shades from light to dark wood, each barn having its own colour. I noticed a large crane at the side of one wood pile; I suspected it was for lifting the wood.'

'Jess, do you remember speaking to the little girl?'

'I thought I was dreaming!' she exclaimed and looked at me in surprise. 'It felt so different from anything else. Everything else felt clear and solid, but this felt surreal.' She jumped out of her chair and spun around as if looking for something. Then she turned to me looking shocked and whispered, 'she spoke, didn't she?' I nodded my head to affirm. 'Jane,' she exclaimed. 'Oh my god, I got a name. She said 'Jane.' 'Yes,' I said, gesturing for her to continue. 'The little girl, I mean Jane, said 'it wasn't his fault. She said it twice; it was like I needed to know that, and he also needed to know that.'

'Who do you think she was referring to?'

'She said Stephen's son, maybe it was him, whoever he is? I can't wait to see Harold. I now have two new names to give him that must be connected to the woodyard.'

Jess sat back down, perching on the edge of her seat. I could see her mind was racing ahead of her with enthusiasm.

'The feeling of love was so strong. I felt connected to both of them. I might be wrong, but I have a strong feeling that Jojo is also trying to connect with me. If he is my grandad Joseph, then he has something to tell me. I feel it is him that has led me here. Maybe he has been leading me here for a long time. Bradbury was not a forgotten memory; it was Joseph leading me towards a certain path. A path that would bring me to you and a path that will in time reveal some hidden information that I need to know. Caroline, we must continue. Something tells me that this journey of discovery is just beginning.'

Jess was no longer talking to me; she was in her head and the cogs were turning at full speed.

'Jojo must be Grandad. What do you think, Caroline?'

'If Jojo is your grandad, then you indeed have a lot of information to help you move forward.'

'Yes, I'm sure Grandad will lead me to discover who Jane was. If I am her reincarnation, then I would love to know all about her life. It would be amazing to learn about the life of someone I possibly once was. I can see I'm going to be keeping Harold busy for some time to come.'

I smiled, stood up, and lifted her coat down from the back of the door.

'Before I go, I want to say, I can't thank you enough. You have been amazing.' She gave me a big hug before saying, 'I'll let you know how I get on with Harold.'

I wasn't sure I wanted to know what Harold had found out. Jess had given Harold Joe's full name. I was worried that this could lead to her discovering that Joseph Metcalf was indeed my father, and that would leave me with a lot of explaining to do. I knew I needed to tell her and to do it soon. I was feeling guilty for not telling her that Stephen's son was actually Stevenson, the name of the company my father had worked all his life. Tonight, I will speak to Malgo, and tomorrow I will contact Jess and come clean.

Chapter 11 Caroline April 2000

April 2000. By the time I got home, I was starting to change my mind about phoning Malgo. I knew she would tell me to stop, but my curiosity was getting the better of me and urging me to continue. The proof of reincarnation was tangible. I didn't want to let this opportunity slip through my fingers. I had this feeling I was on the brink of a major discovery that could change the way people think about life and death. Nothing in life is coincidence; I had taken this path for a reason, and I owed it to society to uncover the truth. I'll sleep on it tonight and I'll call Malgo tomorrow, but for now I need time to think. I opened a bottle of red wine and poured myself a large glass. Simon and Gail ordered a Chinese takeaway and watched TV for a short while. Enough time for them to finish their meal and leave me to clear up the mess. Feeling annoyed, I poured myself another large glass of wine and opened another bottle. Tonight, I need a drink, and I didn't care that tomorrow I would have a banging head.

Later that evening, and a little bit tipsy, I was still feeling guilty for not correcting Jess when she said Stephen's son. More than once, I found my hand hovering over my mobile; I even got as far as typing in her number. I stopped myself because I wouldn't know where to start to explain my actions. Instead, I sent her a text message, suggesting that the name could be Stevenson. I would rather her go chasing down that rabbit hole than down my father's.

I remember Mr Stevenson very well, but I never met his wife. She had died when I was too young to remember. Mr Stevenson was a tall man, very straight-backed and well-spoken. He would often call round to the house with parcels of food. Mum said it was because he was lonely and wanted the company. He would always stay to take tea and cakes with us. I used to feel sorry for him because he lived on his own and didn't have any family. Our house was always full of laughter, and I couldn't imagine how lonely it must feel to go home to an empty house.

My mum had started doing a little cleaning for him when she went over to check his accounts. She complained that the girl he employed to do his cleaning wasn't doing a particularly good job. So, she took it upon herself to rectify her sloppiness. Sometimes she would take me with her. I used to love going with her because Mr Stevenson's house was vast. There was a large bedroom at the top of the house which was full of wonderful toys. I would head straight there as soon as we got through the door. There was a large rocking horse, and I would rock backwards and forwards as fast as I could, pretending I was a jockey winning a race. A large Pinocchio puppet hung on the wall, that I wasn't allowed to play with. Mum told me that my dad had made it for Mr Stevenson's daughter Jane. Jane had a beautiful baby doll, and I longed to take her home with me, but mum could be stern. I could play with most of the toys, but I must always put them back exactly where I found them. When I asked where Jane was, mum would say that she had died a long time ago. There was never any mention of the train accident.

It struck me that one day Jess would want to see the home Jane had lived in. It wouldn't matter how much I tried to keep my connection to her a secret; one day she would find out. My family were going to be furious with me for bringing her to our door. There would be the inevitable questions about her claim to the Stevenson inheritance. After all, she is my father's granddaughter, and as such could make a claim against the estate, if she chose to. And then there was Christine, Jess's mother. She would be owed years of backdated dividends if she were to make a claim. As the Nat King Cole song says, 'There will be trouble ahead.'

Chapter 12 Jess April 2000

I knocked on the porta-cabin door, a bit more confidently this time. Beth welcomed me inside with her natural warmth.

'Jess, how lovely to see you again,' she said with a smile. 'Would you like a cup of tea?

I accepted gratefully, and we settled in, chatting casually as the others arrived. Harold was the last to walk through the door, his face lit up with excitement.

'Jess! I'm so pleased you're here,' he said, his grin widening. 'I have so much to tell you.'

As Harold spread his papers across the table, we all fell silent. We were like school kids waiting for the teacher to start the lesson.

'I knew the name *Joseph Metcalf* sounded familiar,' Harold began, staring at me with a twinkle in his eye. 'Jess, your grandfather is quite famous. His work, and the work of his father, James Metcalf, can fetch a high price at auction. Both of them worked for Stevenson's Joinery in Bradbury, just as you thought. And did you know that James restored woodcut panels at St Paul's Cathedral in the early 1930s? His talent for matching the style of the original work was praised as nothing short of masterful.'

Harold passed around a black-and-white photograph of an elaborate biblical wall panel. As we took it in, he continued, his voice high and commanding.

'James Metcalf quickly earned a reputation for his meticulous attention to detail. He transformed wood into intricate works of art, becoming the go-to craftsman for the British nobility. He created custom decorative panels that adorned the grandest estates. Hand-carved floral motifs, mythical creatures, classical scenes. These weren't just panels; they were masterpieces in mahogany, walnut, and oak, each carving brimming with life and texture.'

Beth, sensing my eagerness to learn about my grandfather, raised her hand.

'And what about Joseph, Harold? I bet young Jess here would rather hear about her *grandfather*.'

'Absolutely,' Harold agreed, his eyes sparkling. He cleared his throat theatrically as he turned to a new page. We all simultaneously leaned forward with anticipation.

'Joseph Metcalf followed in his father's footsteps and became a celebrated master craftsman in his own right. Joseph inherited his father's meticulous eye for detail and passion for the craft. He developed a reputation for his innovative techniques and modern approach to woodworking. After the Second World War, his reputation skyrocketed.'

'In the 1950s, Joseph was commissioned to create a series of hand-carved panels for the Houses of Parliament. These panels were praised for their innovative design and craftsmanship. Thus, cementing Joseph's status as a leading figure in the woodworking world. Joseph was frequently commissioned by European royalty to design and craft bespoke wooden interiors for their palaces. His skill in blending traditional crafts with modern styles made his work popular with the modern aristocracy. Joseph pioneered new methods of wood inlay and veneer work, often using rare and exotic woods. No one could match his ability to manipulate wood into flowing, almost sculptural forms. His techniques pushed the boundaries of traditional woodworking, and his designs were like nothing anyone had ever seen. The Stevensons' success made their name synonymous with top craftsmanship. Even after the company closed their name continued. Synonymous with names like Chippendale, Hepplewhite, Sheraton, and Adams.'

Harold paused, beaming with delight at his own ability to discover something monumental. His audience hanging on his every word. We sat, spellbound, as Harold passed around two more photographs. Each one capturing the elegance and fluidity of Joseph's designs.

'After Joseph's death in 1975,' Harold said, his voice softening, 'his work only grew in prestige. Today, his pieces are considered 20th-century masterpieces. A few of his works have even sold at auction for staggering amounts. In 1990, for instance, a set of his handcrafted panels fetched a record price. These pieces are a testament to his legacy, one of innovation and elegance. Picture one, from Westcott Manor in Suffolk sold at Sotheby's for a record 1 million pounds. This made headlines in the art world. In late 1998, a unique dining table, picture two, was auctioned. It was designed by Joseph and sold for three million pounds.

He leaned back, satisfied, as the room fell silent, each of us lost in thought. I couldn't help but feel a swell of pride, knowing that this legacy ran in my blood.

'We have my crib at home, that my grandfather made. I wonder if that's worth something?'

Harold gasped, 'It most certainly will be! Joseph Metcalf signed and dated all his work, so look for that when you get home. That's most important to establish its authenticity.'

There was lots of excitement in the room and speculation about how wealthy I could become. 'Ha ha,' I joked, 'if I become a millionaire, I'll hire you some better premises.' 'I'll hold you to that,' Harold joked back.

'I've been to see Caroline Manning again; she's the hypnotherapist I told you about. When she took me back this time, I got a name. The name was Jane. From what you have told me today; I think her surname might have been Stevenson. Is there any chance you could find something about her?'

'I'll give it a try, lass,' said Harold, raising his eyebrows.

Caprice turned to me and added, 'If there's information out there to be found, then you can rest assured that Harold will find it.'

Chapter 13 Christine April 2000

Christine is alone in the kitchen chattering away to herself as she cleans the table and re-sets it ready for the evening. Her table needs to look inviting. A clean starched tablecloth, white crockery, polished cutlery, and a wine glass placed, as it should be, above the knife. Her slight build and dark blonde hair cut into a smart bob make her look younger than her 60 years. She is obsessed with fitness and keeping her weight in check, but to look at her you wouldn't think weight would ever be an issue. Often, she has the radio playing and will dance as she works, but today she is dreaming of times gone by. Her mind is full of her late husband Frank, whom she misses dearly. When she is alone, she expresses her thoughts out loud, hoping that somehow Frank can hear her. She likes to imagine that his spirit is still present in the house and doesn't only exist in her head.

'What do you think, dear, should I have one of those blogs, like our Jess? Or should I continue talking to you, even though you never answer me,' she says, tutting at him. 'She calls it a journal, but it's all over the internet for anyone to read. I'm not sure I have anything interesting to say. But Jess has thousands reading her blog. It's all about her obsession with her past life. She's learning all sorts about my father's life. I hope she doesn't want me to get involved with that family. I never needed them then and I don't need them now. Where are you now, my love?' There's a longing in her voice for the piece of her that she has lost but keeps searching for.

'Anyway, I can't hang around talking to you; I have a busy day ahead. I have the gym this morning and the Women's Institute this afternoon, so dinner tonight will have to be a takeaway. What do you think, Frank, Chinese or Indian? Okay, Chinese it is. I'll get Jess her favourite 'special fried rice.' That was your favourite as well if I remember correctly.' Christine makes a note in her phone to call at the 'Oriental Garden' on her way home.

'One thing you taught me, love, is to live every day to the full. I wish you were still here, my darling, and that your poor heart hadn't failed and taken you from me. You going so soon woke me up. It urged me to live in the moment.' She grabs her gym bag and checks her purse for enough cash for coffee and cake this afternoon.

'I wish you could see Jess's salon; it's so beautiful and she's making a go of it. She's named the shop after you; it's called 'Frank Confessions.' I thought it was a strange name for a hairdresser, but Jess says that the hairdresser's chair is like a confessional booth. People like to share their secrets. She said it was only right that your name should be above the door. After all, it was your insurance money that paid for it.' She scoops up her car keys and locks up.

Christine always meets her friend Linda outside the gym. They both help motivate each other, but also, it's to catch up and have a gossip. Linda's tall, lean stature towers above Christine, making her feel short and dumpy.

'Hi Christine, how are you today? Are you ready for a good workout?' Linda always tries to sound enthusiastic, but they both know it is a bit of a slog.

'To be truthful, Linda, I'm feeling rather melancholy today. Frank has been on my mind a lot. I miss him so much.'

'I understand, she says,' linking her arm through hers. 'How about we have a coffee first, and if we don't feel like lifting weights in the gym, we could go for a swim instead.'

'I like the sound of that; come on, my treat.' They head straight to the coffee lounge and order two black Americanos. They settle into bucket chairs near the window overlooking the duck pond. There's an icy sparkle to the water from the spring frost that is still lingering. Christine gives a little shiver and hugs her cup for warmth.

'Tell me about Frank; sometimes it does you good to talk about them,' says Linda, reclining back in her chair not looking at all eager to go into the gym room.

'Where to start, let me think... Well, we were childhood sweethearts; we met at school. He was a quiet kid, and I guess I felt sorry for him. The other lads used to bully him because he preferred books to football. 'Specky four-eyes Frank' the other kids called him. His real name was Franklin; his mother named him after Franklin Roosevelt; God knows why. Oh, you would laugh, he wore those thick-rimmed NHS spectacles, and they were always stuck together with Elastoplast.'

'Sounds like a real catch,' says Linda, laughing.

'Ha ha, that's true, but we were drawn to each other. We had a lot in common. I never had it easy at school. My mum was a single mother, and as you can imagine, that was frowned upon back then. I would sometimes catch the girls whispering behind my back, and I heard the word 'bastard' more than once. Kids could be so cruel.' Linda nods in agreement. 'My mum was quite a looker and would always turn up at school dressed up to the nines. You could see the other mothers looking and snarling at her. Mum used to say they were jealous of her looks. Everyone thought she was the spitting image of the actress Diana Dors, as she was in her 'heyday' of the 1950s. I remember her taking immense pleasure in winding up the other mothers. She did this by wearing tight pencil skirts and bleaching her long, curly hair blonde. Frank and I were always safe from the bullies when she arrived at the school gates. She had an attitude and a mouth to back it up; nobody messed with Mum and got away with it.'

'Good for her,' said Linda, punching the air.

'You know, I knew straight away that Frank was the only boy for me. He was sweet and always caring, with good morals and a total gentleman. We married in our early twenties; I was twenty and Frank was twenty-one. Our dream was to start a family as early as possible. For the next ten years, we both tried.' Christine started laughing, 'We tried rather a lot.'

'You little tart,' Linda says with a playful tone.

'When I was thirty, I consulted my doctor for advice, and you'll never guess what she said to me. She said I was too old to be having a baby, and we should learn to accept that it's always just going to be the two of us. Cheeky cow, how can you be too old at thirty?'

'I was twenty-seven when I had Bobby, and they said I was too old then. 'Thank goodness attitudes have changed,' Linda said, her voice filled with indignation.

'Well, you'll never guess what happened next. Frank took me for a romantic weekend in Paris for my 30th birthday. The pressure of trying for a baby was gone; we could relax and enjoy each other. We stayed in a beautiful hotel overlooking the Eiffel Tower. There was something so romantic about strolling hand in hand down the Champs-Élysées. I'd love to go back again if you ever fancy a weekend away...? Lo and behold, two months after Paris, I realised I hadn't had a period for some time. I had a local clinic perform a pregnancy test, and one week later, they told me it was positive. When Frank got home from work, I had a neatly wrapped parcel for him to open. His eyes lit up when he saw it was a little white baby grow.'

'Oh, how sweet! I wish I'd thought of doing something like that. Let's get another coffee; I'm enjoying all this reminiscing. You will laugh your head off when I tell you how I met David.'

Linda went to order coffee, leaving Christine with her head in the clouds.

Chapter 14 Joe 1939 - 1945

By September 1939, we were at war. After Hitler invaded Poland, it was inevitable that we would go to war. I was quickly conscripted and my talents assessed. They decided my carpentry skills would help in building tunnels and trenches. From then on, I was called the 'chippy'. I was shipped off to Belgium to do my duty for king and country. Our orders were to quickly establish defensive positions in fields, towns, and along rivers to slow the German advance. These defences were rudimentary to say the least, and highly exposed. We were under a constant threat of artillery bombardments and air attacks from the Lufte underwaffe. We would often receive orders to fall back and abandon our position to avoid being encircled by the Germans.

One day we reached the outskirts of a small Belgian village. Our orders were to dig in and defend our position. The locals had fled, leaving behind empty houses and abandoned livestock. We used whatever we could find to fortify our positions. We used farm tools, furniture, and planks from nearby barns. We dug trenches in the fields and set up makeshift barricades along the roads. It was backbreaking work, and with the ground still soft from the spring rains, mud clung to everything, making our uniforms heavy and stiff. The German advance was far more rapid than anyone could have predicted. We would crouch as low as possible as the planes screamed overhead. The bombardment was relentless. The noise was deafening, and it was hard to hear the commands from the officers over the din.

The memories of war are so painful, and it felt like a bit of me died every day. I thought I would never be the same again, if I survived, which was looking more unlikely by the day. The stench of death was all around me, and I was weak, hungry, and so very cold. The only fighting I was doing was for my basic survival. The only thing that kept up our morale was the occasional letters and parcels from our families back home. Mum would send me warm clothes and underwear, and Jane would send me fruit cake. She said in a letter that she couldn't send me buns or the iced fancies she knew I liked because her mum said they might go mouldy before I received them. But fruit cake would last a long time.

We got the call to withdraw because our losses were becoming too heavy, and we were not equipped to resist the German advance. We moved under the cover of darkness, moving as quietly as possible to avoid detection. The retreat was chaotic, with weary and often wounded soldiers giving each other support the best they could. The march for safety was exhausting, and you could see the pain etched on every soldier's face.

Our goal was to reach the beaches of Dunkirk. The beaches were crowded with soldiers waiting for any vessel that could take them across the Channel to England. At times, the beaches were eerily quiet, and then you would hear a sudden burst of fire whenever a boat approached. We could see the plumes of smoke coming from the city and the distant sound of fighting as the rear guard tried to hold the Germans back.

The evacuation from Dunkirk took days. It was an emotional and heartwarming experience. It looked like anyone who owned a boat had come to our rescue, along with the Royal Navy. It was overwhelmingly emotional to see all these civilians risking their lives for our men. The boat I was rescued on was in fact a civilian boat captained by a Cornish fisherman named Bryher Thomas. He packed that boat so tightly to try to save as many of us as possible, but we didn't complain; the sense of relief was palpable. Seeing the white cliffs of Dover brought cheers and floods of tears. Cheers at being home and tears for those we had lost.

  After Dunkirk, I spent two years in England. I was fortifying air-raid shelters and building the many defences around Southern England. Even though we were being bombed, I somehow felt safer in England. It was much easier to stay connected with family from London. Our commanding officer had a telephone on his desk, and we would take it in turns to receive calls from home. I always knew when it was Mum or Dad calling because I would have to wait for the pips to stop. I could imagine them cramped into the tiny phone box at the end of our street. Whereas when Jane phoned, there were no pips because her parents had their own telephone.

  The people down south were amazing in their generosity. Many didn't have much, and some had lost their homes, but they would share with us what they could. There always seemed to be an endless supply of homemade cakes. We were allowed to go to the local pubs, if we didn't drink too much, and didn't return to our barracks drunk. There was always a piano player and someone willing to sing. 'Run Rabbit Run' was a favourite because it was jolly. 'There'll be bluebirds over the White Cliffs of Dover' was usually sung at the end of the night because it sounded so sad. With the warmth and charm of the people, it was easy to keep our morale high in London, and our hopes for victory even higher.

One day in 1943, General Montgomery himself came to see us. He enlisted my battalion to join other allied troops who were going to push forward in Naples. On our last day in London, hurried parcels and letters for family arrived. It would be the last contact we would have with our loved ones before moving out. Mum and Dad had sent tobacco and rolling papers, and Molly had sent a photograph of her with David sat on her knee. A second parcel was from Jane. She had sent some wool socks and gloves and a balaclava. One of the gloves was heavy, and when I looked inside, there was a gold cigarette case. It was engraved on the back – *'may angels watch over you.'* Inside was a photograph of Jane. She was seated, wearing a long white dress, and her delicate lace-covered hands were resting on her lap. To me, she looked like the most beautiful angel that ever existed. I kissed the case and put it in my breast pocket, knowing I would always keep it with me.

As we moved towards Naples, the signs of war were everywhere. Buildings were destroyed or severely damaged, and roads were cratered from the bombings. The smell of smoke and burning fuel that lay heavy in the air turned my stomach. German forces were everywhere. Snipers and machine-gun nests were hidden in the ruins, and every street corner posed a threat from ambush. We moved cautiously, supported by tanks and artillery, clearing buildings one by one, using grenades and close combat. Once again, I feared for my life and believed I would never see my family again. I moved through each building, my rifle grasped tightly in both hands. I heard a noise behind me and swung around. A young German soldier was standing with his gun pointed at me. His hands were shaking, and he looked uncertain about what to do. I was frozen to the spot, not knowing if he would shoot or run. Then I felt it, a blast to my chest that threw me backwards onto the floor. The blue-sky overhead was turning black. I could feel myself slipping away, and in that moment, I said goodbye to the world.

I woke up in a field hospital. At first, I didn't know where I was. If this was heaven, I thought to myself, then it's pretty shabby and noisy. I tried to sit up to get a better look, but a soaring pain in my chest prevented me from doing so. Two nurses came to my aid and propped me up with a pillow. I stared at each of them in turn, hoping to find answers. The older nurse, who had a formidable sternness about her, said, 'you'll live' and walked away. The younger nurse dipped her hand into her pocket and pulled something out.

'I believe this is yours,' she said, handing it to me. 'You have this to thank for your life.'

I stared at the cigarette case. There was a large hole in the front and a protruding bulge in the back. I managed to force it open. The picture of Jane was now blackened and burnt. All that was left was her little gloved hands, her fingers touching each other, forming the shape of angel's wings. I owed her my life, and I would use it to protect her forever.

After the war, I returned to work as soon as I could. Nothing much had changed. The smell of the wood welcomed me back, and the sound of the machines cutting through the wood was like music to my ears. Colleagues knew I had been in the thick of it, so they knew better than to ask too many questions. If anyone ever mentioned the war, it was always with sadness. It was regret for the people we had lost and the destruction of our beautiful country. I had the cigarette case repaired, which cost me a pretty penny, but it was worth it, and I vowed to always keep it close to me. With my angel by my heart, I felt I could conquer the world. Being around loved ones and helping Stevenson's grow to strength once more healed my soul.

Work started to come in thick and fast. The demand for restoration work was immense, and we soon had to expand our workforce. We built a modern extension onto the existing workshop. We also hired several new employees, mainly lathe operators and trainee carpenters. Jane was now 10 years old and still as pretty as a picture. She didn't come to the workshop as often because of school, but on a weekend, you couldn't keep her away. She would bring me sandwiches and little fondant fancies. We would sit on the railway embankment to eat our lunch together. We would always try to time it so we could wave at the 12.45 train as it went past. The driver would always blow his horn to acknowledge us. Times were good once more, and the future was becoming one to look forward to rather than dread.

Chapter 15 Jane 1942 – 1945

In 1942, a lady brought two children to our home today. They were clutching small bags, and they wore labels around their necks. They looked nervous; their wide anxious eyes darted around the hall. Mummy had called Nanny to meet the children and told her to make beds up for them in the right wing. Nanny is having to help around the house a lot more now since our two maids went to work on a farm. Mummy says we must all pull together and do our bit for the war effort. Which sounds strange because Mummy spends most of her time in bed. I hide behind a curtain when Nanny brings - the children upstairs. I peek from behind the curtain and see that both children are of similar age. They look much younger than me. The girl is very thin with blonde tangled hair, a face covered in freckles and wearing a dirty grey coat. The boy stands a little taller than her; he's round, and the buttons are straining on his coat. His hair is also blonde and is cut close to his head. She takes them to the bedroom and tells them to put all their clothes in the wash basket. Then she gives them towels to wrap themselves in. I hear her running the bath and I can smell the perfume of my favourite bubble bath. I hear them climb into the bath and Nanny comes back out to make their beds. I dash past the half-open bathroom door to ask Nanny why they are here. She tells me they are refugees from London and that they are going to be staying with us for a while. 'Why here?' I ask.

'There are bombs dropping on London, so it's not safe for them there. The poor mites have been sleeping in the air raid shelters every night since the Germans started bombing London. Lots of children have arrived in the village today, so over the next few weeks, I imagine, you will see lots of them. You have a big house, so you have plenty of room for them.' I start to cry, 'but I don't want them here.' She bends down and whispers in my ear, 'neither do I, but we have to do what we are told.'

I run out of the room crying, and I find Mummy in the study. She is still with the woman who brought the children, and she is signing some papers. I waited outside the door until the woman left.

'Mummy, I don't want those strange children in our house; please make them go.' I'm sobbing and pulling at my hair in frustration.

'Jane, don't be so childish. Those poor children have had their house destroyed by those nasty Germans. They need somewhere to live; it won't be for long, I promise. Now you must make them feel welcome, and besides, it will be good for you to have some children to play with.'

The next day I find the two children sitting at the kitchen table. Cook is spooning porridge into bowls, but spills some on the table as I bounce in.

'Miss Jane, can't you walk like a normal child? You made me jump out of my skin. Come and sit down and meet our new house guests. This is Eireen and this is George, and they are twins. Now say hello to each other.' I stare at them, not knowing what to say.

'You can't be twins; you don't look alike and you're not even the same... Er... gender.'

'What's a gender?' asks George, looking at Cook?'

'She means, you're a boy and Eirene is a girl.' Cook looked reproachfully at me. 'Not all twins are identical, Jane. Now be nice to them.'

It was difficult to be nice to two children that I couldn't understand. Their London accents were so strong, they might as well have come from a foreign country. Over the next few months, Nanny tried to get them to talk properly, but I still struggled to understand them. I didn't like them, and they didn't like me either. They would hide from me, and I would hear them giggling and saying things about me. I couldn't tell you what they said, but I got the impression it wasn't nice.

The twins were four years old, but George looked much older. He was tall for his age and almost as round as his height. I imagined him eating all Eirene's food and anything else he could get his chubby hands on. I felt sorry for the timid-looking Eirene, but I was wary of George. His face was always tense and rigid, with furrowed brows pulled tightly together. His narrowed eyes glared at me sharply, and his thin, pressed lips over gritted teeth made him look fierce, like he was constantly ready for a fight. I kept my distance as best I could.

After breakfast, I hurried back to my nursery and climbed onto Neddy, my rocking horse. Rocking always made me feel better. I was about to win the Grand National when the door opened. The children were brought into the room by Nanny, and she told them to sit at the worktable. I sat on Neddy, staring in disbelief that they were in *my* room. Nanny gave them sheets of paper and a pencil. She told them to write a story about where they lived and what their parents were like. George sat there with his arms crossed and refused to write. Eireen looked at Nanny with a vacant expression and scribbled what might have been her name on the paper. It was obvious neither of them could write. Nanny looked dismayed, 'let's try some numbers instead. Write down the numbers 1 to 20.' Eirene tried her best but only managed 1, 2 and 3. George pushed his paper on the floor and glared at Nanny. Nanny looked at me with a troubled expression.

'Jane, come and sit over here and join us. You can show George and Eirene how to form letters. We can start with the alphabet and progress from there.'

The weeks that followed, Nanny tried her best, but in the end, she gave up. She would sit them at the other side of the room in the nursery and give them lines to write. I was learning French, and I would speak loudly to annoy George. My old school had closed because of the war and had been turned into some kind of training centre for new soldiers. The local junior school was open two days a week and all ages were crammed together around desks in the large assembly hall. We were told that we would all have to work together and help each other. The male teachers had gone to war and the females were in short supply. We divided into groups, with us older children teaching the younger ones. I made sure I wasn't in the same group as Eirene and George; I saw enough of them at home. On the days we weren't at school, I would beg Dad to take me to the workshop. The few men that remained were no longer making fine furniture. They were now knocking together packing crates instead. Workers made pile after pile of these crates. Jim said the boxes were for the ammunition for the soldiers. This gave me an idea. I wrote little letters and fastened them with a drawing pin to the insides of the crates. I would write that everybody back home was thinking about them, and we all hoped they came back safely. I would draw trees and flowers on the back of the letters to remind the men of home. I asked Jim if he thought Joe would get one of the crates. He said he hoped so because it would cheer him up no end. I missed Joe deeply; he was my best friend. I'm sure that if he were here, he would send those horrible twin's home.

One day the telephone rang, and it was Joe; he was in London, and he was safe. Finally, I could get to talk to him and tell him how horrible it was back home. I gave him George and Eirene's full names, and he said he would try to locate their family. A few weeks later Joe phoned back and said he had found their mother. She was working as a warden in the air raid shelters. He said she was a fine woman who put herself at risk every day to help others. She asked Joe to tell the twins she missed them very much and couldn't wait for the day they could return home. Joe made me promise to be kind to them and to let them play with my toys. I felt cross with myself for being so mean. I still had my mum and dad, and they were hundreds of miles away from their mother. They didn't even know where their dad was stationed, or if he would ever return. From then on, I tried to be kinder and more tolerant of them. Cook said the war had a way of making children grow up before their time, and I knew exactly how that felt.

In 1945, the war ended. Mummy and Daddy held a large celebratory party in the grounds for all the locals to attend. It was an exciting day. A band played victory songs and there were lots of sandwiches and cakes for everyone. I asked Daddy if the twins could go home. He said they had to stay a bit longer because their house was destroyed. He said as soon as their mother had somewhere to live, he would take them home. For a moment, I felt sad that they would be leaving soon. I'd kind of got used to them being around. I was playing skipping with some of the other children when I saw Jim's car coming up the drive. I stopped and ran over to greet him. I got the surprise of my life when Joe climbed out of the car, followed by Molly. I threw my arms around Joe's neck, and he spun me around. I didn't let go of his arm for the rest of the day. I never wanted him to leave me again.

My school reopened and things began to return to normal. All except for Eirene and George, who were still living with us. Eirene loved to help Cook in the kitchen and she would always be covered from head to toe in flour. George liked to go with me to the workshop. He was incredibly good at hammering nails into things, but I doubted he would be able to do fine carpentry like Jim and Joe. The men didn't like George as they liked me. But they tolerated his sulky behaviour. They gave him lots of menial jobs to do. Sometimes, when there wasn't much to do, George and I would climb to the top of the wood store and play eye-spy. At times, George could be fun, but if he were losing at a game, his mood would shift to anger. Once he kicked me and I had a large red mark on my leg. Joe put him over his knee and spanked him hard. He didn't do it again after that.

Chapter 16 Ivy 1945

Times were tough through the war for the women left back home. Rationing was harsh. We had to stand in long queues to get items such as meat, sugar, and butter. We supplemented our diets by growing vegetables in our small gardens. Plus, there was a weekly market where the allotment owners would sell their vegetables at a low price to the locals. The women rarely looked happy during the war as too many were anxious and fearful that their loved ones wouldn't return. I didn't know where Joe was and whether I would ever see him again. Though the times were tough, I also felt lucky. The men were away fighting in, God knows what, conditions, so who was I to complain? I never wanted to compare my plight to that of our brave young men. But money was always tight, and I felt hard done by.

After the war, I heard through the grapevine that Joe was back with his wife and kids. I know I had promised my mum that I wouldn't ever reveal who Christine's father was, but I felt I had no choice. Christine was getting bigger, and I didn't have enough money to buy her clothes or shoes. It was only fair that Joe should help support her. I was sick of others making me feel dirty. Why was it that women always got all the blame? We were tarts, we had led them on, we had stolen their man. To hell with that. I was angry and proud at the same time. I'll make the bastard pay, I thought, so, with Christine in hand, I made the short walk to where he lived.

I stood at the bottom of Joe's gate and took a deep breath. I was determined to face my fears without feeling scared or intimidated. I marched up the path and banged on the door with an air of confidence. No one answered at first, so I banged again. I heard a voice inside shouting, 'I'm coming, I'm coming, leave the bloody door on its hinges.' Molly answered the door. She looked dumbstruck at first, but then she remembered who I was.

'Ivy, is that you? My goodness, what are you doing here and who's 'this little beauty?'

'This little beauty,' I said, almost shouting and with a degree of anger in my voice, 'is Joe's daughter. Is he in? I want to see him; it's time he took responsibility.'

Molly was aghast and quickly started to call me all the names under the sun, but I wasn't budging. I started shouting Joe's name. 'Get out here and face me.' He sheepishly came to the door. He instantly denied the child was his and that he had ever touched me. What followed next was a lot of shouting and more name-calling, mainly from Molly admonishing Joe. Joe's face was bright red, and he looked absolutely terrified.

'Right,' he said, 'I've had enough of this.' 'You,' he said, glaring at me, 'can bugger off and leave us alone.'

He grabbed my arm and marched me down the path. Poor little Christine tried to keep up as she clung to my coat's hem. At the gate, he whispered, 'meet me outside the Dog and Gun at 9 pm.' He slammed the gate and shouted, 'now piss off.'

I was furious and tempted to go back and have it out some more, but I knew it would be futile with Molly there, so I went on my way. I stopped at the park. I hoped the swings would help Christine forget what had happened. I would be in trouble if she told her grandma, and I didn't fancy another flea in my ear. Mum was always telling me off for something. Usually, the way I dressed. I sat on the park bench and tried to calm myself. I had done what I set out to do, and on reflection it had gone quite well. It had gone well because Joe had arranged to meet me, which gave me hope that he would step up and help. The Joe I knew was a kind and caring man and not the sort to turn his back on his own child. Molly, on the other hand, would slam the door in my face if I went back. She was a hard bitch, so I knew it was no use talking to her.

Later that evening, I read Christine a bedtime story. Then, I quietly went downstairs. As expected, Mum was asleep with the radio playing. Mum would sleep in that chair until I dragged her up to bed. I slipped out of the door and ran all the way to the Dog and Gun. It wasn't easy running in my high heels, but I wasn't going to meet Joe looking anything other than my best. Joe was already there, lurking at the side of the pub smoking a cigarette. When he saw me coming, he beckoned for us to go around the back so no one could see us. Initially, he was churlish, questioning whether she belonged to him.

'Look Joe, she's five years old; her birthday is the 30th of December 1940. Work it out for yourself and at the same time don't you dare deny we weren't getting it on. In fact, from what I remember you couldn't get enough of me.'

My words hit Joe like a double-decker bus. I could see his mind racing, trying to calculate the dates. He was probably wondering why I had never told him about her. He had tears in his eyes, and he struggled to meet my gaze. With his head down and looking broken, he said, 'yes, I know and I'm sorry about earlier. It's come as a bit of a shock, but of course I'll take responsibility. But if Molly finds out, she will turn me out and I will lose everything. I'm only just starting to get back on my feet, but work is picking up, and I can spare a little for you and the bairn each week. But please, please don't tell Molly.'

'If you think I want anyone to know, then you are as stupid as you look. It's bad enough being a single mum; I don't want to be labelled as a homewrecker as well.'

He raised his head and said, 'you know I never stopped caring about you. You left work so abruptly, and then you disappeared.'

'Now you know why,' I said sulkily, 'Mum shipped me off to my uncles as soon as she found out I was pregnant. You had gone to war and there was nobody to turn to. Life was fucking miserable.'

'Well, you survived and you're still looking good,' he said, touching my arm, 'and the bairn looks just like you. I need to see her; I need her to know that I'm sorry for the way I treated you earlier. What must she think of me marching you away the way I did? I'm so sorry.'

'I would like that too, Joe. Christine needs a male influence in her life, and I would never stop you from seeing her. But I warn you, if you mess either of us about, then I will be straight back on your doorstep.'

I smiled at him; I had forgotten how charming he could be, and the old love I had once felt for him was resurfacing.

Joe's eyes were smiling. 'Okay then,' he said, this time taking hold of both my arms. When he pulled me close, my heart skipped a beat. I was sure he would kiss me. Instead, he gazed into my eyes and said, 'If we keep it between us, we can make this work.'

I could feel my face reddening and once again I felt like a young blushing girl on a first date. If he were to flick his fringe out of his eye, I would faint. 'Could you manage a pound a week?' Hastily adding, 'that's fair, don't you think?' I could no longer look him in the eyes; my desire to kiss him was burning inside me. I needed to get this over with and be gone before I did something I would regret.

'Yes, of course, whatever you think. I want a chance to get to know my little girl.'

I turned away in a hurry, shouting after me that he knew where I lived, and I would expect a visit from him tomorrow.

When I told Mum what I had done, she wasn't as angry as I had expected. In fact, she agreed that it was only right he should support us both. The only thing she insisted on was that Christine should call him Uncle Joe. She didn't want shaming in front of the neighbours. Mum wasn't like me. She was a proud woman and what the neighbour's thought was important to her, whereas

I couldn't give a damn anymore. Joe was true to his word and started to call round each week, except for when he was working away. He would bring us parcels of vegetables from his dad's allotment and sweets for Christine. He was brilliant with Christine and her little face would light up whenever he called round. My mum also got used to him calling in whenever he was passing. She was grateful for the extra money he gave us, not that she would ever say so.

Chapter 17 Joe 1946

1946. The shadow of the war no longer loomed over me like a dark cloud. Life had returned to normal, and I was once again my happy, confident self. The company had plenty of work coming in, and there were always laughs and friendly banter in the workshop. I was getting to know Christine, and my visits had other benefits, as Ivy and I rekindled our love for each other. Molly was expecting our third child and was in her element decorating the nursery ready for its arrival. Thelma, who was now Molly's assistant, had shaped up well, and Molly considered her more than capable of running things in her absence when the time came. I was earning good money, and my reputation as a Master of my craft was growing. If there was such a thing as a perfect life, then I felt that I was living it. I was likely one of the jolliest fellows you could wish to meet until that fateful day. The day my heart shattered into a million pieces, the day the sun stopped shining, and all laughter seized.

It was a Saturday, June the 15th, 1946. Jane and I had eaten lunch early because a customer was coming to see me at 12.15. The last time I saw her, she was playing with the Jiminy Cricket puppet I had made. She was patiently waiting for the train to pass so she could wave to the driver. I had given her an umbrella to shade her from the hot sun. But Jane was so delighted with her puppet that she didn't notice the heat. She was determined to learn how to make it wave to the train driver.

Reverend Roberts had come to discuss the design for the new pews for the church. Each row end would have a different carved design depicting the book of Genesis. So far, I had created designs to show him, depicting Adam and Eve, an apple tree, God's hand with rays of light emanating from it, the Tower of Babel and Noah's Ark. Reverend Roberts had brought his Bible and had placed pieces of paper between the relevant pages. I knew the next designs were to be the faces of significant people within the book of Genesis. I loved carving faces, even though these would take me much longer to produce, but the end result was always rewarding, from an artist's point of view. That's how I thought about myself now; I wasn't just a carpenter; I was an artist and a bloody good one at that. While we were reviewing the designs, an almighty screech of the train's brakes pierced the air. The sound of metal against metal pierced the quiet afternoon air. I was frozen for a few seconds. Then, the Reverend grabbed my arm. We ran outside to see what the commotion was and why the train had stopped so violently. The sun was still blazing hot, but the blanket Jane was sat on was now empty. The umbrella had blown across the yard and there was no sign of her. I started calling her name with growing urgency, but there was no answer. Fear and panic were threatening to overtake me when Ted, one of the new labourers, suddenly appeared from down the embankment. For a moment I expected to see Jane climbing up behind him, but the look on his face soon dispelled any hope I had. He was shaking and looked deathly white. He could hardly speak; he was stuttering and crying and spitting out his words one at a

time. 'Jane …. Train….' He didn't need to say any more. I slid down the embankment and ran along the train line. The first thing I saw was a shoe; it belonged to Jane. It was her shiny black patent shoe, but it was no longer shiny; it had become scuffed and dirty. Then I noticed lots of brown liquid on the tracks; at first, I thought it could be a diesel spill from the train. I carried on running and about half a mile down the track I came across her mangled body or what remained of it. The horror of it was indescribable. My heart was racing, and I started to feel faint. My legs started to buckle under me, and I could no longer stand up. The train must have come to a halt further down the line and the driver was running towards me. He was distraught and I was dumbstruck. We stared at each other for a few minutes. Finally, he spoke. He had alerted the Station Master, and the police were on their way. I was still slumped on the floor crying and wailing like a wounded animal. The driver was repeating he was sorry over and over again, but even in my grief I knew it wasn't his fault. But I felt that someone must be to blame. There was no way Jane would put herself in danger; she was a sensible lass.
As soon as the police arrived, they started questioning everyone that was working that day as well as the train driver and all his passengers. The driver said he had turned his gaze to the left, to look for the lass that always waved, but she wasn't there. Seconds later he felt the train shudder and he knew that he had hit something. Sometimes stray sheep would appear on the lines, so he expected that would be the case. Railway procedure dictated that the driver must stop before reporting the incident. He told the police that as soon as

he had jumped down onto the track, he could see hair and clothing stuck to the train's wheels. He knew then that this was a person and not an animal.

Some passengers said they saw a young man running back along the track. They said he looked distressed. I knew that must be Ted because he was coming back up the embankment when I first saw him. I was still distraught and confused, but I had once again found my feet. I headed back to the office, and, to my surprise, I found Ted there. Molly had made him some strong tea with sugar in it and he was sitting there looking forlorn. Anger replaced my grief. I grabbed him by the collar and hurled him to his feet. Molly was screaming at me to let him go, so I released my grip and pushed him back down into the chair.

'What the fuck were you doing down by the line, I snarled at him.' All he could do was stutter and manage to gabble out that he'd been for a fag break. 'You don't go all that fucking way for a fag, you little runt, so tell me the truth before I beat it out of you.'

I hadn't realised that Molly had gone outside and beckoned one of the policemen. The police had set up camp in the yard. The officer charged at me and pulled me off Ted, saying 'he's mine now, son. I have some serious questions for this one. So, leave him with me.' I protested and tried to grab Ted. But the officer made it clear. If I didn't back off, I'd spend the night in a cell for obstructing their enquiries. Ted was bundled into a police car, and I watched them drive away. I didn't know what to do with myself; I felt the need to run. To run and run and not stop. I saw Mr and Mrs Stevenson's car pull up in the yard, but I couldn't face them. Before they could see me, I turned and ran through the fields towards home. I didn't stop running until I got through the door. Then I once again collapsed, and the grief overtook me. I was alone in the house and wailing like a banshee.

Chapter 18 George 1946

I sat at the top of the wood store watching Jane have lunch with Joe. He had made her a wooden puppet and she was trying to make it walk. I saw her stare in my direction a few times with a smug look on her face. I could tell she was trying to taunt me with the stupid puppet. I could imagine her thinking 'Nah nah, I've got a puppet, and you haven't.' Jane always bragged about the toys Joe had made her and I wasn't allowed to touch any of them. Except when she wasn't around, I would take my penknife and scratch my initials on them in a place she wouldn't notice. If she ever did see the scratches, I would be in for a good hiding from Joe for sure. She and Joe always had lunch together, but I wasn't allowed to join them. She treated Joe like one of her special toys; I wasn't allowed to play with. She said Joe was her special friend and she didn't want me ruining their time together. I hated Jane; she was a spoilt brat who had everything. I couldn't wait to get away from here. Mum had received a council house and was busy moving in. She said as soon as it was ready, Eirene and I would join her.

Joe returned to the workshop, leaving Jane alone on the blanket. I was about to slide down and go and join her, but then Ted went up to her and started talking. I sat and watched as Ted pinched her puppet and held it over his head so she couldn't reach it. It was hilarious, Jane crying like a baby and trying to jump up to get the puppet. I saw Ted slide down the embankment, so I slid off the logs and went to get a closer look. Jane followed him down, shouting at him to give it back. This was the funniest thing I had seen in a long time. My sides were bursting with laughter. I crouched down at the top of the embankment behind some long grasses and watched the comedy unfold. Jane ran after Ted, and Ted was making her beg for it back. Jane must have said something that made Ted angry because he threw her puppet onto the train tracks. I could hear the train in the distance, and so could Jane. She was frantically looking towards the train and then back towards her puppet. As the train got closer, I saw her put both arms in front of her face, like she couldn't bear to see what was going to happen. I slid down behind her; she couldn't hear me over the sound of the train.

After the train had hit her, I ran back up the embankment and climbed back up to the top of the wood store. From here I watched everything like it was in slow motion. People running around screaming, the police and ambulance arriving, and then Ted being bundled into the police car and driven away. Mr and Mrs Stevenson arrived and looked distraught. I slid back off the logs and sneaked over to their car. When no one was looking I climbed into the back seat and lay down. I felt sad; nobody was looking for me; they only cared about Jane. It was like I didn't exist. Mr Stevenson's overcoat was on the back seat. I pulled it over me. I must have fallen asleep because when I woke up, I was back at the Hall. I went inside and straight up to my bedroom. I could hear raised voices downstairs, and the door kept opening and shutting as people came and went. Nanny came into the bedroom with a tray of sandwiches. Eireen was following behind.

'Now you two, get some food inside you and when you have finished eating, I want you to pack your cases. Your mum wants you back home.'

Eireen and I were jumping up and down for joy. At long last we were going home. Getting away from this god-awful place. When the car arrived, it was Fred who was driving us home. Other than Nanny and Fred, we didn't get to see or say goodbye to anyone else. They wanted us gone and out of the way as fast as possible. As we drove away, I looked back at the house and stuck two fingers up.

Chapter 19 Ivy June 1946

June 1946, there was a knock on the door. It was 10.30 pm, so I felt a little nervous opening the door. It wasn't normal to get callers at this time of night. I pulled my dressing gown around me and tightened my belt. I edged the door open a little at a time, trying to see who it was. The door suddenly jolted open. Joe fell into me, sobbing like a baby and throwing his arms around me. I could feel his chest heaving and the wet tears running down my neck.

'What on earth has happened, Joe? What's wrong?'

'It's Jane. She's dead.' The sobs were coming louder now, so I rushed to shut the door.

'Come now, my love, come and sit down. I'll fetch you a drink.'

I handed Joe a large glass of brandy and I waited for his sobs to stop. He finally calmed himself, but in all honesty, he looked like a broken man. He told me what had happened the best he could, through sobs of anguish and bursts of anger.

'The day started out like any normal day. Jane and I had an early lunch because I was seeing Reverend Roberts. She was happy. I had made her the Jiminy Cricket puppet she wanted, to go with the Pinocchio puppet I made her when she was little. We heard the deafening sound of the train screeching to a halt. I knew then that something bad had happened. In all my years of working at Stevenson's, that train has never stopped. God, Ivy, it was awful.' Joe was crying once more and was holding his head in his hands. I waited for him to calm down before telling him to go on. 'We ran outside, and then I saw Ted.' That little bastard must have had something to do with it.' Joe was shaking and looking like a wild animal. I had never seen Joe look like this before; he was generally a calm and happy man. But he had got it into his head that Ted Mallinson was somehow to blame for her death. At one stage I had to hold him back from running round to his house and confronting Mrs Mallinson.

'She can't do anything, Joe, it's not her fault her son is a wrong-un. Let the police deal with it.'

'What am I to do, Ivy? I can't go home; I can't face Molly. 'I'm angry with her for stopping me from throttling the bastard.'

Joe went on to tell me how Molly had called a policeman to intervene.

'I'm glad she did, Joe; you would be locked up in a cell now if she hadn't.' Stay here tonight, Joe. You can make up some excuse to Molly tomorrow.'

Joe nodded and let me lead him up to my bedroom. I helped him undress and then I tucked him into bed. 'Please don't go, Ivy. Stay with me,' he pleaded.

I undressed and climbed in beside him. His body was hot and sticky, but I didn't mind. We held each other close all night. Joe must have been exhausted because he soon fell into a deep sleep. I could hear his low snoring, the sound comforting me. My man was in my bed, in my arms. I wanted time to stop, for us to stay like this forever.

In the morning, he turned to me and said, 'You know I still love you, don't you?' 'Yes,' I said, 'and I love you too.'

He kissed me tenderly and held my face in his hands. 'You are so beautiful, Ivy; I don't know what I would do without you.'

He continued to kiss me, starting at my face and then working his way down my body. The electricity between us was ecstatic, and he made love to me more passionately than he had ever done before. We must have been a bit louder than we intended because Christine came running in and jumped on top of us both. She didn't ask any questions, like it was the most natural thing in the world. Mum opened the door and looked at the three of us. 'I'll put the kettle on. I take it you're staying for breakfast?' She didn't wait for an answer before hastily shutting the door. I burst out laughing and threw the blankets over us. If only I could make this moment last.

Over breakfast, Joe told Mum what had happened. 'Poor Mr and Mrs Stevenson; they must be distraught.'

'When they arrived at the works, they looked cut to pieces. I noticed one of the ambulance crew were attending to Mrs Stevenson. I was so caught up in my own grief, I didn't speak to them. What must they think of me? I'll go over to theirs now. I know Mr Stevenson will want me there.'

Joe looked heartbroken all over again. Touching his hand I said, 'Don't worry, Joe. They will understand given the circumstances.'

Joe's face was a picture of scepticism, his furrowed brow screaming uncertainty. His breakfast, once a steaming hot plate of scrambled eggs and crispy bacon, now sat congealing, almost untouched. None of us spoke another word. The tension in the room growing with every silent moment. In his haste to escape the tension, he grabbed his coat and keys. His voice was barely more than a grunt as he turned to thank us. As the door closed behind him, I felt the loneliness of his departure.

Chapter 20 Joe 1946
   Yorkshire Star, Monday, 17 June 1946
POLICE have confirmed a child died on the railway at the weekend.

   Trains were cancelled between Halifax and Bradford on Saturday due to an emergency on the tracks.

   Bradford City Police said officers were called to the line between Bradbury and Ellendale just after 1.30 pm, following a report of a casualty on the tracks.

   Ambulance crews were also sent to the area; however, sadly, a child was pronounced dead at the scene. The child's name has not been released at the present time.

   The police have not yet ruled out foul play, and a local man is being held in police custody.

   The police had held Ted for two days in a cell but had let him go. They said there was insufficient evidence to prove he had committed a crime. They released a statement on day three, saying they had concluded that it was an 'unfortunate accident.' I couldn't accept that. There was no way that Jane would ever go near those tracks of her own accord. I was as angry as hell. I suspected that Ted was somehow involved. He had told the police that he heard the train's brakes screeching and then he saw Jane on the track. Now that couldn't be true because the train driver only braked after he had hit her. This seemed to be an inconsistency that the police had somehow overlooked or, more likely, couldn't be bothered to investigate further. I needed to know what the little toerag had done, so I went looking for him. He only lived a couple of streets away from me, so I hurried there and banged on the door.

'Get out here, you little runt,' I shouted, 'come out and tell me the truth; wait until I get my hands on you.'

He wouldn't open the door, but I knew he was inside. I shouldn't have done it, but the fury in me was too overpowering. I put my shoulder to the door, breaking the lock with one thrust. He saw me and tried to run away, but I grabbed him by his greasy hair, and he fell backwards onto the floor. I started kicking the shit out of him. His mother pushed me off him and blocked my path, which benefited him and likely me too. I had my fist raised, but both she and I knew I would never strike a woman. 'This is not over,' I threatened as I stormed out of the door.

I was still seething with anger, so I went and made a nuisance of myself at the police station. I demanded that Sergeant Smith conduct a thorough investigation into the case. I insisted Ted was to blame. No one else was there. Plus, he had lied about seeing Jane after the train braked. I wanted answers; I needed to know why. Was he jealous of her because her family were wealthy? Was he chasing her? Something had happened between him and Jane, and the police had failed to get to the bottom of it. I was shouting and demanding they re-arrest him.

Sergeant Smith had known me since I was a little boy. 'Look, Joe, don't go doing something you will regret. Let the police handle it.

'But you haven't handled it, have you? You have let the bastard go.' If I get my hands on him, I'll...'

Sergeant Smith stopped me before I could say any more.

'You won't be doing anything of the sort.' He firmly took hold of my arm and directed me through to the back room where the temporary cells were. He pushed me in.

'This is for your own good. You can stay here for the night and cool off. I'll let Molly and your mother know where you are, and you can go home in the morning, as long as you don't give me any more trouble.'

The night in the cell didn't do anything to improve my mood. The cell was dark and smelled of sweat. The walls were covered in what looked like shit and piss. You wouldn't expect even an animal to be locked in something like this. Needless to say, I didn't cool down. In fact, spending a night in a stinking cell because of that little bastard had made me angrier. The first thing I did when I was released was go straight to Ted's house. This time I knocked softly, considering that if I entered with aggression, he would hide. His mum answered the door. She looked angry.

'What do you want, haven't you done enough damage?' she said, looking at the broken door that was still needing repair.

'I'm sorry for the door and I'll get it mended for you, but I'm not sorry I thumped your Ted. He knows more than he is letting on. Where is he? I need to talk to him, and I promise I'll keep my hands to myself.'

'You're too late; he's gone to Maidstone in Kent. His uncle has found him some work down there, so I'm not expecting him back anytime soon.' She sounded apologetic, like she was almost sorry for me.

    I stood, staring at her, not knowing what to say or do. In the end, I said, 'I'll be back tomorrow to fix that door.' I tipped my cap and left.

I took myself straight to the pub; if ever I needed a drink, I needed one now. My blood was boiling; that little runt had got away, and there was nothing I could do about it. The talk in the pub quickly turned to Jane's death when they saw me walk in. Most of the village believed he was somehow involved in her death. Ted wasn't well thought of in the village; he had always been a gambler and a drinker and was always up to no good. There was hardly a man in the village that Ted didn't owe money to. When I told them he'd gone to Maidstone, the general consensus was that he had run away because of the guilt and shame he had brought on his poor mother. Everyone felt sorry for Mrs Mallinson. Most people knew her from her work in the chippy, and they believed she had a heart of gold. I knew in my heart that if I ever saw him again, I would kill him.

Chapter 21 Joe 1961

By May 1961, work had slowed down. The demand for handmade ornate structures was becoming a thing of the past. The trend was for sleek lines, which were easy to turn out on the new machines. We attempted to move with the times by extending the workshop and fitting the new block out with the latest cutting technology. The new block was for making staircases and banisters, to customers' specs. Workers in here could be trained up quickly and the skill involved was minimal. We also moved into making veneered furniture because it was less expensive and more affordable for the general market. The old part of the workshop was still designated for the Master Craftsmen, where the real skill took place. A small number of wealthy clients willing to pay good money for a hand-made one of a kind piece.

It felt like the old days, although old Mike and Harry were no longer with us, and my dad had retired. Not that you would know it because he couldn't stay away. He would stand over poor Fred, tutting and pointing out his mistakes. 'Call yourself a craftsman, Fred, that's not craft, that's butchery,' he would say.

One day, Fred came into the workshop. He said, 'Guess who I've seen strolling down 'Town Street' as bold as brass.' He didn't wait for a reply. 'Ted Mallinson! as large as life and still looking like the little snake that he is. He must be back at his mum's, poor lass. Likely got himself into trouble and had to slither back home.' I didn't say a word; I grabbed my coat and left.

The corner house on Calder Road had been turned into a general store. I went in and bought a packet of Capstan Full Strength. Then I stood outside leaning against the wall and occasionally looking at my watch as if I were waiting for someone. In reality, this corner gave me a direct view of number 27 – the Mallinson house.

I knew Mrs Mallinson worked at the local chippy, so I waited for her to leave her home at 4 pm to start her shift. I wasn't sure if Ted was in, but there was only one way to find out. There was a ginnel that ran between the houses, giving access to the back of the terraces. I waited until the street was quiet, and then I snuck down the ginnel. The backs of the houses had small gardens, mainly laid with vegetables. Mrs Mallinson's was the first through the ginnel. It was quite secluded due to the tall broad beans growing up a trellis and a large apple tree in the centre. I knew that no one locked their doors around here, so the back door wouldn't be locked. I held my breath as I slowly turned the handle. The kitchen was quiet, but I could hear sounds in the distance. Taking each step with caution, I made my way through the kitchen and out into the hallway. The sound of the television was coming from the living room. I stood for a while, looking through the gap in the half-open door, not quite knowing what to do next. My blood was boiling, and I could feel myself shaking. Behind the front door was a row of coats and shoes. An old metal shop weight, used as a doorstop, lay beside them. With a deep breath, I grabbed the weight, pushed open the door, and whacked Ted over the head before he had a chance to realise what was happening. He fell to the floor groaning, but not dead. I turned him onto his back so that I could look him in the eye. He was trying to shuffle backwards away from me, so I grabbed his legs and pulled him back. I took a cushion off the settee and sat on top of him.

Ted started to wriggle, but I held him firmly.

'What the fuck are you playing at? Get the fuck off me.' He looked terrified.

'This cushion is going over your mouth unless you tell me what happened to Jane the day she died. And don't try to bullshit me.' I sounded confident, but inside I was bricking it.

'I don't know what you're talking about. It has nothing to do with me,' he shouted.

I struck him in the face, and he whimpered. Blood was starting to stream out of his nose. 'Now let's start again. What happened to Jane?' I raised my fist to show him I meant business.

'She was being a little brat,' he said, his voice shaking. 'I never touched her; I took her toy from her to teach her a lesson. It wasn't my fault she went on the track.'

I hit him again and he started to splutter blood from his mouth. He seemed like he was having difficulty breathing.

'Why did she go on the track? You were there, so you must know, and I want the truth.'

Through splatters of blood and spitting, he garbled, 'I threw it on the track. That daft bitch, Jane, ran after it. It's not my fault she was fucking stupid.'

My blood was boiling; I had never felt so much anger in my life, not even when I was being shot at by the Germans.

'Shut your filthy mouth, you're not fit to utter her name. She would still be here if it weren't for you.'

I couldn't stop myself; I pressed the cushion with all my weight over Ted's face. I continued to suffocate him until I was sure he was no longer breathing.

To my surprise, I found I was no longer shaking with anger, and a sense of calm had come over me. The tension in my shoulders faded and I felt no remorse. Now I had to work against time. I knew Mrs Mallinson would be back in three hours. So, I dragged his scrawny body down to the cellar. Like the cellar at my parents' house, the floor was lined with Yorkshire stone flags. I remembered my dad burying our old dog, Scrap, under one of them because he couldn't bear to think he was no longer with us. He used to go down to the cellar with his cup of tea and talk to Scrap as if he were still there. Mum said he was a 'sentimental old fool'.

I looked around and found a garden spade and lifted three of the flags in the far corner of the cellar and started digging. The soil was soft, and it didn't take me long to dig a hole deep enough for his body. With sweat dripping off my brow, I rolled him in and shovelled the soil back over his body, before laying the flags back in place. This left me with a pile of spare soil that I needed to get rid of. I found a couple of buckets into which I shovelled the spare soil and then carefully lifted them up to the kitchen, making sure I didn't spill any. I peeked out of the back door to check if anyone was around. There was a young lad kicking his ball against the side of the house two doors down. Panic was trying to take hold; I had to take deep breaths and tell myself to stay calm. It must have been a good half hour of nearly shitting myself before I heard the lad's mother calling him in for his tea. I took the buckets and hurried behind the apple tree. I scattered the soil around the broad beans and raked it over. It would be dark by the time Mrs Mallinson came home, so she was hardly likely to notice. By tomorrow, the soil should have blended in.

I went back to the cellar and swept up, shoving any leftover soil into the corners where it wouldn't be noticed. I then moved some old furniture that was stored down there over the top of the slabs. This would ensure the flags had enough weight to stay down. I gave myself a good brush down to remove any dirt and went back up to the kitchen. Washing my hands in the sink, I noticed that blood and dirt covered them. As I washed it off, I winced; my knuckles were grazed and bleeding. I wiped my hands on my jacket and removed my shoes before I made my way up to the bedrooms. Mrs Mallinson's room was on the left and Ted's room was opposite. His duffle bag was on the floor with a few pieces of scruffy clothing inside it. He had obviously travelled back to his mums with little to show for his time in the big city. His wallet and a few coins were on the bedside cabinet. His wallet was empty except for a bundle of betting slips. I remembered that when he worked for us at Stevenson's, he would head straight to the betting shop on pay day. Nothing had changed, I see. I stuffed what little I could find of his into his duffle bag and went downstairs. In the lounge, I found a packet of fags and a lighter on the coffee table. I shoved these in the bag and switched off the TV. There were splatters of blood on the red floral carpet. They were hardly noticeable among the busy patterns. I scrubbed them with soapy water. Then, I moved the rug a little to the left to cover the damp patch. I was about to leave when I noticed a notepad on the kitchen table. Mrs Mallinson's intended shopping was neatly listed. I couldn't help but feel sorry for her when I saw 'shaving soap' on her list. But then again, I thought, she wouldn't be needing to waste her money on that poor excuse for a son anymore.

    I tore a sheet out from the back of the notepad and, using my left hand, I wrote, 'Gone back to London.' I had no idea what Ted's handwriting would be like; I hoped it would be as scruffy as him. I took his coat and hat from the back door, and I put them on. I put the duffle bag over my shoulder before taking one last look around before slipping my shoes back on and opening the back door. The kid was back outside playing with his ball again, so I turned up the collar on the coat, and with my head down, I shut the door behind me and left. If the kid had noticed me, he would have thought it was Ted.

    I walked the few blocks to where Molly and I lived, making sure I kept my head down, and didn't look in anyone's direction. I went round the back of my house and stuffed Ted's duffle bag and clothes in the corner of the outhouse under a pile of potato sacks. When I got in Molly scolded me for being late. She wasn't working tonight, so she had cooked a meal, and she was angry that it had now dried up in the oven. I ate what was edible and then said I was going for a bath. Soaking in the bath was soothing my body, but my head was confused. I couldn't believe what I had done and the way it had made me feel. Instead of feeling remorse, I was feeling elated, like I had done something good. Ted had forced me to drive to a place of darkness, a part of me I didn't know existed. I swore to myself that I would never go there again. This was a one-off, and it was all down to Ted.

Chapter 22 Caroline 1970 - 1975

In the autumn of 1970, Mr. Stevenson's solicitor called Dad to attend the reading of his will. Mum was filled with excitement.

'Mr Stevenson must have left us something in his will,' she said, jumping up and down for joy.

'Calm yourself down, Molly; it might not be much, so don't go building your hopes up.' Dad was always the pragmatist. But Dad was also smiling, and we all knew we would be in for a treat. I might get that bicycle I've been asking for; I thought to myself.

When Mum and Dad returned home, they didn't look happy. They slumped down next to each other on the settee and we children all gathered round, staring at them. I felt my stomach lurch, expecting bad news.

David was the first to speak. 'Well, come on then, don't keep us in suspense.'

Mum's eyes scanned the room, her gaze lingering on each of us, her face a picture of shock. Her mouth worked silently, opening, and shutting like a fish gasping for air, but no words emerged. Her expression was a mixture of confusion and concern, her brow furrowed in a deep crease. The atmosphere was tense, like the moment before a storm breaks. We all waited, holding our breath, wondering what had caused Mum's sudden loss for words.

Dad took her hand and said, 'Let me lass.' He took a deep breath before saying, 'I don't know where to start; it's mighty complicated. Mr Stevenson has left me everything.' There were screams of delight from us all with questions being fired left, right and centre. Dad raised his hands, 'calm down. Like I said, it's complicated. There are a lot of conditions attached to the will.'

Dad did his best to explain the details of our inheritance. There was something called 'generational wealth.' This meant the house and all Mr Stevenson's assets would be passed down from generation to generation. Dad said it would be the family's responsibility to maintain and further generate the wealth of the estate. There were various tenanted properties, an array of stock, shares, and investments, plus the upkeep of the hall and its grounds. David, who was already a builder, and Jack, who was a trainee carpenter, were told they would be responsible for the maintenance of the estate and the tenanted properties. Sheila, who was a trainee accountant, would help Mum manage the accounts and investments. For now, Daniel and I would continue our education. Dad looked at us all before saying, 'today we pack up and tomorrow we take up residence at Bradbury Hall.'

Bradbury Hall is a magnificent Jacobean house. It dominates the skyline and stands proud in its grand grounds. There's a long winding driveway with lawns either side, and to the rear of the property is a large fishing lake. The interior is vast, with high ceilings and mullioned windows. Every wall is oak panelled and richly decorated with intricate wood carvings. All the furniture is heavy, dark brown wood, mainly oak and walnut. Each piece bears the carpenter's unique decorative skill. The twelve bedrooms are all spacious, each featuring a four-poster bed with a tapestry backdrop and heavy velvet drapes. Living at Bradbury Hall felt like I was living in a museum. The heady smell of beeswax polish permeated the air. Paintings of lost generations stared down at me, and the China vases looked too delicate to touch.

The Hall had a cook, Mrs McGregor, a bulky no-nonsense Scot, and we had two maids, Sally, and Carol. Mrs McGregor lived in the Gate House on the grounds with her husband Sherlock, the groundskeeper. Sally and Carol lived in the area and visited every day except Sundays. It was peculiar hearing them call me Miss and my mother Mam. I felt like a squatter or someone borrowing a house. I couldn't belong here; it was far too grand. As the months went by, I eased myself into the property. Residing myself to the fact that we were here now; I vowed to make the most of it.

My brother Daniel studied agriculture at university and specialised in lawn management. His contribution to the estate was to establish a golf course that attracted the wealthy society. Once everyone was settled into their roles, the estate's wealth went from strength to strength. I went off to Durham University to study Psychology and education. It felt good to be away from the Hall. There was something about its walls that stifled me. University allowed me to spread my wings and make my own mind up about what I wanted to do in the future. I knew I didn't want to work at Bradbury Hall. I knew I needed a career that would take me out of its grasp and allow me to forge my own life. Upon leaving university, I got a job teaching Psychology at Bradford College. My brother David used to say I was spoiled. He would often say, 'We were told what to do.

You got to choose your own path.' But choosing my own path made me feel like an outsider in my own family.

The only money I have ever taken out of the estate was to buy myself a modest house. After that, I determined to make a living for myself. My marriage to Phillip only lasted five years, but it gave me two beautiful children of which I was proud. I was equally determined not to spoil them and to teach them the value of money. Bradbury Hall's doors were always open to me and my kids. We often went there for family weekends, but it never felt like home.

My brothers, my sister and their children all lived at Bradbury Hall with Mum. To them it was home, and they took to the lifestyle like ducks to water. The house had also come with a title. Mum was Lady of the Manor and David took my dad's title as Lord of the Manor after he died in 1975. Each year Mum would throw a garden party for the locals. There would be bouncy castles and clowns for the children and cake stalls and beer stands for the adults. The villagers would all get involved, bringing food for the table, and providing music and entertainment for the day. It was Dad who had started the tradition. He said he wanted to honour their humble upbringings by giving something back to the community. Dad had never changed; he had always been down to earth and spoke to everyone as an equal. Whereas Mum would put on a posh accent and look down her nose at the locals. Mum and Dad had been so different. I often wondered why they had stuck together, but somehow it worked. The majority of the time, we were a happy close-knit family, even after my dad died.

Chapter 23 Jess 2000

When I returned home from work, Mum and Grandma Ivy were busy preparing dinner in the kitchen. Grandma Ivy didn't usually come over mid-week, so I thought it was a little strange; she usually came for Sunday dinner once a month. After we had finished eating, we went to sit in the lounge. I expected Mum to switch on the TV because her favourite programme, Countdown, was about to start.

'Your grandma has come to talk to you about your recent experience with the hypnotherapist, love. She feels you should know more about your grandad.'

I felt surprised but pleased. Grandma has always had a sternness about her, and I know Mum shies away from asking her anything personal. She definitely intimidates mum, and I guess some of that has rubbed off on me too.

Grandma Ivy interjected, 'As you know, Joseph Metcalf was your grandad, your mum's father. But I'd like you to know what he meant to me and what he did for us.'

'Joe was my true love, my 'soulmate.' He never abandoned me or your mother. Yes, he had another family of his own, and we were a secret from them. But believe me, it was far easier back then to keep it hidden. A child out of wedlock was frowned upon. I want you to know that he did not have complete control over the decision. The arrangement we had suited both of us.'

'It's okay, grandma, it's just that Mum never spoke about him much and I never thought to ask. It's only because of recent events that I feel I should have known more about him. Without any knowledge, I was assuming that he had abandoned Mum.'

'No love, it was never like that. Joe consistently supported us, and he loved us all with great affection.

I stood up and went over to give Grandma a big hug. She had tears in her eyes, and I could feel her frail body shaking.

'I don't know how or why you are seeing into Joe's past with that hypnotherapist. But much of what you have learned is very accurate.' So, it's only right that I fill you in on all the details.'

Grandma's eyes sparkled as she delved into the story of how she met Joe through work. Her voice dropping to a whisper as she confessed to having an affair with Joe, who was already married at the time. The consequences of their actions soon became apparent when Grandma discovered she was pregnant with Mum. She was bundled off to have her baby out of the sight of prying neighbours, leaving Joe oblivious to her situation. After the war Grandma said she was struggling for money, so she confessed to Joe that he had a daughter. Joe stepped up, rekindling their love, and becoming a reliable presence in Mum's life.

'Your grandfather was an exceptional master carpenter. He did work for many noble families and royalty. Many wealthy people sought your grandfather's services. So, many would slip him a handsome retainer to jump the queue. And I'm not talking about the odd tenner; I'm talking hundreds of pounds. Whenever Joe got a retainer, he would give it straight to me to put in the bank. If you had ever wondered how I managed to buy my beautiful bungalow, well, that was from the money Joe gave me. Joe always kept a roof over our heads, some spare cash for new clothes, and a yearly holiday to Great Yarmouth.'

'Oh, I always cherished our family holidays to Great Yarmouth when I was a little girl. I distinctly remember riding on the donkeys along the beach. And who could forget the Punch and Judy shows on the beach, the silly antics of Mr Punch. I would laugh so much my belly hurt.'

My memory of those holidays was tinged with a hint of sadness when I thought about Grandad. He had walked those very same beaches with our family, but sadly I was too young to remember.

Grandma smiled and continued, 'Joe was also savvy when it came to his work and the work of his father. He knew that one day their work would be worth a pretty penny. He kept all the design drawings. They are all dated and have the name of the customer on them, and he gave them all to me. You know that large dresser I have in the dining room; well, that alone is worth somewhere in the region of half a million.'

'Wow,' I exclaimed. I couldn't believe Grandma had something that expensive in her possession. I thought to myself, 'if it were me, I would have sold it and lived the life of luxury.'

'I have many more pieces, so when I die you will be an extraordinarily rich young woman if you choose to sell them. But for now, I couldn't bear to part with any of them; they mean too much to me.'

'Grandma, the company that Grandad worked for, Stevenson's. Does it still exist?

'No love, it was sold sometime in the mid-1960s. Joe's health was deteriorating, and Mr Stevenson was getting too old to oversee the company. They got a generous offer to buy them out from large furniture manufacturers called Alexander Herm. They are still producing furniture today. But they sold the Stevenson works and moved their business down to London.'

Grandma started laughing, 'Joe said they turned out a load of 'shite', but still, it was fashionable back then.'

'Grandad died of cancer, didn't he?'

'Yes, but he didn't know it was cancer until the very end. He'd always had a bad chest. He put it down to all the sawdust he inhaled over the years; plus, the twenty-a-day cigarettes didn't help, and he refused to give them up. It was so sad to lose him so young; it left a big hole in my heart.'

Grandma turned to Mum and squeezed her hand. 'Yours as well, love.' Both women had hugged each other and sniffed away their tears.

'Grandma, what do you know about Jane?'

'Jane meant so much to your grandad; it broke his heart when she died. It was so shocking; a train ran over her, poor thing. I met her many times when I worked at Stevenson's. We all called her 'Joe's little Apprentice.' She loved working by his side in the workshop. I don't know how Joe found the time, but he was always making her toys. I remember him presenting her with the most beautiful rocking horse for her birthday. She would have been about 4 or 5 years old at the time.'

'That's young to be in a workshop,' I said, my voice filled with disbelief, 'it couldn't have been a safe environment for a child.'

Grandma laughed, 'Aye, you're right. Health and Safety would have a giddy fit these days. But Jane had been brought up in that workshop. Her mother suffered with her nerves, so she was happy for her to be anywhere other than with her. We all felt sorry for the kid. She was bright and bubbly, and everyone loved her. She used to whisper in my ear and say, 'I love Molly, but I like you more.' Now that always used to cheer me up because Molly was a right bossy cow. She's a few years older than me, but I've heard she's still going strong and lording it up as 'lady of the Manor.'

'What do you mean by "lady of the manor?"'

'When old Mr Stevenson died, he left everything to Joe, including Bradbury Hall.'

'Bradbury Hall, I said, perplexed; I've never heard of it.'

'It's right at the top of Dean Hill, in Bradbury. It's still the Metcalf family residence. You can visit it because it has got a golf club and a café. Look it up on that Google thing you use. I'm sure there will be lots of information on there.'

I turned to Mum. 'So, Mum, you must have half-brothers and sisters?' I said questioningly.

'I've never thought of them as family. My dad never spoke about them, and your grandma was adamant that we would never have anything to do with them.'

'Yes, that's right,' said Grandma, interjecting. Joe had us, but he also had another family, and they were nothing to do with us. I'm not sure how to explain it, but I never wanted Molly to know about Joe and me. If she had known, then everything would have been spoilt. She would have made sure of that.'

'But aren't you curious about them? Wouldn't you like to meet them?'

Grandma spoke before Mum got a chance to answer. 'If you must know, Molly had three boys and two girls. But don't you go looking them up. They're nothing to do with us, I tell you.' Grandma looked stern, so I thought I had better drop the subject. I would talk to Mum about it when Grandma had left.

Chapter 24 Caroline 2000

For the past week I had been a nervous wreck. I was torn between talking to Jess, talking to Malgo, or talking to my family. In the end I decided to consult family first. I told the kids not to make any plans for the weekend because we were going up to Bradbury Hall. Simon would get to play golf with his uncle and Gayle would take her sketchbook. She was creating a sketch for every room in the house. My eldest brother David was trying to encourage her to study architecture at college. He already has her lined up for entering the family business.

On arriving at the Hall, the kids ran straight to their bedrooms to unpack. Whereas I headed for the study, where I was certain to find Sheila.

'Hello there,' said Sheila, looking surprised. 'I didn't know you were coming.'

Sheila is short and chubby, like me. There is no mistaking that we are sisters. 'I thought I would surprise you all. The kids are unpacking, but I thought I would come and see my favourite sister.' We both laughed because, of course, Sheila is my only sister. Although I wondered if that might not be the case for much longer.

We chatted about the estate and the accounts. Sheila obsessed over the financial side of the estate, so you could talk about little else with her.

'I wanted to talk to you about the wages, Sheila said, opening a spreadsheet on her computer. 'As you know, we all get paid a wage from the estate, and although you have always said you don't want anything, I have you on the books as a director.'

'Yes, I know, and I'm grateful you include me in the decision-making process, even though my contributions are minimal, aren't they?'

'You always sell yourself short. You are brilliant at our meetings; you always have great ideas. Don't ever think you are somehow less than us because you don't live and work here.' She got up and gave me a hug.

'Thanks,' I said, 'that means a lot to me; I do feel guilty sometimes for taking a different path.'

'Don't be silly. We are all doing jobs we love. Anyway, back to the wages. As you can see from the spreadsheet, Mum, David, Jack, Daniel, and myself all get paid the same each month. The amount we get is based on the estate's income, which is calculated after we take all the outgoings into consideration. It's simply basic profit and loss. We also set aside money for investments and future growth. Here is what you get paid; it's a third of what the rest of us get.' She clicked on my name and a full account for me appeared. She pointed to a figure of £120,000. 'This is when you bought your cottage. This put you in the red for a while, but since then the account has been growing, and you ought to decide what you want to do with it. I could transfer it into a trust for Simon and Gayle if you like. Or you could draw some out. The balance in your account stands at £600,000.'

I had never taken any interest in the accounts, so the figure she was showing me came as a shock. It also switched a light bulb on in me, one that illuminated all the possibilities.

I hesitated, not knowing how Sheila would respond. 'I have been considering giving up teaching and doing psychotherapy full time.'

'So why don't you? There's plenty of money there to see you through until you get established. You could even buy some premises to work from.' I was surprised at her enthusiasm and wasn't sure if it was genuine or not. The family had always previously pooh-poohed it.

'Talking about psychotherapy. There's something I need to tell you.' I was as nervous as hell to bring up the subject, but I knew it had to be done.

Sheila looked confused. 'Go ahead, what is it?'

'Remember when you were looking into the family history, you tried to find out if Dad had another child.'

'Yes, but I couldn't find anything. If there was a child, it wasn't registered under his name.'

'I had a young woman come to me for therapy.' I didn't mention past life regression, as I thought that would complicate matters. So, I lied a little. 'During our sessions, it came to light that her grandfather was called Joseph Metcalf. He had been a master carpenter, and he had worked for Stevenson's. Now I haven't said anything to her about our connection because I felt I should talk to the family first.'

'Oh, my goodness,' said Sheila, looking shocked. We will have to call a meeting and discuss it. Everyone has a right to know. Mum won't be best pleased, as you know.'

Later that day, the dong sounded, calling us all to dinner. We all congregated in the drawing room, which was next to the dining hall. Mum had embraced the lifestyle of being a Lady with great enthusiasm. She insisted on us all taking an aperitif before going through to dine. Sheila pulled me to one side. 'I've arranged a meeting for 10 am tomorrow. Mum doesn't want it discussed in front of the grandkids. So, not a word.' She put her forefinger to her mouth.

The next day, Gayle and Simon went horse riding with David's two sons, Andrew, and Peter. David had clearly arranged this to remove them from the situation. We all went into the library, where a large round mahogany table had been installed especially for family meetings. I stuck to the same story I had told Sheila; except this time, I added the names of Jess's mother and grandmother.

'Ivy Thornton, I knew it,' said Mum in disgust, getting up and pouring herself a large brandy. 'She came to the house with this scrap of a kid hanging onto her skirt tail, shouting blue murder about your dad being its father. I sent her away with a flea in her ear. Joe swore blind to me that it wasn't his kid, but to tell you the truth I never really believed him. I'd seen the way he looked at her when she worked at Stevenson's.'

'So, what are we to do?' asked David, looking straight at Mum.

'Nothing,' Mum snarled. We do nothing unless any of them come knocking at our door. At the moment there isn't a problem, so we're not about to create one. She turned to me, shaking her finger. 'Don't you dare tell this girl that we are related. You keep your mouth shut. Do you hear me?'

'Yes, Mum. 'I'll do whatever is best for the family; you know I will.' Her words hurt me. She wouldn't have said that to the others. Mum often treats me like an outsider.'

'That's it then, meeting over,' said Mum, storming out of the room.'

We all looked at each other, raising our eyebrows. There was no point in discussing it any further. Mum had made up her mind, and we all had to do what she said. She might be getting older, and her body starting to look frail, but her mind and will are as sharp as they have always been.

I went up to my bedroom and phoned Malgo. Thinking I might as well get this over with. Malgo's wrath couldn't be half as bad as Mum's. It was almost lunchtime, and I knew she wouldn't be seeing clients over lunch; she valued her time-out too much.

'Well, it's about time you called,' she said, not sounding too pleased. I expected you to call me after your last session with Jess.'

'Sorry, I needed to get my head straight, and I needed to speak to my family. Oh Malgo, there's no doubt about it, Jess is my niece and Christine is my half-sister.'

I went on to tell her about my meeting with the family and the fact that I had left out the bit about past-life regression.

'I take it you are not going to tell Jess who you are, then?'

My mother has forbidden me to do so, and if you knew her, you would realise that life would be unbearable if I defied her.

'And what about Jess now, are you going to see her again?'

No, I don't think so. She is meeting the people at the historical society and looking into the Stevenson history. She is focused on Jane for the time being.'

'Um, for the time being,' she sounded sceptical. 'But in the future, she could look into your family line and what will you do then?'

'I have thought about it. My only hope is, if she does look, then she doesn't find me. It will be pretty easy for her to check births and marriages, but she doesn't know my real name. I use Caroline for my therapy but that's my middle name; she doesn't know me as Margaret, or Maggie, as I get called at college.'

'You are in a difficult situation, my angel, but there's nothing in the rules that says you must disclose who you are. She was a client who has now been and gone. Keep it that way. If she asks to see you again, pretend you are too busy. You can't continue with her now that you know for certain. That would not be ethical.'

'I hear what you are saying, and I agree. As unlikely as it is, if she ever did discover who I am, I will have to cross that bridge when I come to it. Thanks, Malgo, I always feel better when I have spoken to you.'

After we ended the call, I couldn't help but feel I had dodged a bullet from both Malgo and my family. Yes, there had been the underlying telling off, but I felt relieved at it all being out in the open. The door was now open for me to both talk about my work and to pursue it further. A tinge of excitement ran down my spine. My future hopes and dreams were lining up and slipping neatly into place.

Chapter 25 Joe 1966

It was a bleak and rainy day in 1966. The lads and I were sat having a tea break when Fred piped up, 'I saw Joan Mallinson today; she's back staying at her mum's house. The poor old lass died last week, so I guess Joan will sort out the house. 'I can't imagine she'll get help from her useless brother.'

This made my blood run cold. Fear and guilt, thought long gone, surged back. My hands began to tremble as I sipped my tea, the sweet liquid doing nothing to soothe my nerves. If Joan sold her mother's house, the new owners could unearth the body. Those cellars were big, and many of the houses on that block had converted them into kitchens. There was every possibility that any new owner of number 27 would want to do the same.

All day, the thought of someone discovering Ted's body consumed my mind. I couldn't concentrate on my work. I was thinking about the possibility of someone finding out. If Ted's body were found, then there would be a police investigation. My name would come up as someone who had an axe to grind with Ted Mallinson. The only solution I could come up with was to go and see Joan and offer to buy the house. Stevenson's had paid me some generous bonuses over the years, so the money wasn't an issue. My problem would be convincing Molly that investing in property was a good move.

At 5pm, when everyone had gone home, I locked up the workshop and hurried over to Calder Road. I stood looking at the shabby house for a while.

Its windows looked to be rotting, and the bow in the roof indicated that it would need replacing. It was far from a buyer's dream. I opened the creaking gate and walked up the path. I tentatively knocked on the decaying wooden door. A trickle of sweat ran down my face, and I wiped it away with my hanky. After a few moments, Joan opened the door. I hadn't seen her since I was a child. She looked older than I expected. But she resembled Mrs Mallinson. She was small, stick-thin, and had a large, dominating nose.

'Hi Joan, I don't know if you remember me. I'm Joe Metcalf; I used to live around the corner.' I was making a strong effort to keep my voice steady and prevent myself from shaking.

'Joe, of course I remember you,' she replied, her face softening with her smile. 'What can I do for you?'

'I wanted to pay my respects and say how sorry I am for your loss. Your mother was a lovely woman,' I said as sincerely as possible. Joan nodded, her eyes glistening with the tears that were starting to form.

'Thank you, that means a lot,' she said, taking her hanky out of her sleeve and blowing her nose. 'Would you like to come in? The neighbours have been bringing me cakes and biscuits all day. You would be doing me a favour if you would stop for a cuppa,' she said, stepping aside and beckoning me in.

We walked through to the kitchen. 'Please excuse all the mess. My mum wasn't in the best of shape these past few years, so the house has got a little dilapidated. There's so much junk to get rid of; I don't know where to start. But come in, sit down, I'll put the kettle on.'

'Well, I could help you with that.' She spun around and gave me a quizzical look. 'Are you planning to sell the house by any chance? And I apologise if this isn't the best time to bring it up.'

Joan put the kettle down without filling it. 'I will have to at some stage. Mum left it to me in her will, but I was hoping that Ted would want it. My husband and I have a place in York, so it's no use to us.' Joan looked around, her arms waving as she pointed out, 'As you can see, Joe, it's not in the best of shapes.'

'Like I said, I could help. I'm looking to invest in property, and this would be a nice little starting project for me.'

'Not so little Joe,' she said with a sigh. 'It needs a lot of work, and I would have to clear it all out first.'

'I could do that for you. Take what you want, I'm sure lots of your mum's possessions will be dear to you, and what you don't want I could clear out later. Take all the time you need to think about it. I can imagine you have a lot on your plate right now.'

Joan sat opposite me at the table. She put her head in her hands and then looked me straight in the eye. 'If you want it, it will make my life easier, but I will have to get a valuation. I can't give it away.' Her demeanour had become brisker and businesslike. 'I'll make that tea, and we can discuss it in more detail,' she said, patting the table with a determination of someone on a mission.

Over tea and cake, we discussed the practicalities, and Joan made a list of things she needed to do. Like contact the estate agent and contacting her solicitor. We talked about a house further down the road that had recently sold for nine hundred pounds. I put my offer of one thousand pounds on the table, knowing it was too much, but I couldn't risk someone else getting it. We agreed that if the offer was close to the valuation, then she would happily sell it to me.

'As long as Ted doesn't want it, of course. But I haven't been able to get hold of him. I reported him missing to the police three months back. Nobody has seen either hide nor hair of him, and he hasn't been in contact with me or my mum for years. He'll be off doing his own thing and living the life of Riley somewhere. He always was a selfish man,' she added with a scowl.

As I walked away, I couldn't help but feel a mixture of relief and nervousness. It wasn't a done deal yet, but I was confident it soon would be. Molly hadn't been easy to persuade, but she relented in the end. Telling me it was on my head if anything went wrong. She made it clear she wouldn't be lending a helping hand because she was too busy with the kids and work. The weeks that followed were a strain on my nerves. I knew I wouldn't feel safe until I got those keys in my hand.

Three months later, they handed me the keys, and I could finally breathe a sigh of relief. One of the first jobs I did in the house was to lay one foot deep of concrete over that cellar floor. I thought to myself, 'Nobody is ever going to dig that up.'

Chapter 26 Joe 1969

In the March of 1969, I received a call from my tenant at Calder Road. 'Hi Joe, it's Michael Stone here. I had an official-looking letter drop through the letterbox today. It's addressed to you. Do you want to come and get it?'

'Thanks, Michael, I can't think what it could be, but I'll come over after work.'

I arrived at Michael's at 6 pm and indeed the letter did look rather daunting. 'I'll take it home with me and read it later,' I said, trying to sound upbeat and not to give him cause for concern.

I sat down with Molly at the kitchen table and opened the letter. I couldn't believe my eyes. It was a compulsory purchase letter.

Bradford and District Council
26 March 1969
Mr J Metcalf
27 Calder Road
Low Dean, Bradford
West Yorkshire

Dear Mr Metcalf
Notice of Compulsory Purchase Order: Property at 27 Calder Road.
I am writing to inform you of an important development concerning your property at 27 Calder Road. As part of the planned improvements to the highway between Bradford and Halifax, the council has determined the need to widen Calder Road. This project is essential for improving traffic flow, reducing congestion, and enhancing road safety in the area. Regrettably, the scope of these improvements necessitates the demolition of the first row of houses facing directly onto Calder Road. Consequently, the council is issuing a Compulsory Purchase Order (CPO) for your property under the provisions of the Highways Act 1980.
Objections: If you have any objections to the CPO, you have the right to submit them in writing within 21 days from the date of this letter.
We will make every effort to provide the necessary support during this transition.
Thank you for your attention to this matter.

Yours sincerely,
J. Fielding, Property Acquisition Officer

A sudden chill swept through me, as if someone had walked over my grave. It was as if my instincts were screaming at me to be cautious, to be on high alert. But Molly, on the other hand, didn't seem the least bit fazed. In fact, she looked positively delighted, a small, self-satisfied smile playing on her lips.

'Well, it wasn't in the best area; we could use the money to buy something in a better area that will bring in more revenue.' Molly could always get excited where money was concerned. Whereas money was the last thing on my mind. If they demolish the houses, then there's a good chance that Ted's body would be found.

'I will have to speak to the neighbours. They might want to contest it.'

'I don't see the point; once the Council has made its mind up, then it's going to happen no matter how much you protest. All you will do is delay the process for compensation.'

'It won't harm to find out what the rest of the street thinks, and I will take my lead from them, I said, sterner than I had meant to.

'Please yourself then,' said Molly, walking away in a huff.

The first house I went to was Mr Fretwell's. He said he was quite keen to move. He had it on good authority that a new housing estate was being built in the field at the opposite side of the road, and the residents of Calder Road would be given first options to buy as well as a generous discount. 'Our lass can't wait to have a shiny new house, with all new appliances. This place is dropping to bits.'

I discovered a few more neighbours at home but they shared the same sentiment. They believed that they would receive a better deal through compulsory purchase, than if they had attempted to sell their properties.

For months I was on edge. Molly said I'd turned into a grumpy old man, always snapping at people over the slightest thing. It was hard to keep the strain under wraps. It's horrible what nerves can do to the body; I felt persistent fatigue, my body ached as if I had the flu, and my brain felt clouded. I was almost at breaking point; I needed to tell someone what I had done. I needed to get this burden off my chest.

It was a lovely sunny June day and Ivy suggested that we take Christine up to Grassington and have a picnic. It sounded like a good idea; some fresh air might do me good. We bought Christine a little fishing net from a gift shop, which kept her busy for most of the day fishing in the river for tiddlers. Ivy knew there was something wrong with me.

'You have been off it for months now, Joe. Don't you think it's about time you told me what is wrong? I'm worried about you.'

'Ivy, love, I have done something terrible, and if anyone knew, I would go to prison.' I hung my head in shame.

'Joe, you are one of the kindest people I have ever met; you couldn't have done anything so bad that it's worth making you ill. What did you do, forget to post your tax return?' she said, laughing.

I looked her straight in the eyes and took hold of her hands. I looked around to double-check that no one was in earshot, and then I told her, 'Ivy, I've killed a man.'

Ivy pulled away in shock. 'Don't be ridiculous; you don't have it in you. Please tell me it's not true.'

I could see a tear in her eye, so I passed her my hanky. 'I'm sorry, love, but it is true. He was an evil man, and he deserved all he got, but the police won't see it that way; I'll go down for murder.'

Ivy was quiet for a while; I could see she was trying to contain her emotions. 'Joe, there's only one person I know of who could drive you to do such a thing. It was Ted Mallinson, wasn't it.'

'How did you guess?'

'I've had my suspicions for a long time; ever since Ted disappeared. I knew Mrs Mallinson from the spiritualist church. She was quite a spiritual woman, you know, and she told me she could feel it in her bones that Ted was no longer alive. She went to the church in the hope of contacting him through the spirits, but no one ever came though. I thought she was being foolish, but something in my gut ached with worry when I thought you might have something to do with it. I remember how angry you were back then, and you threatened to kill him more than once in conversation. But I never thought you would go through with it.'

'I will have to go to the police; will you come with me? I don't think I can do it alone.'

Ivy sounded angry. 'We will do nothing of the sort. No one else knows what you did, and I intend to keep it that way. I'm not prepared to lose you over a rat like him. I love you, Joe, and look at Christine; she needs you too. No, we will not tell a soul. This will be our secret.' She threw her arms around my neck. 'I'm begging you, Joe, please don't do this.'

'Ivy, calm yourself, love. You know you and Christine mean the world to me. But I fear the police will come knocking at my door. I'll be suspect number one. Everyone knew I hated Ted for what he did to Jane. He as much as admitted it, you know. He said he tossed the puppet I had made for her onto the train track, and she went to retrieve it. 'The poor little love must have been so distressed.' I paused for a few minutes to fight back the tears and to regain my composure.

'I didn't go with the intention of killing him, but when he started calling her names, I lost it. I suffocated the bastard to prevent him from speaking another evil word.' Ivy nodded in silence, indicating her understanding. We hugged for a long time, watching Christine play. I felt a calmness come over me. Together we can get through this.

Later that day, I took my usual soak in the bath. The warmth of the water was soothing, and I started to relax. The aches in my body had eased, and my thoughts were clearer. Ivy was right; why should I throw away everything I have over Ted Mallinson? Ted should never have walked this earth. I did everyone a kindness by getting rid of him. I have lived with the guilt up to now, so I'm sure I can carry it a little longer. If it hadn't been for the pending demolition, I wouldn't be thinking about him at all. What I'm feeling isn't guilt or remorse; it's the fear of getting caught. But they haven't caught me yet, and they might never catch me. I have a life to live, I have people I love, and I won't let him take that away from me.

Chapter 27 Joan Turner 1970

One Sunday morning in 1970, Joan was sat reading the Daily Express over breakfast. The headlines were all about Edward Heath's surprise victory over the Labour Party. Joan wasn't interested in politics, so she turned over the page without hesitation. A report caught her eye. The heading was 'Colder Road'; it was a play on the name Calder Road. The report read:

'Colder' Road Bodies

A chilling discovery has sent shockwaves through the quiet village of Low Dean in Bradford. Authorities have so far unearthed three bodies in the rubble from Calder Road. This grisly find came to light when workers were breaking up the concrete and stone slabs for landfill. The site had recently been used to dispose of the rubble from a recently demolished row of houses on Calder Road. Sergeant Morrison gave a brief statement saying:

The identities of the deceased and the cause of death are yet to be determined. Preliminary investigations suggest that the bodies could have been buried there for several years and have only just been discovered due to the demolition works in the area. The houses had recently been demolished as part of the Bradford 'road improvement scheme.' The houses had been repossessed to widen the road into a dual carriageway, to improve the road network between Halifax and Bradford. We are

> *looking into missing persons reports from the past decade and we also urge anyone with information to come forward.*

Joan's blood ran cold; she had an awful feeling that one of the bodies was going to be Ted's. I must tell the police, she thought anxiously. She went over to the sideboard and ruffled through the various items to find her old diaries. Joan never threw her diaries away. She shuffled them until she found the one for 1966, the year she had reported Ted missing. There on the page she had written the name of the officer she had spoken to at the time. Next to his name was the telephone number for the police station.

The young sergeant Smith thanked her for her call. He knew it was really his father she wanted to talk to, but his dad had retired two years ago. She wasn't the only caller that got the two of them confused. Not correcting her, he told her the forensics were examining the bodies, and he would pass the information about Ted to the pathologist. If it was Edward Mallinson, then they would be able to check his dental records. He said it would take two or three days, but he would get back to her immediately after he knew the results.

On the third day, Joan received the call she was dreading. Sergeant Smith was very sympathetic. He was well experienced in giving families this kind of news. He said the cause of death was suffocation. However, there were other signs on the body of a fight having taken place. He told her that the police would be opening the case as a murder investigation. Sergeant Smith couldn't tell Joan when his body would be released. He said, when murder is suspected, it might take some time.

Joan cried for hours, partly through grief and partly through anger. 'Who,' she thought, 'would do such a thing? Yes, Ted wasn't perfect, but he didn't deserve to die in this way.' It didn't take Joan too long to put two and two together. Joe Metcalf had attacked Ted, and it was well known in the village that people thought Ted was responsible for the death of Jane Stevenson. One person in particular hated Ted's guts, and that was Joe. She had always felt it strange that Joe should want to buy the house where a suspected murderer lived. It seemed clear to her that the only reason Joe would want the house was to protect the hiding place of Ted's body. Joe had insisted on her leaving everything to him to clear out. She had believed he was doing her a favour, but now her perspective had changed. Joan got herself more and more worked up and more and more convinced of Joe's guilt.

Chapter 28 Joe 1970

1970. The telephone shrilled loudly in my study, its sudden ring piercing the silence and making me jump. 'Joe Metcalfe speaking,' There was a long silence. It sounded like a call coming through from a phone box.

'Hello Joe, this is Joan Mallinson. I've spoken to the police. They confirmed one body on Calder Road was my brother, Ted. Joan sounded agitated. 'I think you and I should speak, don't you?'

'I'm not sure how I can help you, Joan, but I am very sorry for your loss.'

'You will be more than sorry by the time I've finished with you.'

'Joan, I don't know what you are trying to imply. I haven't seen Ted since he left. Frankly, I was glad to see the back of him. My whole body tensed. Tingles ran through my legs and arms. Fear was gripping me. I must try to sound calm at all costs.

'Joe do not even try to pull the wool over my eyes. It all stacks up: you attack Ted, and then you being so desperate to buy my house. I could go to the police with my suspicions, and they would take it seriously. All the evidence points to you.'

'Joan, why don't you get to the point and say what it is you expect me to do?'

Joan was almost shouting down the line. 'You owe me, you owe my mother, and you owe Ted. If you want me to stay quiet, so you can get on with your family life,' she said, sneeringly, 'then I want money; £50,000 buys my silence, and you will never hear from me again.'

'That's a rather large amount of money for something I didn't do. I could take my chances with the police.'

'That's your choice, Joe Metcalf, but the press will have a field day, and the scandal will follow you. I'm sure the reporter at the Express would love to hear my story; and my story will be the complete truth. People will decide for themselves, and you'll be ruined.' Her voice held a clear threat. This woman means business.

'This is a lot to take in; I need time to think about it. How can I contact you?'

'You can't,' she said with a fierce tone. 'At the moment this is between you and me. I haven't told anyone yet, but I will if I have to go to the police and the newspaper. 'I'll call you at the same time tomorrow. 'You have today to decide if this stays between me and you; and I don't care which option you take. Either way, I *will* get retribution.'

The line went abruptly dead. Nausea was building. I rushed to the toilet and threw up. I was like a cat on a hot tin roof; I didn't know what to do or which way to turn. I had a thought and grabbed the pile of telephone directories off the bookshelf. I found the one for the York area and threw the others on the floor. I knew Joan's married name was Turner, so I combed through the pages for anyone with the name Turner in the York area. I had no idea what they called her husband, but he had died a few years ago, so hopefully the listing would be under her name. I found three S Turners in the area. I had to find out where she lived, and I had no time to spare, so I jotted down the addresses and made a call. I thumped my chest in frustration; this damn COPD has wrecked my body. Asking for help is the last thing I want to do. He is loyal, so he will do what I ask, but I hate involving him. If this comes back to bite, then I want it to be on my head only.

Our conversation was tense, but he was a good lad, so he didn't hesitate in following my instructions. We would drive to York and check out the addresses I had found.

'Do you think you will be okay driving all that way? The lad asked looking concerned.

'Of course,' I snarled, 'plus I have no choice. This needs to be done.'

'Let me get your tablets and inhaler, just in case.' He hurriedly grabbed everything I would need. We didn't have much time.

The traffic on the A64 was horrendous as usual. Why a major road like this was always congested is beyond me. By the time we reached the first address, it was almost 3:00 pm. We sat in the car opposite a neat semi with a bright yellow door. We waited, pretending to look at a map in case we looked suspicious. Around 3:30 pm, a young woman walked up the drive holding hands with two young children in school uniform. I wondered whether to wait longer, but my intuition told me this wasn't the right address. I could be wrong because these children could be Joan's grandchildren. Time wasn't on my side, so I put the car in gear and drove to the next address; we could come back to this later if necessary. The next address was a smart detached house with two Audis parked in the driveway. Somehow, I couldn't envision Joan in an Audi, but we waited around in case. At about 5:30 pm, a man drove his car up behind the other cars in the drive. It was yet another Audi. The man who stepped out was Asian in appearance. Again, intuition told me this wasn't her house either. The third house we drove to was a neat bungalow on a nice tree-lined avenue. It was now starting to get dark with the autumn night's drawing in early. A light was on in the front room, and I could see someone moving around. I wasn't sure if it were her, but I had a good feeling it could be. We waited and watched, the tension growing in me; time was slipping away, soon everyone would be settling down for the evening. Then it would become almost impossible to identify her house. A woman appeared at the window and reached up to close the curtains. It had been a few years since I'd seen her, but it was her all right. She looked even more like Mrs Mallinson now that her hair was grey.

'That's her,' I said. 'No doubt, she is her mother's spitting image.' The lad looked nervous but asked, 'What do you want me to do?' I suggested we wait until the streets were quieter before making any moves.

As the night descended, enveloping the street in darkness except for a few dimly lit streetlamps, we made our plans.

'You stay here, he said, 'I'll go and scout around and see what I can learn.'

He double-checked that the street was quiet before plucking up courage to get out of the car. He crossed over the road, and I soon lost sight of him. Feeling breathless, I reached for my inhaler and took three sharp puffs. I then popped one of my bronchodilator tablets in my mouth and tried to steady my breathing. He returned, filling the car with cold air and rubbing his hands to warm himself.

'I've had a good look, well as much as I could see in the dark. Joan luckily doesn't have a security light, so I'm quite confident that no one saw me. There were no cars, but there's a garage, so there could be one in there. The entrance to the kitchen is at the side. I tried the door, but it was locked.'

I gave him a reproachful look. 'Don't worry, I was careful not to make a sound. Outside the door was a small milk bottle holder, you know, the type with a lid on it to keep the birds off the milk. Two empty bottles were in there waiting to be collected, so we can safely guess she gets her milk delivered.' I nodded in agreement. 'I had a quick look around the back of the house. Up against the side of the garage were two bins. So, I shuffled through each bin, grabbing hold of anything that felt like paper.' He unzipped his jacket to reveal a pile of paper rubbish.

'Let's get away from here and find somewhere quiet to have a look at those.' I checked the map, 'there's a park around the corner, according to this. I'll drive there and let's see if we can find a secluded place to park.'

The lad nodded. We drove a few hundred yards before coming to a deserted dirt road at the side of the park. We pulled over and switched on the interior light. We examined the array of rubbish he had grabbed. There were a couple of newspapers, some circulars, and an electric bill.

'Mrs Joan Turner, Bingo, we have found her,' I said, patting the lad on the arm.

Joan wasn't as clever as she thought she was. A dark thought overcame me, 'Joan Turner had to go, and she needed to go before she told anyone else.'

The next day, Joan rang me at 10:00 am on the dot. 'Right, what is it to be, your reputation or the money?'

'How can I be sure you haven't spoken to anyone else about this? I asked.'

'You will have to take my word for it, won't you?' she said, sounding cocksure of herself.'

'£50,000 is a lot of money; how do I know you won't take the cash and then go to the police?'

'For a man of your means, Joe Metcalf, you are not very bright, are you? If I take your money and then go to the police, I would be arrested for blackmail. No one else suspects you except me, and that money will buy my silence. I'm a God-fearing woman, and I swear on the Bible, I shan't tell a soul.'

'I didn't know God-fearing women engaged in blackmail,' I said with a sarcastic tone.

'Well, needs must. I have things I want to do and places I want to see. Life is getting shorter by the minute, but your hush money will make my bucket list a reality.' Laughter evident in her voice.

'And what's to stop you from coming back for more in the future?'

Joan laughed, 'I'll be too busy cruising around the world with your blood money. Think yourself lucky that I'm not a greedy woman. £50,000 is more than enough to see my days out.'

'Okay, I will pay you, but this is not an admission of guilt; I only want to protect my family from any scandal.'

'Sure,' she said with a smug laugh.

'We will need to meet because I will be giving it to you in cash. I can't risk a cheque going through the bank; Molly would pick up on it. I will have to call in some favours to get the cash under the radar. It will take me a couple of weeks to pull it all together.'

'Okay then, two weeks it is. I'll call you on the 25th, and it better be ready by then. I'll give you the name of a café, but it will be in York, so you will have to come here; I'm not chasing after you.'

The call ended without warning. A sinister idea ran through my head, but I was not sure whether it would work.

Chapter 29 Joe 1970

The next two weeks I thought of nothing else; I would be naive to trust the word of an angry and greedy woman. There would be nothing to stop her from coming back for more or from telling someone. I wouldn't be able to rest; I'd be constantly on edge, dreading every knock at the door and every phone call. I have never considered myself a bad man; Ted Mallinson had got away with Jane's murder; he deserved to die. If Joan really cared about Ted, she would have gone straight to the police. Instead, she chose to exploit the situation through greed and selfishness. I was angry. Why should she gain from Ted's death. if I pay her, it will be like Jane paying for the murderous actions of Ted Mallinson. I owed it to Jane to make sure Ted paid for his evil actions. And now I owe it to Jane to make sure Joan doesn't profit from her death. Joan and Ted were alike, both selfish and uncaring people. Joan has to go!

Joan phoned bang on time, as I knew she would.

'So, this is D-Day for you, Joe Metcalf; have you got the money or am I going to the police?'

'I have your money, but I want more than reassurances from you.'

'What do you mean my word is my honour and it is all I have to give?' she said with indignation.

'Not quite. This is what I want you to do. You will write a letter to the police telling them that Ted used to steal money off your mother and make her life hell with his gambling and heavy drinking. Tell them you suspect she must have hit him over the head in a fit of rage and unintentionally killed him.'

'Not a chance, I'm not accusing my own mother of murder.' She sounded outraged at the idea.

'You won't be accusing her; you are only voicing your suspicions. The police would never be able to prove she did it. All you will be doing is helping them look in the opposite direction, away from me and away from my family.'

'I won't do it; my mum was a good woman. I won't tarnish her name, so our deal's off.

'Wait, don't be so hasty. I have a briefcase in front of me holding £80,000 in cash. This money is yours if you do what I ask.'

There was a deathly silence, but I could hear her breathing. She finally spoke, her voice filled with uncertainty. 'I'm not sure…. I need time to process this…. I'll call you back when I've had time to think.'

The phone went dead without warning. I poured myself a large glass of whisky and waited. Thirty minutes later, she called back.

'Okay, I'll do it.'

'I'm glad you appreciated my situation, Joan. Your word I'm sure is honest and good, but I need a little more to be able to sleep easily at night. The letter will become your story; it is what you will tell everyone who asks you. Remember it's only suspicion.'

'Okay, but £80,000, right?'

'Yes, I will hand it over after I have read the letter. Do not seal the envelope. I will take it from you, and I will post it myself.

'You do not trust me, do you? But you should remember that I am doing you a favour by saving you from jail.'

'Then everything is agreed; where shall we meet?'

'I'll meet you at the café in Roundtree Park. Make sure you sit outside. I'll be there tomorrow at 2:30 pm; the café is quieter at that time. Don't be late and don't try to trick me, as you know Joe; I hold all the cards. I felt so angry towards Joan, the arrogance and audacity of the woman. How could anyone use a child's death to extract money from someone? She was truly an evil woman, and she deserved what was coming to her.

A plan had formed in my head. It would be dangerous, but if I pulled it off, then all my troubles would be over. Our groundsman keeps cyanide in his shed; he uses it to control our rat problem in the tunnels that run under the house. I have a box full of syringes that I use for treating small areas of woodworm. I would fill a syringe with the cyanide and slip it into her drink.

I wasn't sure I'd be able to make the walk from the park entrance to the café, so the lad lifted my electric wheelchair into the back of the Land Rover. We arrived at the café 15 minutes early. I took the first table I came to, and he took a seat a little further away. I ordered a pot of tea for two. The guy behind the counter said, 'we only do mugs.' 'Okay, I'll have 2 mugs of black tea with a small jug of milk on the side, please.' The man tutted and poured the teas into polystyrene cups and a third cup half full of milk. 'Take a seat, I'll bring them over.' As he turned his back to return to the café, I felt in my pocket for the syringe. Joan arrived as I was slipping it back into my pocket.

'I've ordered tea,' I said, my voice trembling.

'I'm not here to take tea with you; I'm only here for the money.' She stood hovering over me.

'Sit down first and try to act normal.' I hissed at her. 'Here is the money.' I said, tapping the large paper bag on my knee.

'You're not looking too good, Joe Metcalf; what's with the wheelchair?'

'COPD! Now give me the letter.'

She handed me the letter and I took it out and read it. She had kept her word and had simply expressed her suspicions of her mother. I saw her pour some milk into her cup, then put it to her lips and take a sip.

'Let's head over towards the park exit; as soon as we pass that large oak tree, I will discreetly pass you this package, and then we can both go our own way. Bring your tea or it will look strange if we leave them.'

As we got up from the table, I deliberately knocked over the cup of milk. I didn't want to risk it being served to anyone else.

'Walk slowly and try to look casual, like a regular couple of friends out for a stroll in the park.'

She looked down at me, 'Do you need pushing?'

'No, it's electric; I can do it myself.'

'Fancy,' she said, raising her eyebrows.

We set off on the path in the direction of the tree. The path wound around the tree's large trunk. I lifted the package like I was going to give it to her, but then I stopped short of handing it over. I raised my cup to my lips.

'It's only tea, but we should still toast our agreement.' She followed suit. 'Good luck to you, Joan, and no hard feelings,' laughing, she said, 'I'm happy to drink to no hard feelings.'

She raised the mug triumphantly and then drank the remainder of her tea before grabbing the package out of my hands. As she walked away, I kept my distance, but I could see the lad was following her. I wasn't sure how long it would take for the poison to take effect. She walked a little way and then I saw her slump down onto a bench. The lad moved swiftly and sat by her side, and I rode over and joined them. 'Are you okay, Joan?' I said with mock concern. She couldn't speak and she was struggling to breathe. The lad put his arm around her shoulder and pulled her into him. I leaned forward to wipe the dribble from her mouth. I could smell the sweet almond of the cyanide on her breath, which was now coming in long rasps, and then she went still and floppy. He held her tight. If anyone saw them, they'd think they were a couple enjoying the late autumn sun. I got out of my chair and hid it behind the bench before sitting down at the opposite side of Joan. The lad looked away every time someone passed, and I pretended to be reading a newspaper, effectively hiding my face.

Five hours we sat there with her lifeless body wedged between the two of us. It had become dark, so I considered now was the safest time to make our move. I looked around one more time to make sure that no one was about, and then I said, 'let's go.' He knelt and positioned her over his shoulder. Her small body, limp and lifeless, hung from him like a rag doll. We headed for the boating lake, and then I nodded at him. He heaved her forward and she landed in the water with a loud splash. I was horrified to see her floating away towards the centre of the lake. Please, please Lord, make her sink, I silently prayed. It was dark and no one was around. The moonlight was glistening on her body like a heavenly light leading the way for her soul. After what seemed like an eternity, she finally sank below the surface. Exhausted, we returned to the car. I had both the letter and the money. I would post the letter in the first post box we drove past. I hoped and prayed that her body wouldn't be discovered too soon.

As we drove away from the scene, the silence between us was palpable. I glanced in the rearview mirror, the image of what we had left behind still etched in my mind. I turned to the lad, his eyes fixed on the road ahead. 'We will never speak about this again.' My words were firm, but gentle. He nodded solemnly, his serious expression a testament to the gravity of the situation. I knew I could trust him, that he would never utter a word of this. The weight of our actions hung in the air as the car chugged its was home. We both knew we would carry this heavy burden with us for the rest of our lives.

I never heard anything more about Joan. If someone had found her body, it never made the national news. A body found in a lake obviously wasn't as newsworthy as the growing knife crime, trouble between the mods and the rockers, or the miners' strike. Poor Joan was gone like she had never existed, and good riddance to her.

Chapter 30 Sergeant Smith 1970

In 1970 Low Dean was only a small village. Sergeant John Smith had trod the beat of this village for over 10 years, like his father had trod these streets for 25 years before him. He knew the villagers well and had his ear to the ground. Everything that happened in and around the village was analysed by the clientele at the Dog and Gun, and rumour about the Calder Road bodies was rife. The police had set up an incident room in the local community centre, and many of the villagers had come forward with their theories of who the bodies belonged to. The remains had been pulled from the rubble that had been dumped in a landfill. So, there was no way of identifying which houses the remains had come from. But that didn't stop the locals speculating on who did what to whom. People guessed that the baby could have been an unwanted pregnancy of one of the local lasses who lived on Calder Road. People thought one body belonged to George Kellet. His wife had reported to the police that he had fallen off a cliff and had been washed away by the sea at Scarborough. Ironically, Mrs Kellet moved to a pretty apartment in Scarborough after collecting his life insurance. The third body had been in the ground for a shorter time than the others, so it was easier to identify.

Sergeant Smith leaned back in his chair, his eyes scanning the circle of local men gathered around the worn, wooden table. The dim lighting of the taproom casting dark shadows over their weathered faces. Having listened intently to their theories, he raised his head, his young features set in a thoughtful expression.

'I can't help but feel guilty. It was my father who had handled the case back then. It was 1966 when Mrs Mallinson's daughter, Joan, reported Ted missing. Mrs Mallinson was dying, and she begged her daughter to try to find Ted so she could say her goodbyes. His disappearance was never taken seriously at the time. Everyone knew what Ted was like, so my father dismissed her concerns and assumed he was off somewhere up to no good. If he had investigated his disappearance at the time, who knows, they might have caught the killer.'

Old Jake spoke first. 'Nay, don't blame your father, John; any of us would have thought the same thing.' The others agreed, and Jake bought a round of drinks to lighten the atmosphere.

'So,' said Jake, 'what do you know so far?'

'We can't identify where the baby came from because it's been in the ground too long. The coroner said there was little chance of getting any DNA off the body. Unless the woman comes forward, it will have to remain a mystery. The second body again has been in the ground for over 40 years. There might be speculation about who it was, but we would never be able to prove it. And then of course there's Ted's body. He had only been in the ground for approximately 9 years, so we were able to check his dental records, and we got a match. In fact, it was his sister Joan who gave us the lead. She had telephoned me asking me to check if the body was Ted's.'

Frank, one of the regulars said, that when he heard the news about Ted's body being found, he suspected it was Ted's mother who had killed him. He thought she had probably had enough of bankrolling his gambling addiction and had taken drastic measures to cut her losses. Frank's theory wasn't entirely far-fetched, given the whispers about Ted's deepening debt. It was no secret that Ted's addiction had been spiralling out of control. Some said they had seen him placing bet after bet in the local Betting Office before leaving with empty pockets. It was just a matter of time before his mother would lose her patience.

'Well, it's strange you should say that. Last week I received a letter from Joan, and she thinks the same thing. Ted was a proper little loser, so I guess that is a possibility,' said Sergeant Smith, shaking his head in disbelief. 'We won't ever be able to prove it was her, so for the foreseeable future, the case will remain open.'

Frank continued. 'And what's this about the police setting up a 'crisis counselling centre for residents?' he said, raising both hands and signing question marks with his fingers. 'It all happened years ago. It's not like we still have a murderer in our midst. I can't understand these people who are blaming the police and protesting outside the station.'

Jake cut in. 'It's all the inbreeding in this village. Half the residents are bonkers.' Everyone laughed. 'My round,' said Sergeant Smith.

Chapter 31 Joe 1975

1975. I've been bedridden now for four weeks. I haven't been able to see Ivy, but I have sneaked a few telephone conversations between us. I know I will die soon, and it breaks my heart that I won't be able to hug Ivy and Christine before I go. I can't take this secret to the grave; I must tell someone, but not Ivy; I have burdened her enough. I ring the bell at the side of my bed, and Molly comes to see what I want.

'Molly, sit down, there's something I need to tell you. When I've gone, Mr Franklin will give you an envelope. It contains a bank account that you know nothing about. Don't worry, it's in my name, so you will be able to get hold of what's in there easily enough.'

'Joe, why would you have a separate account? I thought we kept all the finances transparent.'

'It was for emergencies; in case I needed to get hold of money quickly.' I wasn't sounding at all convincing, and Molly didn't look impressed one bit. 'Anyway, I did need it. I needed to pay a blackmailer.'

'Christ, Joe, you paid a blackmailer. Why on earth don't I know anything about this?

'Well, technically, I didn't pay them, and I put the money back. It's just that when you see the account, it will show money coming out and then money going back in again.'

'How much are we talking about?'

'The amount I took out and put back in was £80,000, but there's a nice round £100,000 in there.'

'I'm annoyed you felt it necessary to have a separate account. But that's the last thing I'm worrying about now. You had better start at the beginning and tell me about this blackmailer.'

Molly paced the bedroom floor, her face red as she tried to contain her anger.

'Do you remember Ted Mallinson?' I asked, knowing full well that she would.

'Yes, of course I do.'

'The blackmailer was Joan Turner, Ted Mallinson's sister.'

'Why on earth would she be trying to blackmail you?'

'She got it into her stupid head that I had killed Ted.'

'And did you?' She looked at me with an accusing expression, as if she thought it could be true.

'Of course not.'

'Then you had better try to convince me otherwise. Tell me what she wanted and why she thought you had done it.'

'She had seen the article in the paper about the discovery of the bodies on Calder Road. She made enquiries with the police, and it turned out that one of the bodies was Ted's. She'd got it into her head that the only reason I wanted to buy the house was to conceal the body.'

'I wondered why you wanted that scruffy little house. You bastard Joe Metcalf, you fucking did it, didn't you?'

'Keep your voice down; does it matter if it was me or someone else? The world was a better place without him,' I retorted angrily.

Molly was pacing even faster now. Her arms flying in the air with indignation. 'Oh, please carry on, I can't wait to hear the rest of this.' Her sarcasm was undeniably hanging in the air.

'She was threatening to go to the police and the bloody newspapers and tell them she suspected me. That kind of scandal would have ruined us. I did what I thought was best at the time.'

'And what exactly did you do? You didn't pay her, so how did you get her off your back?'

'I killed her.' I let the statement hang there, giving Molly time to adjust to the news.

She sat on the end of the bed with her head in her hands. She looked up a few times but was unable to speak. She took out a hanky and blew her nose. 'You fucking stupid bastard,' she threw at me before storming out of the room.

It was several hours later before Molly returned with a tray of food. 'Your dinner,' she said, almost throwing it down on my lap.

'Molly, please don't go. I need to tell you everything that happened.'

She stood leaning against the wall, unable to look at me. I told her all about meeting her in the park, poisoning her drink and throwing her body in the boating lake. 'I've never heard anything since. I don't know if her body is still there or whether they found her and put it down to an accident.'

'Joe, there's only one thing I want to know. Is this going to come back and bite us?

'No, it was five years ago. No one will ever know; I promise you.'

'Why, Joe, why not just pay her? Why murder her?'

'She was a greedy, evil cow, like her brother. They both got what they deserved. I would never have been able to trust her. Her type keeps coming back and bleeding you dry.'

'Okay, you have said what you have said, and we will talk about it no more. I wish you had kept it to yourself.'

'I needed to get it off my chest; I want to be honest before I meet my maker. Surely you can understand that.'

'Oh, so it's all right, as long as your conscience is clear, but you are happy to saddle me with it. I hope you burn in hell.'

I tried to call after her, but she was out of the door in a shot. I knew that would be the last of it; Molly would never want me to talk about it again. I felt guilty, but there are some things you can't take to your grave.

Chapter 32 Caroline 2000 session 3

It was May 2000. I had received a call from Jess asking if I could see her again. I knew I shouldn't have said yes, but my curiosity was overpowering me. And more than that, I had achieved something quite spectacular with Jess. The past life regression had worked, and Jess was proof that we have lived before; that we do come back again in the future. It was a mixture of pride and the feeling I was on the verge of a new discovery that was driving me forward. This was my calling, a path of discovery that I needed to follow. During the past two weeks, I have been getting lots of requests from people for past life regression. Somehow word had got out that I was some kind of expert in this field.

Jess arrived at 4.30 pm after my earlier clients had all been seen.

'Hi Caroline, thank you for seeing me again. I hope you don't mind, but I can't get it out of my head that there's something unfinished, something I need to learn.'

'You're very welcome, Jess; I'm more than happy to take you through the process again. Intuition is a powerful driver, so you must go along with it. Whatever you get from this experience will be what you need. What have you learnt since I last saw you?'

'Harold has been amazing. Mr and Mrs Stevenson had a daughter called Jane who had been killed in a train accident. They were a wealthy family who lived in a grand house in Bradbury. She was only eleven when she died. Harold showed me a newspaper article from the time. The death was originally viewed as suspicious circumstances. It was believed that Jane was not the type of girl to go wandering onto the train track because she was too sensible and old enough to be aware of the dangers. One man in particular, a local man called Edward Mallinson, was being questioned by the police. Her death still carries an open verdict because they couldn't prove his guilt.'

'So, there was no closure for her family and the people who loved her. Given the circumstances, I can fully understand you feeling like there's something unsaid. It seems there's more to learn. I hope during this session you get the answers that you need. I've been thinking about it a lot since you asked to see me again. I have an idea, and I want to know how you feel about it.

'Go ahead, I'm listening,' said Jess, leaning forward and inching her chair a little closer.

'My idea is that when you have gone back and you can see Jane, I then ask you to go inside her and look and experience everything through her eyes. I will hold you in time before the train hits her. This way, you will learn the precise circumstances of how the tragedy happened. I will not let you experience the accident itself; that would be counterproductive and potentially harmful.'

'Knowing what caused her death might give me the closure I'm looking for. So, yes, I'm willing to give it a try.' She took a deep breath and released it slowly in a faint whistle. 'Caroline, I trust you and I'm willing to follow your lead. Yes, I'm a little nervous, but this is something I want to do.' She stood up and put her arms around me. 'Thank you for everything you have done so far.' She held that hug like a little child hanging onto her mother for comfort and reassurance.

I guided Jess back in our usual way, presupposing that she could communicate with me at all times and describe her journey as she went back in time.

'I'm back,' she said in a low voice. I'm looking through the railings and I can see Jane and Jo Jo together. Jane has a bright smile on her face.... Her mum and dad are there.... They are stood next to the handsome black car.... Her mum is climbing into the car, and her father has turned, and he is heading towards the building.' She paused for a few moments and then said, 'yes, he's gone inside.'

'Focus your attention on Jane; is she still looking happy?' I asked.

'Oh yes, she looks overjoyed at something; she is holding up a large doll. Oh, I see now it is a puppet with lots of strings.'

Jane was happy, so I considered this a good time for Jess to integrate with her.

'Float above, high into the sky and move to a position directly above Jane. Look down and see her there below you; she is happy and relaxed. Take a moment to feel that love and happiness inside you.... Now slowly descend and feel the love as you merge with Jane.... You and she have become one and you can see through her eyes, and you can feel what she feels. Let me know when you have done that?'

I waited with bated breath as I watched her face go through the emotions of struggle. Then she started to smile, and there was a glow about her that I can only describe as pure joy and serenity.

'Jane, describe to me what you see and how you are feeling?' I used the name Jane, presupposing that she had merged into her and was no longer in the observer position.

'I'm so happy, I could cry. Jojo has made me a Jiminy Cricket puppet. He knew how much I wanted one to go with the Pinocchio puppet he made me. I love Jojo so much; he is my best friend and the bestest person in the whole world.' Her voice had gone childlike, and Jess no longer sounded like herself.

'I lean over and give him a big hug and he kisses me on the top of my head like he always does…. We are sat on a blanket; it's our favourite spot overlooking the railway line and across from the poppy field…. We love this spot because we can wave at the train as it goes by, and the driver will blow his horn.' She giggles, becoming even more childlike.

'I've got sandwiches and cake for us. Jojo's favourite dripping sandwiches. Martha made it from the fat when we had a lamb dinner. We never eat dripping at home, but Mum tells Martha, our cook, to save it for Jojo. I take a bite of JoJo's sandwich, but I spit it out because I don't like it. Urgh! I say, 'How can you eat that?'

'I'm so happy sitting here with Jojo and my beautiful Jiminy Cricket; I wish this day could last forever…. I hear my dad calling Jojo; he wants him to join him in the office.'

'I won't be long,' says Jojo, planting another kiss on my head. 'And don't you go eating my cake, missy,' he adds.

'Jojo is only teasing me; he knows I wouldn't eat his cake.... One of the joiners, Ted, comes over to me and asks me what I've got, pointing to my puppet.'

Jane's voice starts to sound angry. 'I don't like Ted; he is always mean to me. He calls me 'a stuck-up madam' and then he grabs Jiminy Cricket from me.... I am so angry, how dare he.... 'Give it back!' I shout or I'll tell on you.' Ted is holding the puppet as high as he can and I'm jumping to try to reach it.... He starts sliding down the embankment and is shouting 'come and get it.' I'm furious with him, 'Give it back.' I scream again as I slide down the embankment after him. He is laughing at me and I'm trying hard not to cry. I chase after him along the side of the railway lines.... I hate Ted. I shout, 'you are a dirty little scoundrel, Ted Mallinson, and I'm going to tell my dad to sack you.'

'Will you now, brat,' he shouts, 'then fuck you and fuck your stupid puppet.' He has thrown my puppet on the railway line before turning and running away.

My eyes are full of tears, and I can hardly see. I hope Jiminy Cricket isn't broken. I must get him back. I don't want Jojo to be cross with me for losing him.

Jess has tears running down her face and she is looking very distressed, so I decide it's time to bring her back. I fear if I wait any longer, it will be too late.

'Jess, listen to my voice and follow my voice as you float back up high into the sky. See a still frozen scene below you. Float to a position where you feel safe and let me know when you have done that?' I get a finger signal and a faint yes. 'Now turn to the past and float back to the time when Jojo and Jane are sat on the blanket, and they are both happy. Let me know when you have done that?'

'I'm back; I see them laughing.'

'Float back down so you are stood a few feet away from Jojo and Jane. Feel your feet firmly on the ground.... smell the air.... feel the heat from the sun on your body.... Turn to look at Jane.... take her hand.... Is there anything you want to say to her?' I could see that Jess was looking down and accessing her emotions; then she looked up and spoke in a gentle voice.

'Remember, Jane, that you are loved; your parents love you, and Jojo loves you, and now I love you. You need to know that it wasn't your fault; you were trying to save something you treasured. After you had gone, your loved ones continued to carry your memory with them; you were never forgotten. Now you and I are one, and I carry your joy with me. Jane, I don't want to say goodbye because you are a part of me now that lives on. Just know that in the future you go on to have a good life, a life surrounded by love. Be happy, little one, and keep the joy in your heart.'

The heartfelt message Jess gave to Jane impressed me. This Yorkshire lass was mature and caring, and I felt proud of her.

'Now Jess, turn and face Jojo. Put your arms around Jojo and reassure him that Jane already knows it wasn't his fault.... Tell him that Jane is living a good and happy life.... Tell him you will prove it to him.... Now in a moment I am going to give you some information that might seem strange. I want you to accept this information without judgement and to relay this to Jojo as if you know this to be true. Take his hand and together float up above your current position on the timeline. As you look below, you can see two timelines, one is yours and the other is Jojo's. Now tell Jojo that very soon, you are going to take him on a journey into his future. Tell him that along the way he will experience many events. From leaving school and starting work…. to taking a wife and having children…. Tell him to connect with that love once again, the love he felt for his friend Jane…. and to carry the essence of her with him on this journey…. Tell him to let go of the guilt he felt over Jane's death, reassure him that it wasn't his fault…. Tell him to step forward now having those experiences and coming forward to a place where the essence of Jane is at its strongest.

Ask him to let you know when he has arrived…. 'Yes.' Now look down at that event and ask him to show you what he is seeing? … 'It's a child being born.' Tell him that this child is proof that Jane lives on. Tell him, if he is happy for you to do so, you will leave him here so he can once again experience his life in the knowledge that Jane is safe and happy.

'He says yes.'

'Now once more put your arms around him and imagine you are both being bathed in a healing white light. Allow the energy from the light to permeate every cell in your body…. Now it is time to say goodbye…. You watch as the image of Jojo fades away…. Turn to face your future and travel back along your own timeline and back to the here and now…. See yourself sitting in this chair, hear my voice getting louder, feel your eyes starting to flicker. Open your eyes. Welcome back.'

I leave Jess to process her thoughts while I make us both a cup of tea. I remain quiet and wait for her to speak, allowing time for her to gather her thoughts.

'That was beautiful. I feel so peaceful. That little girl was so full of love and joy. I could feel it all around her. She and Jojo were close. It's so sad she had to leave him,' Jess said, shaking her head.

'But did she leave him? Isn't she here now? He got to experience your birth once again. I believe that Jojo knew in his heart that Jane had come back to him. Your birth would have given him closure. He could allow himself to let go of the guilt of not protecting her, because you are here now.'

'It was all that lad's fault,' she said, sounding angry. 'It was him, Caroline, the one the newspaper said was being interviewed. If he hadn't thrown her puppet onto the railway line, then she would still be here and living a wonderful life.'

'But she is living a wonderful life. You will carry her with you forever.'

'Yes, it's strange, but I can feel her, or at least, I feel her love and joy for life.'

'And do you feel you got the answers and closure you were looking for?'

'I'm not sure; there is something that is puzzling me. I understand the need for him to let go of the guilt around Jane. But what about the guilt he must have felt in later life, when he had to keep my mother a secret from the rest of his family?'

'I think I know the answer to that, but I'm not going to influence you by expressing my thoughts. Once you discuss this with your mother, the answer will come to you.'

'One more question: How can you be sure he knew Jane was in me when I was born?'

'Because Jane is in his 'spirit circle', he will always find her in the many lives he goes on to have.'

Jess looks puzzled but accepts this.

'Caroline, I know this is a big question: where is our soul? What part of us is it that lives on?'

'Nobody knows, so we can only theorise. Let me ask you a question: where in your body do you feel your soul? Move your hand now to where you think it is?' Jess puts her hand on her heart.

'Yes, that's where we would expect it to be because our soul is responsible for our feelings. We say things like, 'I love you with all my heart' or 'I've put my heart and soul into this' or 'follow your heart.' But if we had a heart transplant, our thoughts, likes, dislikes, prejudices, loves, wouldn't change. So, the soul can't be the heart. When the soul leaves the body, it does so in the form of an intelligent energy. So, please don't quote me on this, but my theory would be that it's in the brain. Our brains are like computers, full of electrical impulses, firing neurons in different directions.' I fire my hands like I have two guns shooting in different directions. 'These are sending electrical and chemical signals to each other. These electrical impulses coordinate our behaviour, our thoughts, our sensations, and our emotions.

'Do you think everyone has lived before?'

'No, because we must consider the growth in population. So, some souls must be new. Now again, don't quote me, but energy, as far as I know, can't be destroyed, but it can be transformed. So maybe when our soul leaves the body, it can transform and multiply, thus creating new souls.'

'Yes, that makes sense. That means when you do this work with other people, there's no guarantee they will have a past life to experience.'

'That's true. And of course, people will come to me expecting an experience, and then when it doesn't work, they will blame me and say I'm a fraud.' I laugh at the irony. 'Talking about other people coming for past life regression, I think I owe you, my gratitude. I have got a lot of new clients recently, so I guess you must have passed my details on to your customers at the salon.'

'Oh, that will be because of my online journal. A friend helped me set up a blog to talk about my journey and to connect with others who believe they have lived before. There's been an amazing amount of interest, so of course I have posted your details. That's fantastic if you are getting work because of it.'

'A blog, that's interesting. Will you be continuing with it?

'Yes, it's a captivating subject. I will email you the link. There are people on there who have had a similar experience to me, but there are few who have had the help of a hypnotherapist to help them see their past. I'm also able to promote the work of the Historical Society. It's important to understand the context of your past life; what it was like back then, how people lived, and the mindset at the time.'

I was almost lost for words. This bright, intelligent woman was writing her story and, without knowing it, she was also writing my story, the story of my family. Fumbling for words, I said, 'When I said, don't quote me, will you?'

'No,' she said, hesitating, 'not everything. I'll put the bit in about new souls, so people know they might not necessarily have a past life, and that this could be their first life.'

'And will that be your next chapter in your journal?'

'Partly. I'll write up today's session in my journal and then I will continue to write about my family and Jane's family. I'm learning more each day from both Grandma Ivy and Harold. Please read my blog if you get the time, and feel free to contribute to it.'

'Thank you, I will definitely have a look.' I pass Jess her coat, and she hugs me again. Jess walks towards the door. 'Do you want me to come again?' she turns and asks.

'As much as I will miss our sessions, Jess, I think this journey has come to an end.' Jess smiles and waves as she leaves.

I have no idea where this is going to lead, but I fear it's not going to be appreciated by my family. All the skeletons are coming out of the cupboard. The great Joseph Metcalf, master carpenter to royalty, has had a secret family for many years. The scandal will infuriate my mother. I could be in for a bumpy ride.

Chapter 33. Jess 2000

May 2000. When I arrive home, Mum is waiting for me with a bottle of white wine opened and ready. 'Tell me all,' she says, sounding excited. It took me some time to recount the process, everything I'd seen and the feelings I had when I was inside Jane. Then there was the journey with Grandad. My brain was hurting, and I still felt a little confused.

'Caroline thinks that Grandad knew I was Jane, or at least knew Jane's soul was in me. She seemed to suggest that my birth allowed him to let go of his guilt around her death and to move on.'

'Well, maybe it did. He was certainly besotted with you when you were little.'

'I wish he had lived longer; I would have loved to get to know him. I did have one question I didn't get answered, but Caroline said it would become clear when I had spoken to you about it.'

'What was it?'

'Didn't he feel guilty for keeping you a secret all those years? I'm annoyed; didn't he feel like he needed to apologise or make amends?'

My mum burst out laughing, 'what's so funny?' I said, feeling annoyed.

'you're the one who thinks Jane is in you, and you are my child. So, if Jane is part of Joe's spirit circle, then she was always going to come back to him somehow. Your grandad was a very poorly man for a long time, but he hung on until you were born, and he cherished you during your early years. I thought I would never have a child, but out of the blue, you came along.'

'Oh my god, I get it, so that's what she meant, yes of course, I can be so stupid! Grandad did make amends; he waited for Jane, and he brought her to you, a baby for you to love, and look at us now, 30 years later and you are still stuck with me.'

'You have given me so much happiness, my love; you have been the best daughter a mother could have.'

We both hugged each other with tears in our eyes. I broke away from Mum's embrace and went to the kitchen on the pretence of getting some nibbles. In reality, I needed time to consider what was running through my head.

'Why the hell am I looking for a place of my own when I'm exactly where I am meant to be?'

I grabbed some crisps from the cupboard and went back to Mum. I sat down and in a timid, childlike voice I said, 'I don't think I will take that flat; I think I will stay here with you if that's okay – pretty please.'

'Thank goodness for that,' Mum said with obvious relief. 'I like you being here; this is where you belong.'

'That's exactly what I was thinking. Cheers.' We raised a glass to each other, holding eye contact and feeling the love between us.

Chapter 34 Jess 2000

I was sitting at the dining table with my computer open. Mum came in and asked what I was up to.

'I'm looking at Bradbury Hall. Did you know it's got accommodation and it's available for anyone to book, not only golfers? How do you fancy a weekend break? It's £80 per room per night and that includes breakfast for two.'

'Oh, love, I wouldn't dare. Your grandma wouldn't approve.'

'Then don't tell her. It can be our secret.'

'I'm not sure. I always promised her I would stay away.'

'Please, Mum, I want to see where Jane lived, and I don't want to go on my own.'

'It would be okay if it were only Jane that had lived there, but as you now know, my dad's other family still live there.'

'So, they don't know you, do they? What harm can there be in having a look around? The photographs look beautiful. It will be a nice tranquil break and there are lots of woodlands around the house for us to walk in. I'll pay,' I added as an extra incentive.'

'Is the house open to the public?'

'Only the bar and the dining room, but still, it would be nice to get a feel for the place.'

'You will get me into trouble. If my mum found out, there would be hell to pay.'

Mum, you're a grown woman; you don't have to be scared of Grandma Ivy.'

'Well, I'll only agree to come if you promise not to tell her. If she asks where we are going, tell her we're off to Blackpool for the weekend.'

'Okay, I promise,' I said, blowing Mum a kiss.

As we entered the gates to Bradbury Hall, a long winding drive stretched out ahead. As we turned a corner, the house came into view. It was a large, imposing stone-built manor house, with broad stone steps leading up to the entrance, guarded by two enormous lion statues. Mullioned leaded windows were nearly obscured by the creeping ivy, which was in sharp contrast to the neatly manicured lawns.

My jealousy was hard to contain; I couldn't help but wonder what it would be like to live in such grandeur. We parked up and headed for the reception. A young woman in her mid-twenties, wearing a smart black skirt and a starched white blouse, greeted us with a smile. Her auburn hair was pulled into a high bun, giving her a professional look. I handed over our booking form and was promptly presented with the keys and the directions to the guest accommodation block. The room was smartly furnished, and our window overlooked the golf course. It was an idyllic setting, soothingly quiet except for the sound of the birds.

Mum switched on the kettle. 'Let's have a cuppa while we unpack, and then we can go and explore.' She spoke with the excitement of a child in her voice.

I couldn't draw my attention away from the golf course, which stretched out in front of me as far as the eye could see. 'Oh mum, it's stunning here. I don't think I've ever seen anywhere so perfect.'

With a map of the grounds, we set off to follow the path that flanks the golf course. Mum takes a deep breath, 'smell that, Jess.' Clean air and freshly cut grass filled our nostrils. 'It's a bit different from the car fumes and takeaways.' I laughed. The path leads us to a large lake. Bubbles and splashes on the surface of the water tell me it's well stocked with fish. A family of ducks sets out in a single line across the water. A squirrel darts across a lawn and into a nearby tree.

'Mum, if this gets any more perfect, I'm going to cry.'

'I must admit,' says Mum, looking gloomy. 'It's far grander than I had expected. I don't know exactly what I did expect, but whatever it was, this beats it.'

'I know what you mean. To me, it feels like stepping back in time to another era. I could imagine women in crinoline skirts and lace umbrellas strolling along, hoping to meet a beau.'

The path continued and swept back on itself, bringing us to the rear of the hall. Two boys in their early teens were playing at throwing a ball into a basketball hoop attached to the side of the house.

'I'm not sure we should be round here. This looks like it's private,' Mum said, looking timid.

'Don't be silly, Mum, we're only following the path. You worry too much.' I couldn't help but wonder if these boys were part of the family, perhaps my own young cousins.

'They look a bit posh,' said Mum, 'not unlike the young princes William and Harry.' I silently agreed. Their clothes were smart, and they were both fresh-faced. It was hard to imagine a family who originated from the terrace houses of Low Dean, residing in this grand setting, with all its trappings of wealth.

There was an array of cars parked in the gravel courtyard, a Mercedes, a Jaguar, and a couple of Land Rovers. 'Even the cars are posh,' whispered Mum. A tall man wearing Wellington boots and a waxed jacket stepped out of a side door. 'Your mum says you have to go in and get a shower and change before dinner,' he instructed the boys. They started pulling faces of frustration. 'Where are you going to, Dad?' one of the boys asked. 'I'm going to pick your cousin Matthew up from the station; he's down from Edinburgh for the weekend. 'Can we come with you?' the smallest boy asked. Their father looked at them, and without speaking, he pointed to the door. They followed his directions with obedience, even though their disappointment was clear.

The path continued round the side of the house. We both had to stop as the man drove his Land Rover out of the courtyard. He smiled and pipped his horn in gratitude for us stopping. We were about to move on when we saw another car headed our way. We waited for the car to pass.

'Mum, that woman in the car, it looks like Caroline.' Christine stared in the direction of the driver.

The woman got out of the car, but her back was turned away from us, so we couldn't get a good look. The woman opened the boot of her car and took out three shopping bags. As she closed the boot, I got a better look at her. 'It fucking is her,' I said, stepping forwards to confront her, but Mum pulled me back. 'Wait. You can't go charging in.'

An older woman came out of the side door, so we stooped down behind the low wall that surrounded the courtyard.

'Margaret, darling, do you need a hand?' 'No, it's okay, I've got it.' They both turned and walked into the house.

I turned to look at Mum. 'Mum, I tell you, it's her.'

Mum looked bewildered, 'but love, it can't be you heard the woman, she called her Margaret.'

I thought for a moment before saying, 'I don't care what she called her; I would recognise that voice anywhere.'

Mum took my arm, 'Look, let's get away from here, and then we can talk.'

We continued following the path in silence. We came to a woodland area that had a circular bench that bordered a large willow tree and sat down.

'Why had Caroline never mentioned that she knew the family? It doesn't make sense. That woman called her darling, so she's not delivering something; she is close to the family. I have shared everything with her; she knows all the details of my life. I mistakenly thought we had become close. But we obviously weren't close at all. She has lied to me, and I feel betrayed.'

'She was seeing you on a professional basis. Her code of conduct probably forbids sharing personal info.' Mum takes my hand and tries to console me.

'I feel there's more to it than that. There are things she doesn't want me to know.'

'Let's take a drive; we can find a nice restaurant, and tonight you can sleep on it. Tomorrow you can decide what you want to do.' I know that Mum is trying to distract me, but it's not working. Tonight, I'll be lucky if I sleep at all.

The next morning, I got up early and went outside to smoke a cigarette. Looking at the hall in all its splendour, I couldn't help but feel envious of the family living within its walls. Today I needed to find out what Caroline's connection was with this family. Was she one of them or was she a friend of the family? Either way, she had lied to me, and I needed to know why. I finished my cigarette and went back inside to wake Mum. I put the kettle on and the noise it made woke her up.

'Would you like a tea?' I said cheerily, not wanting her to see how I was really feeling.

Mum sat up in bed and I gave her the cup. We avoided talking about the event of yesterday. We planned to re-visit the woods before heading in for breakfast. If Mum knew what I had planned, I don't think I would have got her into the dining room.

The people we met at breakfast were either visitors or staff. The family obviously didn't get involved with the day-to-day running of the guests staying in the lodge. The breakfast was substantial. Cereal to start with, followed by a full English plus toast and jam. Mum said she was stuffed and wanted to go back to the room for a lie down before going out for the day.

I walked back as far as the accommodation block with Mum, and then I said, 'Oh no, I've left my purse on the table. I'll run back, and I'll see you in a bit.'

Mum went up to the room and I returned to the hall. Instead of using the main entrance to the dining hall, I went straight to the back of the house. The courtyard was empty apart from the parked cars. I took a few deep breaths and went up to the door and knocked loudly. An elderly woman wearing an apron opened the door.

'Is Caro...,' I broke off, 'I mean, is Margaret in, please?' 'Who will I say is calling?' the woman asked. 'I'm a friend of hers; my name is Sally.' I thought if I used my own name that she might not come to the door. 'I'll go and fetch her, one minute.'

I could feel myself starting to shiver. I wasn't sure if it was because of the cool morning air or whether it was my nerves. Caroline approached the door with a huge smile on her face until she saw that it was me.

'Jess, what are you doing here?' She now looked flustered.

'Shouldn't I be the one asking you that question?' I said, standing with my arms folded across my chest.

'Look, let me get my coat and we can go for a walk. I promise I will tell you everything.' She disappeared inside for a minute and came back out holding her coat. 'Come, follow me,' she said, setting off at a fast pace away from the entrance.

'I think you owe me an explanation. All this time I have been telling you about my past life, and you have never once mentioned that you knew the family.'

'I'm sorry. I didn't know how to tell you. By the time I realised there was a connection, I was in too deep. Please believe me, I have wanted to tell you, but the time has never seemed right. I would have told you in due course.'

'So, what is your connection here?' I was still being defensive, but I wanted to hear her out.

'Joseph Metcalf was my father.' She could see the shock on my face, so she took my hand. 'Please, Jess, I promise I was going to tell you, but I needed to speak to my family first. Your story has come as a shock to us all.'

'Oh, so they all know then.' Anger was creeping into my voice, no matter how hard I was trying to stay calm.

'Yes. You must believe me when I say that none of us knew you or your mother existed. This has come as a big shock to the family and especially my mother, as I'm sure you can appreciate. Look, we are all excited at having found you; please don't think we don't want you. But for my mother's sake, we need to manage this delicately.'

'When I was growing up, I always wanted a sister or cousins to play with. It was lonely being an only child.' All the emotion swelled to the surface, and my tears began to fall.

Caroline put her arms around me and hugged me tight. 'You have cousins now; in fact, you have quite a few,' she laughed. I swear, Jess, I was always going to tell you, but you have beaten me to it. We can be a family now, I promise you.'

We sat on the bench in front of the duck pond and held each other. There no longer seemed to be any need for words. As the sun glistened on the pond and the gentle breeze blew away my sorrow, I had a feeling that everything was going to be all right.

Chapter 35 Jess 2000

By the time Mum and I returned home, we had already decided that we would tell Grandma Ivy everything. I was happy and excited at having a new family to get to know, but Mum was apprehensive. She wasn't looking forward to Grandma's wrath.

'Look, Mum, it wasn't fair of Grandma to keep this from you all these years. You were an only child, like me. You could have had a family. Imagine you could have been spending weekends in that beautiful house with lots of children to play with.'

'You don't miss what you never had. I'm sixty years old now; I have had my family, and I have been contented with that. It feels too late to be getting to know a new family. To me, they are a set of strangers.' Mum sounded defensive.

'They are strangers now but give them a chance; they might turn out to be lovely people. Look at Caroline; she is the sweetest person I have ever met.'

'Don't you mean Margaret?'

'I don't know that I'll ever get used to calling her that.' I laughed. 'She doesn't look like a Margaret or a Maggie,' I say, frowning. 'But I will have to try because Caroline is her professional name, and now she is going to be my aunty. 'Your sister,' I say with emphasis, giving Mum a gentle shake of her shoulders. 'Cheer up and look at it as an adventure.'

Tuesday night we make plans to go over to Grandma's. We decide to tell her that it was me that went to stay at the Hall, to keep mum out of the firing line. I'm much stronger-willed than mum; I can take whatever grandma throws at me. I take two bottles of grandma's favourite Shiraz with me, hoping a couple of glasses might loosen her up. We sit in her lounge. She is watching a quiz programme on TV and getting annoyed with the contestants when they get the answers wrong. I pour the wine into three glasses, and she sips it with enthusiasm. We join in with the quiz and wait for it to finish before mum goes over and switches the TV off. Grandma looks up at us both and then turns to look directly at me. 'So, this isn't a social call then. What have you been up to now, Jess?' she inquired, her voice filled with accusation.

'I went to stay at Bradbury Hall at the weekend.'

'I thought I had asked you to stay away. I've told you that family has nothing to do with us.' Grandma said sneeringly.

'That's not exactly true, Grandma. That family are my mum's brothers and sisters, which makes them my aunties and uncles. I have a right to get to know them.'

'There are things about that family you don't want to know. Skeletons should be left in the cupboard.' She turned away grabbing her glass and topping it up.

'What on earth are you talking about,' I say, annoyed with her. They already know about Mum and me, so there's nothing to hide. Carol... I mean Margaret has told me that the family are accepting of the situation, and they will welcome us with open arms.' My voice was a little louder than intended.

Grandma turned to Mum. She was angry now and started shouting. 'Is this what you really want,

Christine? After all these years and all the promises, we made to Joe, are you going to betray him now?'

'This is not about me, Mum; it's about Jess. If she wants to get to know her family, because that's what they are, then I'm not going to stand in her way.' Mum crossed her arms and slumped back into the chair like an indignant teenager.

'And what about you, are you going to get to know them as well?' Grandma was still shouting at Mum.

'I don't care one way or the other. I've lived this long without them, so I don't expect we will become bosom buddies. But Jess is young, so it's different for her. There will likely be cousins her own age, and she has already formed a bond with Margaret.

'Seems like you have both made your minds up and what I want doesn't count.'

'Look, Grandma, we haven't even met them yet. So far, I've only spoken to Margaret. But from what she tells me, her sister and brothers are happy to meet me. Well, not only me, they want to meet all of us.'

'When is this going to happen? I guess you have made plans; otherwise, you wouldn't be telling me this now.'

'They have invited us up to the Hall, to meet them on Sunday at 2 pm. Mum has reluctantly agreed to go with me. You can come as well if you want.'

'Oh, you bet I will. It's time that Molly learned a few home truths.'

'Grandma, I don't want any trouble. If you come, you will have to promise to be nice to them.'

'I will be nice. I'm always nice. But I won't hold back. My relationship with Joe will be laid bare. I won't be ashamed to tell them how it was. I'm not being painted as some bit on the side. Joe and I were in love. If it wasn't for Molly popping out babies like a rabbit, then Joe would have left her and been with us. She deliberately had so many children to tie him down, and it wouldn't surprise me if some of them aren't Joe's.'

'Grandma, you can't go up there making accusations; it's not fair. I don't want you to ruin this for me.'

'I'm sorry, Jess. I'm only saying I will be honest and if the truth hurts then so be it. But yes, you're right, I won't go making any unfounded accusations. Now if you don't mind, I'm going to watch Morse. It's time you two were going home.' The click of the remote control told us the conversation was over.

The next day I was feeling guilty at upsetting Grandma, so I called in after work to see if she was okay. Grandma seemed a lot calmer, and we both hugged each other and apologised if either of us had upset each other. She asked me to stay and have something to eat with her, so I called Mum and told her I wouldn't be home for tea. Grandma opened a bottle of wine, and I sat chatting to her at the kitchen table, while she prepared some food. I could tell she had already been on the wine because she was very vocal and looked a bit wobbly. After we had eaten, we took our wine into the lounge.

'I have got some photographs to show you.'

She reached over and grabbed a small photo album that she had on the floor at the side of the settee. We sat side by side, and she opened the first page. There was a strip of black-and-white photos taken in a photo booth of her and Joe. They had their heads together smiling, and on the last photo, they were kissing.

'This was taken in 1946. Joe and I had just got back together.'

The next page had a photo of her sitting at a desk with a child sitting on her knee.

'This was taken in 1939 when I was working at Stevenson's. The little girl is Jane. She would be about four or five years old.'

During the past life regression, Jane was older, but there was no mistaking that this was her. The next page had a photo of Joe, Grandma, and Mum.

'This was taken at Blackpool. We had gone for a day trip.' She turned the photo over to look at the date on the back. '1948, so your mum was just eight years old.' I looked closely at the picture.

'Mum doesn't look like your grandma, but I can see Joe in her.'

'Yes, she definitely takes after Joe. She has got his nose and his sticky-out ears.' She laughed.

The next page contained a photo of Jane wearing a school uniform. Again, Grandma turned it over to check the date '1945. 'Joe loved this photo of her. It was taken when she was at Upper Dene Independent School.

I stared at the picture for quite some time, taking in everything about her. Her hair, the Alice band, her grey pinafore dress. This was exactly as I saw her when she was sitting on the picnic blanket with Joe.

'Grandma, would you mind if I kept this? She looks exactly like she did when I saw her during the past life experience. This adds to the proof that what I was seeing was real. There's no way I could have dreamt all this.'

'Yes, take it, love, I guess I don't have any need for it.'

The other photos in the album were of Mum, Joe, and Grandma. We looked at them all as Grandma recounted her memories of the events. All these scenes looked perfectly natural. You would have thought they were a married couple with their daughter. I was still finding it hard to get my head around Joe leading a double life.

'Grandma, tell me more about Joe and what he was like.' I said snuggling up a little closer.

'Where to start. Well, he was handsome, funny, and caring. He loved jazz music: Louis Armstrong, Duke Ellington, and Bix Beiderbecke. He had quite a collection of their LPs. We used to play them when he came to visit. Even your great grandma, my mum, would join in the dancing.' Grandma started singing a song that sounded vaguely familiar; 'It don't mean a thing if it ain't got that swing,' Grandma got up and tried to dance a few moves, but she soon sat down again complaining about her bad back. 'I was quite a mover in the day and had great legs.' She lifted one leg up to show me. 'Still not bad, if I say so myself.'

Grandma was in a great mood. The wine had loosened her up, and she was in her element telling me tales of her and Joe. Days out, dancing, and sneaking nights together. She had even stayed with him a few times when he was working away; booking into the best hotels and pretending to be his wife.

'You paint a fabulous picture, Grandma; it sounds like you and Joe have had some amazing times together.'

'We did, but not everything was as rosy as it seemed. Joe had a dark secret that could have ruined everything.'

I was taken by surprise. 'What do you mean by a dark secret?'

'A secret is a secret.' Grandma was slurring her words by now with the effects of the wine.

'You can't throw something out there and not tell me the whole story.'

'I'm sorry; I shouldn't have said anything. Forget about it.'

'Easier said than done.'

'Look, I'm tired; isn't it time you went back home? 'Forget I spoke; I'm a silly old woman babbling on.'

She got up and went to the door and opened it for me to leave. This seemed to be grandma's response to confrontation, to walk away from it. I left, annoyed, and upset. How could she say that and then refuse to say more?

Chapter 36 Caroline (Margaret) Year 2000. Session 4

It was 7.30 am on a Thursday morning, and I was getting ready to go to work. I answered it, trying to put my trousers on at the same time. 'Hello,' I said, almost falling over.

'Margaret, it's me, Jess. I need to see you.'

'Why, what's happened? Is everything okay? Are you still coming on Sunday?'

'Yes, it's not that. We are all coming, me, Mum, and Grandma. It's something Grandma said that is bothering me. Look, I know this isn't the best time to call, so I'll make it quick. She told me that Joe had a dark secret. I think she regretted saying anything, so she clammed up and refused to tell me what it was. Do you remember when I first met Joe, through the regression therapy? I had the feeling that he was trying to communicate with me. I'm sure he has something to tell me, something I need to know. The last session I had with you; I got to speak to Joe. Not that he said much, mainly yes and no. But I wondered if we could do it again, and this time I could ask him about his dark secret.'

'Jess, now that we know we are related, it would be unethical for me to work with you. It's strictly against the code of conduct. I could be struck off.'

'No one needs to know; only you and I.'
'What about your blog, won't you want to post it on there?'

'No, this is different. This is a secret that might affect us both; it might affect the whole family. I promise I won't blog about it. I haven't slept all night worrying about what it could be. Please, Margaret, I need to know.'

'I'm about to leave for work, so I don't have time to decide right now. Come to my house tonight. I'll be home after 5 pm. I'll text you, my address.'
'Okay. I can get there for 6 pm, after my last appointment. Thanks. I'll see you tonight.'

I couldn't help but think, 'here I go again. I'm risking my career.' I couldn't imagine my father having a dark secret. He could be cantankerous at times, but nothing dark. It couldn't be anything to do with the finances; Mum and Sheila keep everything above board, or at least I think they do. Maybe it is something from when he was younger. I can't believe I am letting myself get drawn into this, but both personal and professional curiosity, I know, will win out.

I went downstairs and Gail was searching through the tumble dryer with a piece of toast stuck in her mouth. 'What are you looking for?' I asked impatiently. I knew she would be searching for something to wear, and I would get the blame if she couldn't find it.

'My Led Zeppelin T-shirt.' I can't find it anywhere.'

'That's because it's in the wash; you will have to wear something else and hurry up or we're going to be late.'

Gail stomped out of the room. I always drop her at school before making my way to work, and she makes me late every bloody day. Why she can't be more like Simon, I don't know. He's up and about at the crack of dawn and will have left the house long before Gail and I appear.

When I got home from work, I changed into my jeans and a baggy top. I was meeting Jess (my niece), so I didn't want to look professional. I decided to make us both some sandwiches, tuna mayonnaise. She's coming straight from work, so she might be hungry, and the last thing we want during hypnosis is a rumbling tummy.

Jess arrived early at 5.45 pm. She came in and looked around, her expression showing approval. 'What a lovely cottage you have here. I love the beamed ceiling, and you have it so cosy.'

I had lit the coal fire because the evenings were still cold. The glow from the fire did make my home look cosy, and I felt quite proud to be able to show it off to Jess.

'Come sit down, Jess, I've made us some sandwiches. What would you like to drink?' 'I guess alcohol is out of the question?'

'Yes, or at least until we have finished.'

'So, you're going to do it then?'

'How can I refuse? Like you say, this could affect all of us. I'll make you a cup of tea, and you can tell me what your grandma had to say.'

We talked and ate at the same time. Jess told me about the photographs and some of the tales her grandma had told her. It was interesting hearing about how my dad was with Ivy and Christine. Jess described it like him leading a double life, and I guess she is right. Mum did say she suspected he had another child, but the truth is only just coming out. We should have known about Christine 60 years ago.

When we were both ready, I got Jess to relax in my reclining chair. I switched off the ceiling light. The dim light from the reading lamp and the gentle glow from the fire were enough.

I started speaking in a lower, more hypnotic voice. 'Jess, I would like to invite you now to relax.... and close your eyes. And with your eyes closed you can become more aware of your body inside and outside.... Notice the weight of your body that is gently supported by the chair... your arms... your legs... your feet.... and head.... and now open your eyes and look up as high as you can without moving your head, and look down and close your eyes, that's right.... now take a deep breath in and release.... Now that the muscles behind your eyes are relaxed, and your breathing is steady, you don't have to think about your heart beating... it just happens. Your subconscious mind takes care of all your inner sensory system... And your mind is beginning to wonder... how will this work this time...what new discoveries will I make... and it's good to be curious. Now you are relaxing more and more.... becoming calmer and calmer... And I know you can deepen that sense of relaxation even further, as you count down from 10 to zero. 10 – noticing the part of your body that feels the most relaxed... 9 – letting that sense of relaxation spread to every cell in your body... 8 – now see the number eight and double your state of relaxation as you follow the shape of the numbers with your eyes comfortably closed. 7 – try to say the number... deeper into relaxation. 6 – going down now... 5 – down ... down... down.... 4 – time to relax... 3 – time to enjoy... 2 – yet becoming more aware... More fully in control... 1 – drifting down now to zero... zero... zero to a pleasant working level of relaxation. Now allow your awareness to float above your body to a distance where you can see yourself sitting comfortably in the chair... see the glow from the fire... and hear my voice guiding you. See how relaxed you look and know that you are perfectly safe.'

I can see that Jess is fully relaxed. I guide her along her timeline, stopping off wherever she feels appropriate. I let it be her choice to access the times in her life that have been the most important to her. Jess travels back through her younger years and to the time of her birth. Then we go into the womb and through to an earlier time.

'Jess, tell me what you see?'

'I see Jane and Joe.'

'That's good... Now float up to a place where you are directly above Joe and look down. Joe is waiting to talk to you.... Float down and stand beside Joe.... Tell Joe you would like to go on a journey with him through his life... Tell Joe you love him, and you want to know all about his life.... Tell him to take your hand... and together float up above the place you are now.... See Joe's timeline spread out in both directions. Take Joe to the beginning of his timeline, so you can start his life journey together.... and let me know when you have done that?' I get a faint 'yes.' 'Now turn to face Joe's future and ask him to tell you what he is seeing.... Where are you now?

'In a house.... it's his birthday.... he blows out five candles.'

'Now move on slowly…. tell me, where are you now?'

'In a workshop…. he is being praised by his dad for doing a good job.'

'Again, move slowly forward…. Tell me where are you now?

'A railway line…. There is blood…. Jane….

'Take Joe's hand and move higher above the event, so that you are observing the event from a distance. Reassure Joe that he is perfectly safe. Move forward past the event to another time in his future…. Where are you now?'

'He is with Ivy…. They are laughing…. He says he is happy.'

'Ask Joe to show you an event when he wasn't so happy…'

There's a longer pause and I am about to end the session and bring her back when she speaks. 'There's blood on his hands…. He says he can't wash it off….'

'Ask him whose blood it is?'

'Ted…. he says it's Ted's blood. He's dead…. I killed him…'

I can see that Jess is struggling. 'Move forward once more to a time after this event to a happier time…. let me know when you have done that?...

'Yes.'

'What do you see?'

'Bradbury Hall…. there are children running around, happy and playing games….'

'Now slowly move forward along the timeline to another significant event.... let me know when you have done that?'

'Joe is holding a baby in his arms.... There's a white light surrounding us... He's looking at me and smiling.... He's telling me that the baby is me.... He's taking me for a ride in his chair... It's a wheelchair. He's happy.... Love.... Intense love all around us....'

Now move forward to the next significant event.... And tell me when you are there....?'

'There's a body floating on water.... she's dead.... she was evil.... she deserved what she got. Joe is angry.... the blood has returned.... It is all around us.... engulfing us....'

'I could see Jess was in distress. 'Jess, take Joe's hand, and once again float higher and higher above this event.... Tell Joe you are with him, and he is safe.'

I got a faint 'yes,' but Jess still looks in distress. 'Now Jess, it's time to say goodbye to Joe, but before you do I want you to float down once again to the place where you first saw him.... a place where Joe is with Jane, and they are happy.... let me know when you have done that.'

The colour in Jess's cheeks is returning, and she is looking more relaxed. I breathe a sigh of relief; I was worried I might not be able to get her back from that traumatic place.

'Now take Joe's hand and tell him you are happy.... Tell him you love him... Tell him you will carry his memory forever in your heart.... Tell Joe to never go to those hurtful places again.... Tell him to stay with Jane and to be happy.... Now let go... Float above this place until you see your own timeline stretched out before you...'

'Yes.'

'Now travel back along your timeline until you can see yourself sitting in this chair....'

There was a long pause, and then I got a 'yes'.

'Float down so that you are back in your body... back in this room... hear my voice getting louder.... Come back, Jess.... come back to the here and now.... open your eyes.... welcome back.'

Jess opens her eyes and immediately starts crying; tears are flooding down her face, and her sobs are uncontrollable. I don't touch her; I let her get it out of her system and wait for her to compose herself.

'Can I have that drink now?' she says with a pained smile.

'Yes, you can. I think we both need one after that.'

'Jess, I don't think it's safe for you to drive home tonight. I'd like you to stay here; I have a spare room in the attic.'

'I don't want to put you to any trouble.' She sniffs.

'Don't be silly; you are my niece; you will never be any trouble.'

'Where are your kids?'

'Your cousins are staying at the Hall for a few days. After your call this morning, I thought it best to get them out of the house.' I pour us both a glass of wine, and we sit staring at the fire.

'That was quite some journey you went through; are you sure you're, okay?'

'Yes, I think so.'

'Your responses were very clear. We might have got to the bottom of Joe's dark secret. What do you think?

'It's all a bit fuzzy; you will need to explain it to me.'

I'm not surprised it's fuzzy; I took you into a very deep trance. And I have to say there were times when I was worried about you; you looked quite distressed.'

I relayed the things she had said, and the things Joe had shown her. The realisation that this was my father we were talking about was starting to get to me. I walked into the kitchen and retrieved another bottle of wine.

'Everything you have seen in your past journeys has been correct. There is no reason not to believe that this journey is also true. Which creates a bit of a dilemma. What do we do with this information?'

'Does anyone else need to know?' the question was rhetorical. 'You and I both know, so maybe that's enough. So many people would be hurt if we told them. Grandma must know; that's what she must have been on about, Joe's dark secret. We could talk to her about it, but I don't think we should tell anyone else.'

'I agree. We have our meeting on Sunday with the family. We mustn't breathe a word. Ivy won't say anything, will she?'

'She promised me she wouldn't. I believe she regretted letting it slip, so I don't think she will speak about it in front of the others.'

'Good. Let's see how Sunday goes. After that, we can both see Ivy together and find out if what you saw matches what she knows.'

Chapter 37 Jess 2000

That morning, I was nervous, so I set about cleaning my bedroom to take my mind off the meeting. After a light lunch, I went to get a shower and put my make-up on. I chose a black knitted dress, which I dressed up with a gold buckle belt. I appraised my reflection in the mirror. I looked smart but not over-dressed. I popped on my new pair of flat black pumps and finished the look off with a gold chain handbag. By the time I got downstairs, Mum was flapping, thinking we were going to be late. Mum had been to the hairdressers, and her neat bob was looking very smart. She was wearing a knee-length black skirt with a pink satin blouse tucked in.

'You look good, Mum,' I said, admiring her.

We drove over to grandma's house to find her waiting at the door. Grandma had gone to town with her looks. She had full make-up on, with bright red lips and was wearing a red floral dress underneath her black wool coat.

'Wow, Grandma, you look glamorous,' I said, and she gave a twirl to show she was pleased too.

'Let's see who looks better, me or that Molly,' she said, climbing into the back seat.

'It's not a competition, Grandma,' I said, tilting my head to see her through the mirror. Grandma shrugged her shoulders and said, 'Let's see.' I felt myself tense at the thought of her being tetchy with them.

It was exactly 2.30 pm when we arrived at the hall. Margaret was standing in the doorway, waving, and smiling at us. Two young people were standing by her side. We got out and I ran over to give her a hug, as Mum and Grandma followed behind.

'Jess, I'd like you to meet my two. This is Simon, and this is Gayle.'

'It is a real pleasure to meet you.' Said Gayle before they both stepped forward and gave me an awkward hug.

I turned to Mum and Grandma. 'This is my mother, Christine, and this is my grandma, Ivy.'

Margaret stepped forward and gave Mum a big hug. 'I'm so looking forward to us getting to know each other. We have lost out on a lot of years. I can't wait to introduce you to your other sister and your brothers,' she said, taking Mum by the arm. 'Please come in. There's quite a gathering of us, so don't be overwhelmed; none of them bite.'

Margaret led us through to a rather grand room with an enormous fireplace. A fire was burning brightly in the hearth and a tall, good-looking man stood with his elbow resting on the top of the mantelpiece. Um, I thought I hoped he was single.

Margaret started with the introductions. 'This is my mother, Molly.' Molly shook my and Mum's hands. Then she turned to Ivy. 'It's been a long time,' she said. There was no warmth in her voice.

'This is David, the eldest, and these are his two sons, Andrew, and Peter. David leaned forward and gave Mum a hug. 'I guess I'll be calling you sis from now on,' he said, a grin spreading across his face.

'This is Sheila, the brains of the family.' 'Don't be silly, Margaret. Come here, Christine, let me have a look at you. Oh my, you have a look of Dad, doesn't she, David?' 'Yes, absolutely,' David agreed.

'This is Jack, and those two sat in the window, engrossed in their mobiles as usual, are his two, Katie and Matthew.' Jack gave Mum a hug and then turned to me. 'I take it you are responsible for this reunion,' he said with affection. 'I guess I am,' I said, laughing.'

'And, last but not least, this is Daniel, the golfer in the family, and this is his friend Peter.' 'I'll be happy to show you the ropes,' Daniel said, looking at the three of us before giving Mum and me a hug and shaking Grandma's hand.

'Please come and sit down,' said Molly. 'I'll have refreshments brought through to us.' She moved to the corner of the room and pulled a long cord that rang a bell.

We nibbled on sandwiches, salmon and cream cheese on tiny crackers and chunks of stilton cheese. All washed down with port for Grandma and wine for me and Mum. We chatted politely, mainly about the Stevensons and this house and how it came into their possession. I was glad of the noise of children babbling away in the background. They brought a softer edge to the atmosphere. Sheila asked me about how I had discovered the family connection, and I told her about the past life regression.

'Wow, sis, you really have a hidden talent; you should take it up full-time.' She said, winking at Margaret.

'I'd like to have a look around if that's okay,' I asked. 'Sure, let me,' said Daniel, jumping up out of his chair. 'What about you, Christine, would you like to join us?' 'No, it's okay, you go ahead, Jess.' 'I'll come with you,' said Margaret. 'I know Jess will find the nursery fascinating.'

The first room we entered was a large dining room which was dominated by a huge oak table with leather-backed dining chairs. The ceiling was beautiful with plasterwork decorated with flowers and cherubs. The walls were dark wood panelled from floor to ceiling. The next room we entered looked like a library with bookshelves full to the brim adorning all the walls. The musty smell of old books permeated the air making me sneeze. Next, we entered another large room. There was a desk in the centre with a computer and piles of paperwork.

'This is where Sheila works her magic with the finances,' says Danielle. 'Don't touch anything or we will be in trouble,' he laughs.

We move back out into the hall. They call it the grand hall, and this I am told is where the balls or grand parties are held. From the hall, a grand staircase made of intricately carved wood spirals leads up to the next floor.

'Come, I'll show you the bedrooms,' Daniel says, skipping up the stairs like an athlete.

Margaret and I follow at a more leisurely pace. We turn left and come across five bedrooms. Each is similar in style, with a four-poster bed and heavy drapes at the windows. The bathroom is long and narrow, with a claw-foot bath positioned underneath the window. The taps are in gold, and the walls are tiled in a black and white check pattern. There's another smaller bathroom with a shower, which looks like a modern addition. We move back to the landing, which opens out to what Daniel calls 'The Long Gallery.' I can see why; it is a long room with windows looking out over the front of the house. The walls are covered with family portraits and pieces of artwork. From there, we find five more bedrooms.

'These are where the children sleep. We like to keep them on the opposite side of the house,' jokes Margaret.

Then we turn a corner and there's another smaller staircase winding upwards.

'Come follow me, Jess,' says Margaret, her voice filled with excitement.

There is a long corridor with doors leading into two more rooms.

'This is the nursery,' announces Margaret.

It's a large room with a wooden floor and wood-panelled walls. There are nursery rhyme pictures on the wall and a puppet, a kite and other toys suspended from the beams. A colourful rocking horse sits in the window and a large dolls' house stands proudly to one side. There's a smaller version of the four-poster beds that I had seen in the other bedrooms. This one has white calico drapes tied back at each corner. The wooden bedposts are decorated with carved fairies. The decoration of the bed reminds me of my crib back home. I wonder if Joe had done this one as well. What was really charming about the room was the number of toys, prams, dolls, teddy bears and an abundance of children's books. I would have happily stayed here exploring all the room had to offer.

'This was Jane's nursery, and next door is where her Nanny would sleep. Mr Stevenson had it written in his will that this room should remain unchanged. So, it's as it was when Jane was alive.'

'I love it,' I say. 'It feels so cosy. Even though it is cluttered with toys, it still has a cosiness about it. It's warm and inviting, do you know what I mean?' I turn to look at Margaret.

'Yes, I do. It's the only room in the house that I like. All the other rooms seem pretentious, but not this room. This room is simply a child's room; it somehow has an innocence about it.'

'Yes, an innocence, that's the word. Jane must have been incredibly happy in here.'

I suddenly feel melancholy, like I have lost something. I sit on the bed taking in the atmosphere. Then, something compels me to slide off the bed onto the floor and reach underneath. I pull out a whip and top. I hold it close to my heart, feeling its energy. Then I open my hands, and the top starts to spin in the palm of my hand. I hear a noise behind me, and I turn to see the rocking horse gently rocking backwards and forwards. Daniel runs from the room, but Margaret stays. The room appears to be illuminated now, and all the colours of the toys are vivid. I can see a faint image of Jane sat atop the horse. I hear Margaret's voice saying, 'Tell me, Jess, what are you seeing?' I tell her it's Jane on her horse. Then the adjoining door slowly opens, and I see the faint image of a young man entering the room and going to sit on the rug. I hear Margaret's voice again asking me to describe what I am seeing.

'It's Jo Jo.' Jane joins him on the rug, and they both sit cross-legged. The picture is flickering in and out like there's a loose circuit. There's a large book on the floor in front of them, and the pages start to turn. There's an energy in the room; it's joyous and inviting, not at all scary. Then the picture flickers once more and it is gone. The colours in the room dim and once more it is back like it was when we first entered.

Margaret and I go back down and join the others. Daniel is already telling them what he saw. He is drinking a large brandy and looks pale. Everyone in the room is staring at Margaret and me. I'm the first to speak.

'It wasn't scary; the room felt alive with love and happiness.'

'Well, you won't get me back in there again,' says Daniel, gulping down his brandy.

Margaret tells them what she saw. She hadn't seen the images of Jane and Joe, but she had seen the top spinning, the rocking horse moving, and the pages of the book turning.

Molly stands up and says, 'I think you three have had too much of the liquid spirits.' She moves over to the cord and once again rings the bell. 'You will all stay for dinner, won't you? We are having roast lamb.' I eagerly agree; I don't feel ready to go home.

David and Jack's wives join us. Madelaine is David's wife and looks a good thirty years younger than him. She's tall, slim, and glamorous, with a mass of curly auburn hair. Her face is pretty, but it has a hardness to it. That must account for his children being so young, I think to myself. Jack's wife, Elspeth, is Scottish and exudes warmth and homeliness. She's quite stocky, but she's attractive with it. She talks a lot and is great at keeping the conversation going. The attractive man I saw earlier turns out to be a good friend of Daniel's, and he is called Peter. 'Damn,' I think to myself, 'They are gay. Shame I rather fancied him.'

The conversation inevitably kept coming back to Joe. Grandma was true to her word. She told them what their relationship was like, but she also kept emphasising that he loved both his families. My earlier fears were unfounded. Grandma was making me proud. Molly admitted that she had always suspected that Joe was lying to spare her feelings. She retold the story of Ivy turning up on her doorstep with little Christine in tow and demanding to see Joe. Both women laughed about it. It was like time had healed the pain. Margaret made an announcement that she was going to hand her notice in at college and leave at Christmas. Sheila looked pleased for her. The conversation then turned to where she would set up her practice. Molly suggested that they could extend the guest accommodation, and she could have a room there. This seemed to get the thumbs-up from everyone.

Regrettably, the evening ended, and it was time for us to leave. Hugs were exchanged, and we promised to come back again soon. Before I left, I arranged to meet Margaret again after work on Tuesday. We still wanted to talk to Grandma about Joe's dark secret.

Chapter 38 Jess 2000

Grandma had made us a meal of quiche and salad with a Victoria sponge to finish. Grandma was her usual vocal self and asked Margaret lots of questions about her work. There was quite a list of therapeutic interventions that Margaret did with clients. She described them like tools in a toolbox, and past life regression was only one of her many tools. After we had eaten, we took our coffees into the lounge.

'I'm guessing you two have some questions for me?' She said raising her eyebrows.

'You are such a perceptive person,' I say to Grandma in a teasing manner. Yes, there is something. I couldn't get it out of my head what you said about Joe's dark secret. So, I asked Margaret to take me back in time again, so I could speak with Joe. Grandma, Joe told me something to do with Ted, he said his hands were covered in blood and he couldn't wash it off.'

'I can't begin to comprehend how you are getting this information, but it's clear to me that Joe wants you to know the truth. Though what good it will do, I don't know. Somethings are best left buried.' Grandma looked annoyed. 'I had every intention of taking what I know to my grave. I'm not happy telling you this.'

'Please Ivy.' Margaret pleaded, 'If we didn't think it was important, we wouldn't be asking you. I can see that the memory is painful for you.'

Grandma took a deep breath and placed her cup on the table. 'Joe was convinced that Ted was responsible for Jane's death, and when he confronted him about it, he as much as admitted it. You must understand that Joe never went to see Ted with the intention of killing him. During their fight Ted said some nasty thing about Jane and admitted he had thrown her puppet onto the train track. Joe saw red, and he couldn't control himself. He buried Ted's body in the cellar of his mother's house. When Mrs Mallinson died, Joe bought her house so that no one would find the body. But, a few years later Joe received a compulsory purchase order for the house. The council wanted to demolish the entire row of properties to widen the road. As you can imagine Joe was quite distraught about this. The worry was making him ill and that's when he told me.'

Margaret's eyes had glazed over. 'So, it's true, my father killed someone. It's so hard to believe.'

'Yes, I found it hard to believe it myself. Joe had always been such a gentle man. We need to put it in context and appreciate how much he loved Jane. Ted taking her away from him was almost too much to bear. He loved her like his own child. Any father would have done the same thing, given the chance.'

'I know what you mean. 'If someone hurt my children I would want to kill them.' Margaret added with sympathy, but I could see she was struggling with her emotions.

'So, let me get this straight, I said scratching my head. Ted threw the puppet on to the railway line, but it was Jane that chose to get it. So technically, Ted didn't kill Jane. Yes, he was responsible for the actions that led up to her death, but he didn't kill her.'

'That's the way the police saw it too. But Joe didn't agree. He said he was as guilty as if he had pushed her. I tried to reason with Joe, but his fixation with Ted was immovable.'

'What happened after the houses were demolished. Did they find Ted's body?' I asked.

'Yes, they did. It was all over the newspapers at the time. The year was 1970. It wasn't only Ted's body they found in that row of houses; they found two other bodies. One was of a new-born child, probably some lasses still birth, and the other was of a grown man. Both those bodies had been in the ground for a considerable number of years, so I don't think they ever discovered who they were. Teds, on the other hand, had been in the ground only a few years, I believe they identified him from his dental records. I know Joe was worried about it. He never seemed the same after that.' Grandma threw her arms in the air, 'Anyway, nothing ever came of it. The police didn't seem that interested in investigating it, so Joe was let off the hook.'

'Grandma, when I spoke to Joe during the hypnosis, he also told me about a women's body floating on water. He said the blood had come back and it was all over him. He said she was evil.'

'I can't help you with that one I'm afraid, it's new to me.' Grandma looked perplexed. 'I wouldn't imagine it was anything to do with Joe.' She paused. 'No, I'm sure of it.'

'What makes you so sure. If he could kill once, couldn't he have gone on to kill again?'

I knew I sounded insensitive, but then Grandma hadn't seen what I'd seen. That vision of a body floating on the water was haunting me. Joe had shown me it for a reason. He was telling me that once again he had blood on his hands.

'I'm certain if Joe had killed someone else around the time he killed Ted, then he would have told me. If you are going to admit to one, you might as well admit to two.'

'During the regression therapy, I was travelling along Joe's timeline with him. Ted's death came before the second death. It also came after my birth, so it would have to be sometime after 1970.'

'Then it can't have been Joe. He was a very I'll man. He was on oxygen most of the time and he was struggling to walk. The Doctors said he had COPD; it was only later that he got diagnosed with Cancer.'

'What is COPD? I asked. Margaret answered, 'it stands for chronic obstructive pulmonary disease. Dad was on tablets and oxygen for it.'

'Yes, that's right,' said Grandma. 'He struggled with his breathing, and it got so bad that even walking short distances was too much for him. He started using a wheelchair because he was determined to still get out of the house and to see us. Not much could stop Joe. His body might have been deteriorating but his will and determination stayed strong.'

'Dad never considered his wheelchair was a hindrance in fact he loved it. He moved into the maid's quarter downstairs, at the back of the house. From there he could navigate the whole of the ground floor. It went so fast you had to run to get out of his way. David and Jack built a ramp up to the east wing, it's still there. They also laid him a path that runs all the way around to the back to the west wing. That's the side where the kitchen entrance is, where you saw me when you stayed at the Hall.'

I was feeling confused; nothing was adding up. 'If Joe was in a wheelchair, then how did he get to see you Grandma?'

'David used to bring him. He'd pull up at our house, take the chair from the back of the land rover, and then Joe could manage the rest himself. It was battery operated so all he had to do was move a handle and it propelled itself. David would then go and wait in the Corner Café until Joe phoned him to pick him up. Or if it were a nice day, David would drop him at the park, and Christine and I would meet him there. That wheelchair was a godsend. It gave Joe his independence back. When you were a baby, I used to strap you onto his knee, and he would go whirling round the park with you. You would giggle and giggle.' Grandma is laughing now at the memory.

Margaret has stood up and is pacing the room. 'So, all this time David knew! When Sheila did the family tree, he could have given her a name, we could have been reunited years ago. And when he met you at the house, he behaved like it was the first time you had met.'

'Well technically, it was the first time he had met me. David always stayed in the background; we never actually spoke. I couldn't even have described what he looked like; I only ever saw him from a distance.'

'This feels so wrong. I can't understand why he would keep something so monumental from us.' Her arms were flying in the air like she was fighting with the revelation.

'Please don't blame your brother, he was only doing what he was told. Joe was the patriarch of that family and what he said was the law. There were two side to Joe. The jolly, sociable side, and the proud determined side. Joe was a self-made man in many ways. He had built a reputation for himself, and people looked up to him. He expected the same from his children. He was particularly hard on those boys. There would be no slacking, he expected them to make a name for themselves and to make him proud. Joe ruled them with an iron fist, and by that I don't mean he was ever violent towards them, but Joe had a way of keeping them in line. A look or a gesture was enough to tell them to step in line, or else. The 'or else' was never spoken. He could control them through their desire for his approval. And I'm sure when he got Bradbury Hall, the money and power that came with it, was also used like a carrot and stick.'

'You are right Ivy, I never thought of it like that. David and Jack would spring into action at dads every request, it was like they hero worshiped him. When Daniel returned from university, he was just as bad. He was full of ideas for a golf course. The men would always have their heads together planning the project out in full. It's not surprising I felt like an outsider. The men were glued together, and Sheila and mum were always working on the finances together. My desire to be a teacher meant that I never had a role in the family. It's sad, but I always felt like an observer looking at what was happening and never being a part of it. David always said I was the lucky one, the one who got away. I never felt lucky if anything I just felt lonely.' Margaret sat back down and took a sip of her wine. I found it hard to imagine feeling lonely with a bustling family around you.

'You could never underestimate Joe. He was the boss, and he always got his own way. That's likely the reason he and Molly made such a good team. They were both driven and both full of their own self-importance.' Grandma sounded scornful.

'Grandma, I can't help but think you are painting a vastly different picture of him than you have before. What happened to the loving, kind, sensitive Joe?'

'Oh, he was still there. I loved all Joe's qualities. I loved his vulnerability, and I also loved his power to be in control. He was reliable in more ways than one. Family was everything to Joe and he would have gone to any lengths to protect them. And I'm not only talking about your family Margaret, but I'm also talking about our little family as well. Joe was our rock.'

Margaret turned to me. 'It would appear then that the woman in the water, is nothing for us to worry about. Like Ivy says, dad wasn't in any fit state to be physically hurting anyone. As we know, memories can get muddled up with things we have seen, so Joe could have been mistaken. Maybe what he was showing you was a memory of something that had had a lasting impact on him but wasn't necessarily true. It could have been a recurring dream.'

I wasn't sure Margaret believed what she was saying but I gathered it was to put Grandma's mind at rest. We changed the subject and Margaret asked if she could see some of the photographs of Joe and our family. Grandma was once again in her element, reminiscing about the old days.

As we walked to our cars, I asked Margaret what she thought we should do with the information about Ted. 'It's enough that you and I know. I don't see what good it will do telling the rest of the family.'

'I agree.' I said, 'what's the saying? 'Let sleeping dogs lie? And what do you think about the woman in the water? I find that quite puzzling.
'Me too, but I don't see that there's any way we could really know for certain. Joe presented it to you, so it was important to him, but it might not have happened in the same sequence we took it to happen. It could be a memory of something he saw when he was a child, and that memory haunted him throughout his life?'

'Well, like you say, I guess we will never know.'

Chapter 39 Jess 2001

2001. My salon is closed on Mondays, so I spent the morning in Bradford central library looking through the local papers for 1970 on microfilm. It was slow work; I had to go back to the first of January and scan every page until I came across what I was looking for. I found a piece from the Telegraph and Argus, dated 16th September 1970. It related to the Calder Road bodies found in the rubble of the demolished houses. I continued scanning, but more slowly this time. I found a piece five weeks later that named one of the bodies as that of Ted Mallinson. It mentioned that he had a sister called Joan Turner, who was his only living relative. I printed off each piece and folded them into my handbag. I felt exhausted, and my back hurt from leaning over the microfilm machine for so long. This research is hard work; I don't know how Harold makes it seem so easy; I thought to myself. I had spent eight hours in the library and didn't feel I was much further along. I still didn't know Ted's mum's first name or his dad's name, and I didn't know Joan's date of birth. I knew I would have to spend hours more trying to find Joan. Even when I do find her, I wasn't sure what I would do with the information. I was feeling torn over Ted's death. Was he responsible? And if he wasn't, did Joan have a right to know? For now, I would collect the information, and later, the right thing to do will come to me.

  I grabbed a sandwich to eat on my drive home, and as soon I was in the door I was straight back to work on my blog. The blog was demanding more of my time, and I was starting to feel exhausted managing two jobs. What had started with a handful of views had now exploded into thousands of followers from all around the globe. Every day, I got hundreds of comments and requests to include people's stories. I also started getting sponsorship offers. It was so time-consuming, but I was pulled along by its allure. It was all too easy to become captured by the glamour of having so many fans. My evenings stretched into the small hours of the morning and my weekends were non-existent. The demand for more content was expanding into other realms. People wanted to talk about their experiences with spirits and to get my opinion on the subject. Some believed in fairies, or spirit guides, or mediums. I was expected to have an answer to all their questions or at least my own theory on it. I never imagined, when I started this blog, that I would need to do so much research to respond intelligently to my readers. Brands began reaching out, offering me serious money for collaborations. I was surprised that brands found my blog relevant. But I guess that's what good marketing is, tapping into new markets. The offers were varied. They ranged from soothing medications to Buddha statues, to beds, all to enhance your relaxation. Brands would pay me to promote their products. If I'd tell my readers, I used a cream or slept on a certain mattress.

     I felt like I was at a crossroads in my career. Do I continue with hairdressing, or do I become a full-time blogger? I felt an obligation to my mum to continue with the salon. I worried that she would be disappointed in me if I threw everything away. And as much as I like hairdressing, the money isn't that good.

The blog, on the other hand, could earn me serious money. The dilemma was tearing me to pieces. I considered cutting back on the amount of time I blogged, but it had me hooked like a drug; I couldn't break the habit. The potential was enormous, and the lure of fame and fortune had me dangling like a fish on a hook. Was I being selfish to want more?

The door opened, jolting me from my thoughts. It was Mum. 'Love, it's 1 am in the morning, don't you think you should be trying to get some sleep? I'm worried about you. You're burning the candle at both ends, and I'm scared you will burn yourself out.'

I felt defensive. 'It's something I love doing and I have followers relying on me.'

'Yes, I can see that, but something must give; you can't continue like this. Everyone needs a certain amount of sleep to be able to function. It's not healthy staying up so late night after night.'

'So, what am I supposed to do, give it up?' I knew I was sounding grumpy, but I couldn't help it. I felt tired; I had deadlines to meet, and I resented the salon full of customers I had booked in for tomorrow.

'Only you can decide what you want. If this is more important to you than the salon, then give the salon up.'

'But I can't, can I? You paid for that salon for me; how can I give it up? It would feel like I was throwing it all back in your face.'

'Jess, it's just a job. People change careers all the time. Sell the salon, do something different if that's what you want? We need to take the opportunities in life as they present themselves. It can't be helped if two or more come along at the same time. Look, hold out your hands. Mum touched my left hand. 'On this hand you have the salon and a career as a hairdresser.' Then she touched my right hand. 'On this hand you have your blog and the potential it can bring. Look at them carefully, and ask yourself which one brings you the most satisfaction? Now close the hand holding the one that brings you the least satisfaction.' I closed my left hand and looked at her hoping for approval. 'Then that's settled. Don't book any more clients in and cancel or pass on the ones that you can. Tomorrow I'll get busy putting the salon on the market. We are a team, you, and I, and I will support you in anything you want to do.' Mum reaches over and gives me a long hug. I start crying from relief and from Mum being so sweet. 'When did you turn into a therapist?' We are both now sobbing and laughing at the same time.

    Within the space of a week, I had made the decision to leave the salon. Mum, ever efficient, had put it on the market and buyers were lining up. It felt surreal to step away from a place that I had once thought was going to be my whole world. But things were changing rapidly. Margaret and I grew closer as we worked on the blog together. She would connect me with details of her clients from regression therapy sessions. She also generously shared her insights and experiences from her perspective as a therapist. This new collaboration brought depth and dimension to the blog.

    Our sessions, discussions, and Margaret's perspective transformed the blog. From a simple recounting of experiences to something much more dynamic and multifaceted. The stories no longer felt flat or one-sided. They had layers, perspectives, and a richness that drew readers in. Each post offered a glimpse not only into the client's experience but also into the therapist's insights. Creating a balanced narrative that set my blog apart from anything else out there. This made the blog stand out, and the response was astounding. My followers rapidly grew, and quickly, the blog became financially rewarding. What started as a personal project had transformed into a platform with a growing audience, providing a steady income. It was exciting to see this new chapter unfold, filled with possibilities I'd never envisaged.

Chapter 40 Caroline (Margaret) 2002

2002. My new therapy centre stands proudly completed and fitting neatly alongside the Bradbury Hall Golf Centre. Mum and Sheila's eye on the purse strings ensured that its position was not only practical but also financially strategic, attracting wealthy clients from the golfing community. As they cross the threshold, they enter a space I've carefully designed to enable healing. It is calm and welcoming, with soft furnishings in a healing purple colour and touches of dream-inspiring artwork. There're two therapy rooms, a reception area, and a wash area. I also have a full-time receptionist who doubles as my PA.

My living space, which is above the therapy centre, is as meticulously designed as the therapy centre. The space is open-plan and feels both spacious and personal. My own little sanctuary overlooking the grounds and woodland beyond. I went for a modern minimalist style, a rebellion against the Tradition of the Jacobean Hall. White walls, natural light, and an absence of clutter create an openness I find relaxing. A vast contrast to the heavy, dark interiors of Bradbury Hall. My father would have scorned at this choice of décor. A traditional man, he would have rolled his eyes at the white walls and the sleek lines. And he would turn in his grave if he knew I had painted a sideboard he had made. Yet, as I made each decision about the décor, I had a feeling that he would understand that I needed to make this space my own. The sideboard, despite its new look, remains an important piece, a quiet reminder of his work and care, now seamlessly woven into my life.

The kitchen continues this minimalist look. It has white gloss cabinets, stainless steel fixtures, and glossy white laminate floors that catch the light. Just beyond the kitchen area is a cosy seating area with a wood-burning stove as its focal point. The glow from the fire offers warmth and a certain rustic charm. An extra-large, white sheepskin rug stretches across the floor. I love to kick off my shoes and sink my toes into its softness. It's a small luxury, but one that gives me a daily dose of comfort after a hard day's work. I've also placed a few small, tasteful pieces of artwork here and there. They add a touch of vibrant colour to break up the predominantly white room.

The real masterpiece of the living area, however, is the picture window. Spanning almost the entire wall, it reveals the woodland and duck pond beyond. This view never fails to captivate me, and each morning, I am drawn to this window. The scene changes, from spring's lush greenery to autumn's golden foliage. It's enchanting. I've placed a small dining table with four chairs beneath this window, and it's here I do most of my work. I like to set up my laptop, with coffee in hand, and feel blessed to have this stunning view. It's become my haven, a place where ideas flow, and inspiration takes hold. I've come to realise that this space, both calming and beautiful, is where I can dream of all the good things that have happened in my life and all the good things still to come. I never felt relaxed in Bradbury Hall itself, but here next to the modern golf centre, I feel completely at home.

Financially, the therapy centre is stable, allowing me to contribute directly to our family's shared coffers. In line with tradition, my siblings and I all receive the same wage, a family policy intended to keep us equal, grounded, and accountable. My additional earnings from lectures and guest appearances, however, are mine to keep. This gives me the freedom to indulge in small luxuries or save for the future. Next week, I'll be appearing on Loose Women, a popular daytime program, where I'll discuss my work on past life regression and promote my new book. It's an exciting opportunity to reach a wider audience. The following week, I've been invited to give a lecture to theology students at Oxford University. The prospect both thrilling and nerve-wracking at the same time.

My preoccupation with past life regression meant that I needed someone for the other therapies. There was only one person I wanted to join me at the centre, and that was my trusted friend Malgo. Her warmth, charm, and exotic presence have made her an instant hit with both clients and the family. She's taken on most of our regular clients, enabling me to focus more on my area of expertise. Despite our close friendship, she hasn't hesitated to remind me of her concerns over my professional relationship with Jess, especially now that we know we're related. But she respects my decisions, and we've moved forward with a renewed sense of trust.

Malgo's presence is also a breath of fresh air at Bradbury Hall. Her personality is vibrant, her laughter infectious, and her style a blend of elegance and eccentricity. She brings life to the otherwise sombre rooms of the House. Every dinner gathering becomes a lively affair when she's around. Conversation flows, laughter echoes, and I can't help but notice the way David's eyes light up when she's nearby. His interest is clear, and while I doubt Malgo would ever entertain the notion, it's amusing to watch her effect on him. Madelaine justifiably has cause for jealousy, as David's admiration for Malgo is overly flirty.

In my personal life, my children are finding their own paths. My daughter Gail is thriving at university, where she's studying architecture. When she's home, she stays in my old cottage, which she now shares with her close friend, Susan. While I'm still not entirely sure about the nature of their relationship, I've learned not to pry. Gail has always been independent, and I respect her need for privacy. Whether Susan is just a friend, or something more doesn't matter to me. What matters is that Gail is happy and surrounded by people who support her. David still encourages her and has already begun involving her in various architectural projects at the Hall. It's clear that he envisions a future and key role for her here. I'm proud to see her stepping into the family business with such confidence and dedication.

Simon, my youngest, is equally driven. His passion for golf hasn't wavered; if anything, it's only grown stronger. He's excelling in school and has set his sights on studying sports turf management, just like his Uncle Daniel. Over the past year, he's won several junior tournaments, and I can't help but beam with pride at his accomplishments. Knowing that he, too, will find his place within Bradbury Hall, gives me a profound sense of peace. Each of my children has chosen their path, yet both paths lead back to Bradbury Hall. I've come to accept the inevitability of the continuing of a tradition. It might not have been my birth-right, but it certainly is theirs.

Now that I'm encompassed into the Bradbury Hall tradition, I can say for the first time that I really do feel at home here. The journey to finding my place, both within the family and within the Hall took its time but it's been worth the wait. This place, with its beauty and its history, has become more than just a residence. It's now woven into who I am, talented, ambitious, but also grounded. A sense of belonging that I once doubted I would ever find. Bradbury Hall is more than a place, it's a legacy, one that lives through each of us who call it home. And now, as I watch the seasons change outside my picture window, I know with certainty that there's nowhere else I'd rather be.

Chapter 41 Jess 2002

April 2002. There was to be a big party at the Hall for Elspeth's 50th birthday. Margaret wanted me to help with the preparations and to film the main birthday event. I had started including a lot of video content in my blog to bring it to life. I had filmed scenes of clients undergoing regression therapy, with consent of course. And I had filmed in Jane's room to add atmosphere to my own journey of discovery. Elspeth's brother, Marcus, was a web developer and had created the webpage for Bradbury Hall, and he was also coming down for the event. Margaret thought it would be a good idea for him to set up a website for me. So, she had arranged for us to meet on the Monday at the Hall before the celebrations on the Saturday. I put a post on my blog telling my followers I would be on holiday for a week. I had made my mind up to take a complete break from the blog and to allow myself to become immersed in the domestic party preparations.

Margaret was there to greet me when I arrived at the Hall. She took my arm saying, 'I'm quite excited for you to meet Marcus; he's rather dishy and single.'

'Oh no, now you have made me nervous,' I complained with a large grin on my face. 'Is he here?'

'Yes, he arrived this morning. I've put him in the nanny's room, and you are sleeping in Jane's room,' she said with a cheeky twinkle in her eye.'

'What about the others? Where are they?'

'Elspeth and Jack are not arriving until Friday, and they will stay in the accommodation block next to her parents. We don't have any outsiders here this week; it's all family. It's going to be spectacular,' said Margaret, unable to contain her excitement. Take your stuff to your room and meet me in the kitchen. I'll let Marcus know you are here.' Margaret skipped away as I headed for the stairs. I had never seen this side of her before. She was like a child waiting for Santa to arrive.

When I got to the kitchen, Margaret and Marcus were sat there talking to Cook about the birthday cake. The kitchen was warm and inviting and a lot less formal than the rest of the Hall. The smell of meat pies cooking in the aga made me feel hungry. The casual chatter resounded off the copper pots and pans. Cook was highly vocal, showing off her drawing. Her chest puffed up with the pride and pleasure she was experiencing over her design. It was to be a traditional two-tier fruitcake with the most beautiful Scottish-themed decoration with thistles running all around the edge and topped with sugar candy Scottish dancers. The napkins for wrapping the cake, for people to take home, were in Elspeth's MacAulay family plaid. The whole theme for the party was to be Scottish and all the men were hiring tartan dress. The women could dress as they chose, but the emphasis was on glamorous ball gowns.

Marcus stood up and turned to greet me. Margaret hadn't lied; he was tall, fair-haired, with penetrating green eyes. Handsome was an understatement; he was positively dishy. How is a girl supposed to act casual when confronted with a Scottish Adonis? His accent was as melting as his looks, deep and sexy. I sat down quickly in fear that my legs would give way if I didn't.

'It's kind of you to agree to meet me. I've been toying with the idea of a webpage for a while. But I wouldn't know where to start.' I almost cringed at my own voice. Did that make me sound like a damsel in distress?

'Let's take these coffees upstairs to the drawing room and I'll run you through it,' he said, clutching both our drinks and leading the way. I saw Margaret wink at me while I followed behind. We sat in the fireside chairs facing each other; this was obviously going to be a casual chat and not a hard sell.

'I love what you have done with the website for Bradbury Hall; it looks so professional, and the artwork is incredible.'

'Thanks, but it's not only me. I have a web development company and the people who work for me are super talented. But you are pretty talented yourself. I've been taking a look at your blog, and there's some amazing content in there; in fact, I found it hard to pull away.'

'Oh, I'm glad you like it. I started it a couple of years back, and although I get a lot of followers, I can't help but feel it looks a bit amateurish. It was Margaret's suggestion that I got myself a professional website. But I'm not that computer literate and there's a lot of technical jargon that I don't have a clue about.'

'Transitioning to a dedicated website is really the way you should go, but you don't have to do it alone; there are companies out there, like mine, which can take care of everything for you. And you can integrate your blog into the same space, so you're not juggling two babies.

'Is it expensive to employ a company to do it for me?'

'Not at all, you are talking about £20 a month and the improvement in sales and income from paid content will more than compensate for it. A professional-looking website will make people sit up and take you seriously. It will promote your books and help you create related merchandise, but sorry, I'm getting carried away. The last thing I want to do is overwhelm you with ideas.'

'Yes, please keep it simple.' There I go again sounding like a dimwit.

'With a website, you can organise your content better. Visitors can navigate more easily to find what they're looking for. For example, I notice you cover a wide subject area, so if a person is searching for 'paranormal activity' they would be sent directly to the relevant section that deals with that subject. If a person is searching for 'what it was like living in the 1930s' they would be sent to your article on the subject. That creates higher engagement and thus higher sales, whether from your own merchandise or from affiliated sellers.'

'You are right, I do have a lot of content that's a bit scattered right now, so people are only seeing my most recent blog.'

'That's the beauty of a website; it will improve your SEO.'

'There you go, acronym alert!' I said, laughing, 'what on earth does that mean?'

'Ha ha, it stands for 'search engine optimisation.' So, when a person types in a keyword, like regression or past life, the search engine sends them to you. The more traffic you have coming your way, and the more professional your webpage looks, the more offers you will get from companies. We call these 'paid collaborations. Your webpage would also include analytical tools for tracking visitor behaviour. Knowing what your audience likes helps you tailor your blog content and helps you to consider marketing strategies.'

'So how would I get started?'

'Well, first choose a company you feel you can trust.'

'That would have to be you because I don't know any other companies, and you do come highly recommended. If you can't trust family, who can you trust? So where do we start?'

'The setting up of the website will be done for you, as well as all the design work, layout, analytics, buying platforms, and so on. My design team will organise all your existing blogs into an easier-to-navigate format. So, to start with, you don't have to do anything. Once you are happy with the design and the layout, we provide training on how to navigate it and upload more content, as and when you like. But it's pretty simple once you get the hang of it.'

'And who would do the training, would that be you?' I said, eager for a positive response.

'It can be if you like.'

'I like,' I said, raising my coffee in a toast.

'Well, I don't know about you, but I'm famished. Let's go and grab some lunch. He took my hand gallantly, helping me up from my chair. I could feel my hand tremble at his touch; it was warm and strong. He kept hold of my hand until we reached the door before stepping to one side to let me through. He exuded effortless charm, and his beautiful green eyes penetrated my soul. I could only murmur a thank you, as I felt an unexpected flutter in my chest.

We went back to the kitchen; the smell of food was wafting through the lower rooms, and I could feel my tummy rumbling. Molly and Jack were sat at the table tucking into pie and chips. 'Hello love,' said Molly, 'come sit down and eat.' Cook slapped a plate in front of me and said, 'what will it be, there's steak pie or there's a lasagne if you would prefer that?' I was torn for a couple of minutes because I love both, but then looking at the pie on the plates made my mind up. 'That looks delicious, I'll have the same, please.'

'Breakfast and lunch are always in the kitchen,' said Molly; 'we only use the dining room for dinner.'

'I love it down here; it's so homely.' It had taken me almost two years to get to this stage. Previously, I had been served sandwiches or cake in the drawing room on my visits, but today, down here, I felt for the first time that I was part of the family.

After lunch, Marcus asked me if I would like to join him in a round of golf. 'I'm afraid I don't play.'

'What have you never played ever?' he said, sounding shocked.

'Well, only pitch and putt at the seaside, but I don't think that counts.'

'Then we will have to rectify that; come on, I'll show you.' He took my hand and once again my heart began to flutter. He led me towards the golfing block, reassuring me as we went that it wasn't that difficult, and I'd soon pick it up. He grabbed a couple of clubs, and we went outside to a flat practice pitch with various holes in the ground.

'Treat this just as you would with pitch and putt. Stand with your feet apart and stroke the ball gently towards the hole.'

On my first attempt, the ball stopped about twelve inches in front.

'Now hit it a little harder and you will soon get the feel for it.' Laughing nervously, I said, 'I'll try.'

We stayed on the practice pitch for about 40 minutes. My nerves were easing, and with each stroke, I was getting better. I punched the air after getting my first hole-in-one. Marcus stood laughing at me.

'You are getting too good; come on time for something a little harder.'

He carried my club, and I followed him over to the driving range. He stood close behind me, adjusting my stance and taking hold of my arms from behind. I could feel his warm breath on my cheek. His sexy Scottish accent was low in my ear as he explained the correct way to grip the club and how to swing naturally. I tried to focus on my posture, but it was almost impossible with him standing so close. 'Relax,' he said softly, leaning in even closer. I swung at the ball, missing it completely. Marcus laughed, stepping even closer. I could feel his chest brushing against my back, the warmth drawing me in. This felt more like foreplay than golf. My attraction towards him was strong, and I hoped he was feeling the same way.

That evening after retiring to bed, it was difficult to relax with him so close in the adjoining room. I kept hoping the door would swing open, and he would take me in his arms and make mad, passionate love to me. I lay in bed drowsy but unable to sleep at the prospect of seeing Marcus again the next day. The room was black except for a warm orange glow from the night light I had plugged in at the side of the bed. I must have been nodding off because I was jolted wide awake by the sound of the adjoining door creaking open. My heart started to race; was Marcus on his way to my bed? A few minutes passed and nothing happened, so I sat up. I could see the door was closed, so maybe Marcus had changed his mind and gone back to bed. Then suddenly I could smell wood, like the fine smell of sawdust lingering in the air. I knew then that Joe was in the room. I whispered, 'Grandad, are you there?' The room was silent, then out of the corner of my eye I noticed a bright ball of light, slowly moving from the curtain over to the adjoining door. The light hovered outside the door for about a minute and then it moved through the door into the room where Marcus was sleeping. I stayed still for about an hour, wondering if Joe would come back. Was he trying to communicate with me? Or was he watching over me? My eyes kept closing and as much as I was trying to stay awake, I fell into a deep sleep.

Over the next few days, Margaret took every opportunity to throw Marcus and I together. She would suggest he take me for a walk around the estate, or pair us up to hang birthday banners in the Grand Hall. Each afternoon, Marcus would take me to play golf. We progressed from the driving range to the course. It was fun and Marcus said I was a natural. I never imagined myself playing golf. I wasn't the sporty type, but I loved the feeling of the wind on my face and the woosh of the ball as it travelled through the air. It was refreshing to be out in the open air; it made me feel closer to nature. In June, Bradbury Hall looks at its best. Everything is so green. The Laburnum trees rained down their yellow blossom, and every now and again I would catch the smell of roses and sweet peas. I started to relax in Marcus's company, his carefree conversation easing me into a sense of security.

More people arrived at the hall. Daniel was first with his partner Peter, followed by various relatives of Elspeth. Jack and Elspeth were last to arrive on the eve of the party, accompanied by her parents, Morag, and Billy, short for William. The house was buzzing with excitement for the main event the next day. Conversation was alive with what the women were going to wear. Plus, whispers of the surprise presentation Jack were going to make to Elspeth on the evening.

Saturday came around in a whirlwind of preparations. The musicians arrived and set up their gear in the far corner of the hall, under the grand staircase. Waiting staff arrived and were put under the direction of Cook. The sound of the bagpipes filled the air around the hall as Billy practiced his piece for the night. A table in the centre of the hall was stacked high with precision-placed champagne glasses. They would be filled later, with the champagne cascading down into each glass. The scene was set and all that was left was to get changed and arrive on time. We all had to be in the hall ten minutes before Jack and Elspeth would make their entrance. Molly was strict about the timing, and we all had to ensure our watches or mobiles were synchronised.

I felt excited to go to my room to prepare. I had bought a beautiful red halter-neck satin dress that clung to my curves in all the right places and a pair of silver sparkly shoes. I wanted to look as beautiful as possible for Marcus. After showering and putting on my dressing gown, a knock came at my door. It was Margaret.

'Come with me,' she said excitedly. I've got something to show you.' Intrigued, I followed her downstairs and into the study.

Margaret removed a large oil painting from the wall to reveal a large safe. She tapped in the numbers and lifted out a beautifully decorated wooden tray. She laid the tray on the desk and opened the lid. There were four stunning diamond necklaces with matching earrings below.

'Choose one, she said with a glint in her eye, 'tonight you will sparkle like a princess. And who knows, you might catch your prince.'

Tentatively, I touched the necklace I liked the best. 'These look mega expensive,' I said, 'I don't know if I dare touch them.'

'I'm wearing one,' she said, roughly grabbing hold of a plain diamond necklace and fastening it around her neck. 'You should wear the one with the rubies; it will go perfectly with your dress.'

Without waiting for a reply, she lifted it out and fastened it in position. She guided me over to a mirror on the wall, and said, 'What do you think?'

I could feel myself shaking; I knew these were real and not paste. Stuttering, I said, 'It's beautiful, but I couldn't... what would Molly think?'

'It was her idea; Sheila will wear the yellow diamonds, so each of us girls get to wear the family jewels tonight. Dad would love it, his daughters, and the granddaughter he so evidently loved, sparkling together, as we always should have been.'

I felt emotional. 'But I'm not Molly's granddaughter; surely these should be for you, Sheila and Jack's daughter?'

'Katie is far too young to be wearing the family jewels, and besides, Mum has accepted you into the family. You might not be her granddaughter, but you are still blood, and that counts for everything in this family.' I stood appraising my reflection. With tears threatening to form, I gave her a hug and said, 'thank you, Aunty Margaret.'

I was ready 20 minutes early, so I sat on the bed nervously twiddling my bracelet, waiting for the right moment to arrive. There was that smell again, like freshly cut trees or sawn wood. I looked around carefully, checking every corner of the room. A book fell from the bookshelf and landed with its pages open. I went over and lifted it up. It was Cinderella. The page was open at the moment her fairy godmother turns her torn clothes into a beautiful gown. I had to laugh out loud. Joe was known for being a joker, and this little message was hilarious. There was a knock on the adjoining door, and it slowly opened. For a moment I wasn't sure if it was going to be Marcus or Joe. Marcus looked so handsome in his kilt, tall and strong and ready for battle.

'I have come to escort you to the ball; is my lady ready?' he said, taking a bow.

I stood and smoothed my dress with my hands and then, taking a deep breath, I said, 'I think so.'

Marcus looked at me appraisingly, 'you look stunning. I had better keep an eye on you; I wouldn't want one of my cousins whisking you away.' He offered his arm for me to link, and together we walked proudly to the Great Hall, which had transformed into a grand ballroom for the evening.

Elspeth and Jack made their entrance. Elspeth looked stunning with her ginger hair in flowing curls and wearing a blue taffeta dress with a plaid sash. As they stood on the bottom step, the champagne was poured into the stacked glasses to a roar of applause. Billy stepped forward playing his bagpipes, followed by the band swinging into action. Everyone mingled as champagne glasses were handed round and swiftly refilled by the waiting staff. Canapés on trays floated with invisible hands through the room. Marcus introduced me to his relatives and some friends of the family who had just arrived.

After a lot of exhausting conversation, Marcus turned to me and said, 'Dance with me. I think this is your song.' I laughed; it was 'Lady in Red' by Chris De Burgh.

He rested his hand on my waist; I knew he would be able to feel the warmth of my body through the thin fabric. A shiver of delight ran down my spine as he looked at me tenderly, singing along to the music. Our eyes locked on each other, and everyone else seemed to disappear. When the music stopped, he grabbed two more glasses of champagne and led me out onto the terrace. It was a warm June evening, with a clear sky and the first of the stars beginning to appear.

He held my hand, 'You look breathtaking,' he said tenderly. 'All I want to do is kiss you.' I said nothing; I gazed into his eyes and let him pull me into him.

His tenderness, the softness of his lips and the warmth of his body made my heart swell. Could this be the perfect man for whom I've been waiting? Has Joe, once again, worked his magic and brought us together? As he kissed me again, I felt like our bodies were swaying to the music, like we were perfectly in tune with each other. He looked deeply into my eyes and, in his soft Scottish accent, said, Jessica Barker, 'I think I'm falling in love with you.' I knew then that this was the start of a new journey in my life.

Chapter 42 Caroline (Margaret) 2003

2003. I'm so pleased for Jess. She and Marcus have been together for ten months now and everything is going swimmingly. He's taken her for a long weekend to Paris and little does she know; he intends to pop the question. Paris is where Jess was conceived, so she will be delighted with the significance and romance of the location. Marcus has been planning this for the last two months and had enlisted me to help him choose a ring and to secretly discover her finger size.

Sunday morning, my telephone rang, and it was Jess announcing that she and Marcus had got engaged the previous evening. They were strolling down the Champs-Élysées when he got down on one knee and proposed. Jess was full of excitement in her voice as she told me how romantic it had been and how she had instantly said 'yes.' I rushed down for breakfast and found Sheila, David, and Mum already there tucking into bacon and eggs.

'He did it,' I announced.

David was grinning from ear to ear, 'Now we will have to guess where they are going to live,' he said. 'I wonder if they will settle in Scotland after all that's where Marcus's business is, and Jess can work from anywhere?'

Molly frowned slightly; 'I'm not sure Christine will want her only daughter living so far away. They could live here,' she said, gesturing towards the estate's grounds. We have more than enough room and she would be close enough to her mum to see her every day if she liked. Cook and Sherlock are retiring soon, so the Gatehouse will be coming free.'

David laughed, 'I somehow can't see them living in that little Gatehouse. I'm sure they will want something a bit bigger, and besides, we need to hire a new cook and groundsman, so the Gatehouse will be needed for them.'

Molly waved her hands dismissively, 'there's plenty of room for them in the old servants' quarters.'

The conversation shifted towards the wedding, a topic I was eager to discuss.

'I've been thinking,' I said, 'wouldn't it be perfect to hold the wedding right here on the estate? Can you imagine it, lanterns strung across the trees, the ceremony under the willow by the lake, and the reception in the grand hall? Or if the guest list is very big, we could hire a marquee for the reception and have the ceremony in the hall.' I knew I was getting carried away wanting the wedding of the century, but Jess had missed out on what this place had to offer for too long. Now was our time to pay her back.

'You must remember, Margaret, that Jess and Christine are not used to such grandeur. They might prefer something more low-key,' suggested Mum.

'Well, they are back tomorrow, so we will find out then,' I said a little deflated. 'I'll work on Marcus,' I thought to myself; I'm sure he would want to give his new wife a spectacular wedding.

I go back to my apartment and sit at the picture window overlooking the lake. Two swans are floating majestically on the water and the sun is making the water glisten like a million crystals. I make myself a coffee and open my computer. Today my head is full of researching marquee hire and bridal décor suppliers. Usually, when guests get married at the Bradbury Hall Golf Centre, they make all their own arrangements, so we don't keep names of suppliers. I find a couple of suppliers in Bradford and make a list of their names and telephone numbers. I then make a list of everything we will need. I know Jess doesn't have much family, so I decide to get quotes based on thirty guests. I phone each company in turn to get an estimate of costs for chair covers, table linen, floral arrangements for the table, and a backdrop. Plus, an exquisite floral arch for the entrance. After comparing the costs, I decided to check Jess's website to see if she had announced her engagement. She hadn't posted anything yet, which wasn't surprising; after all, she would want to tell family first. I opened her latest blog to see what she was currently working on.

Here's a hypothetical scenario for you past-lifers to contemplate:

Imagine you discovered that in a previous life you had killed someone. The case remains unsolved, and the family of the victim are still alive and have never had closure. Do you report your past crime to the police? Do you contact the dead person's family? Or maybe in the past life, you were the victim and can now identify your killer. If you go to the police, they won't be able to take your account as solid evidence, but it might point them in the right direction. If you go to the family, will you be taken seriously and what would the likely consequences be? Have any of you had this experience, and if so, what did you do? And if you haven't had this experience, still comment, and let me know what you would do?

I was taken aback; this felt a little too close to home for comfort. What on earth is Jess up to? Surely, she can't be considering making Joe's actions public. I wonder if she is fighting an internal ethical dilemma; maybe she is torn between what she feels is right and wrong. Will the morals of her readers sway her to decide? We had agreed to keep this between ourselves, but now I'm wondering if she is having second thoughts. This post is making me feel uneasy; it feels dangerous. Who else will read this and put two and two together? This past year, Jess has been giving more and more information out in her blogs. Everyone now knows that Joe Metcalf is her grandfather. Luckily, it never sparked the scandal I was worried it would. I guess times have changed and having an affair or a secret child is no longer considered a major crime. But murder is a different matter altogether; that would cause a scandal and be extremely damaging to the family. It would tarnish the family name, and it could have an impact on the business. It would be highly embarrassing, and we would no longer be able to hold our heads up in the community of Bradbury. God knows what Mum will do if she gets wind of this.

Monday evening, Jess and Marcus arrived back from Paris in time for dinner.

'Sorry we're late,' said Jess, sounding out of breath. 'We called in to see Mum, and I'm afraid we can't stay long because she said she wants me home for a few days. Mum gets very lonely when I'm away.'

'Can you at least stay for dinner and tell us all about Paris?' asked Mum.

'Yes, that would be lovely; we have so much to tell you all.'

The room hummed with excitement as Jess showed us all her ring. Madelaine was openly jealous as she scolded her husband for not having bought her something as beautiful as that. David quizzed them about where they would live. He suggested there was plenty of room at the Hall. But Marcus said they had already decided on that. They were to live with Marcus's family in Scotland.

'But what about Christine?' said Molly in disbelief.'

'We are going to ask her to come and live with us. She can either move into one of the spare rooms in the main house or she can live in the old gardener's cottage. It has sat empty for years, but it could be modernised, and she would be extremely comfortable there,' added Marcus.

'What do you think, Jess?' David asked.

'I'm not sure she will go for it; there's Grandma Ivy to consider, plus she has a lot of friends around here and she is very involved with the WI. I can't see her wanting to give that up. But if she says no, then I will have to come back down here and spend as much time with her as possible. I'm sure whatever happens we can make it work. Mum is really happy for us both, and she wants me to be happy too, so whatever we decide, I'm sure, will be okay.'

I couldn't help but feel that moving to Scotland wasn't such a bad idea. It would create distance between her and the family.

'Maybe you should get married in Scotland, if that's where you intend to live,' I said, bringing a quizzical look from David.

'Or you could have the wedding here?' said Mum, her gaze fixed sternly on me.

'That's kind of you to offer, Molly; there's more room here to house the guests, so that's something we should consider. What do you think, Jess?' Marcus said, taking her hand.

'I'd love to have it here, and I think Jane would like that too.'

By now, everyone was used to Jess talking like Jane was a part of her. Like it gave her more right to be here than everyone else. I thought Jess and I had a strong connection, but now her arrogance was starting to annoy me.

'We don't want anything big or fancy. Just close family and a few friends.' Jess hesitated and looked at Marcus, 'but….' Marcus took over, 'but, we would like to have the wedding soon. We're not getting any younger, so we would like to start a family as soon as possible. We are thinking about June; that will be one year since we first met. To marry in this beautiful place, the place where we fell in love, will be so romantic. Don't you think?'

I could tell by Jess's face there was more to it. If I were a betting person, I'd wager that she's already pregnant.

'Gosh, there's a lot to do in a short time, but I don't see why not. Margaret could help with the preparation, couldn't you, love?' Mum said, turning to me.

'I don't think I can. I'm snowed under with clients for the next two months. I'm sorry, I would love to if I had the time.' Mum won't be so bloody keen once I show her Jess's blog, I thought to myself.

'I'll help,' said Madelaine with a bright smile. I could throw you the perfect wedding; after all, I have a flair for style and glamour. I could turn this museum,' she said, looking around dismayed,' into a wedding fit for a princess.'

'Oh, thank you, Madelaine,' Mum said, still looking at me suspiciously. 'Jess, when you have had a few days with your mum, you could come and stay here for a few days and plan out everything you need with Madelaine. The Clubhouse in the Golfing Centre is already an approved venue, so you could have your ceremony there and your reception here in the Grand Hall. I could ask the vicar when he is free.'

'There's no need; Mum's friend Linda is a registrar, and I know it would mean a lot to Mum if she could officiate at our wedding.'

Madeleine was clapping her hands. 'Oh, this is going to be so exciting; I can't wait to get started.'

After Marcus and Jess left, I pulled Mum to one side and told her I wanted to show her something. We went through to the study, and I opened the computer. Mum typed in the password, saying, 'What is it, Margaret, why all the cloak and dagger?'

'Wait, I'll show you.' I clicked on Jess's website and opened her latest blog. 'There, read that.' Mum put her spectacles on and sat at the computer, taking her time to read the post.

'Why didn't you show me this earlier?' she said, her voice filled with anger.

'There was no time; when I came back to the house, Marcus and Jess had already arrived. I could hardly mention it in front of them.'

'This is worrying; do you think she is planning to expose your father as a murderer?'

I looked at Mum with a puzzled expression. 'Do you know about this...?' 'What do you know...?' Do you know about Edward Mallinson...?

'Sit down and calm yourself. I've known for a few years now. Your father confessed as much before he died.'

'Mum, how...., where...., when....?

I don't know the details... I didn't want to know the details. I only know he is guilty, and if this gets out it will ruin us.' Mum sat staring at the screen rereading the text, over and over again. Then she turned to me, with anger in her eyes. 'Margaret, you need to find a way to stop her. You brought her to this house, so it's your responsibility to make this go away.'

'I'll talk to her, I promise, I'm sure I can persuade her to keep quiet.'

Chapter 43 Jess 2003

April 2003. I had a lovely four days with Mum, talking about wedding outfits and writing a guest list together. Linda had been over the moon about being asked, and we settled on the date of June the twenty-first. We had found a beautiful bridal shop in Bingley, and I had chosen an off-the-peg gown. All it needed was shortening a little, and it would be good to go. Mum gave me a lovely pearl necklace and a matching bracelet she had worn when she married my dad. So that was something borrowed and something old sorted out. The something new could be my dress and tiara, plus I bought a blue garter, so I had covered all bases. Mum had bought a beautiful dress and jacket in pale blue from the same bridal shop. All she needed was some new shoes and a handbag. I don't think I'll have bridesmaids, because we don't have any small children in the family, but I will ask Margaret to be my Maid of Honour. Mum suggested I ask my Uncle Andrew, my dad's brother, to give me away. Other than Mum and Grandma, he's the only living relative I have, and I'm sure Dad would approve.

    I felt guilty leaving Mum so soon to return to Bradbury Hall, but I promised her I'd only be gone for a few days, and then I would be all hers until the wedding. I was a little apprehensive about working with Madelaine on the planning. She's very glamorous and does have great taste, but I also think she could be a bit bossy. I'll have to make it clear, it's my wedding, not hers. Margaret has asked me to arrive at 12 noon. She wants to talk to me about something before lunch. She sounded a bit strange, and I thought her behaviour at dinner a few nights ago was a little odd. I hope she isn't ill. My car wheels crunch loudly over the gravel of the courtyard, and Margaret comes to the door.

'Leave your things in the car for now. Let's go over to my apartment so we can have a chat.' She was smiling and looked well, so I assume it must be something to do with wedding preparations. Maybe she has changed her mind about not having time to help, I thought hopefully. As we walked over to her apartment, I told her about my wedding dress, Mum's outfit, and Uncle Andrew. Margaret stopped walking and turned to face me.

'Can I ask you something? Are you pregnant?'

'How did you guess? 'Please don't tell anyone, at least not until after the wedding. I would hate people to be whispering that it's a shotgun wedding on my special day. They can snigger afterwards when they find out.'

'Then let's hope you're not showing?' she said, raising her eyebrows as if she didn't approve.

We got inside and Margaret poured us a couple of glasses of my favourite Sauvignon Blanc.

'Not too early, I hope,' she said, passing me the glass.

'Definitely not, I will need it if I'm working with Madelaine this afternoon.' I sat down, kicked off my shoes and curled my feet up under me on the settee. 'I love what you have done in here; it's modern but it's still cosy.'

'Thank you, it's the wood-burning stove; it gives the room a focal point, and it's lovely and warm in winter. You know how much I love a real fire.'

'Yes, me too. Margaret, are you okay? I've been worried about you. I didn't think you seemed yourself when I saw you last. I hope there's nothing wrong.' I touched her arm and snuggled a little closer to her.

'I'm fine health-wise, but there is something that has been bothering me, and I need to talk to you about it.'

There was sadness in her eyes and concern in her voice. 'It's about your blog. I'm concerned about where your head is at. Your last blog was a little close to home and I wondered if you were thinking of revealing Joe's secret.'

'To be truthful, I don't know what I'm thinking of doing. It's been bothering me that Ted has family that might be suffering because they don't know who killed him. Imagine if it were the other way round, and he had killed Joe; we would want to know, wouldn't we? Plus, it's been bothering me that Ted only admitted to throwing her puppet on the line, so he didn't actually kill her, did he?'

'We don't know what happened. Maybe he did push her on the line, maybe he didn't, but he still caused her death, whichever way you look at it.'

'I don't see it like that. I'm worried that Joe might have killed an innocent man.'

'Jess, it was a long time ago and if this ever got out, it would ruin our family. Imagine how angry they will all be. They have welcomed you into the family and you go and destroy it? Yes, they would eventually get over it, and ride the wave of condemnation, but our relationship with you would be damaged beyond repair, and I don't want to lose you. You have come to mean a lot to me. Jess, I couldn't love you more if I'd known you all your life. I hope this isn't the end for us?' She took my hand and continued to hold it tight. A little too tight; it was becoming uncomfortable.

'Do you think it would come to that? Would the family really turn their backs on me if I revealed the truth?'

'Yes, of course it would. Our family name and our standing in the community mean a lot to my brothers and sister. I think the revelation would finish Mum off. She's not in the best of health, as you know. I doubt they would be able to forgive you.'

'I guess that's why I posted the scenario on my blog. It's a moral dilemma, and I wanted to get an idea of what the consequences would be. My post has already attracted a lot of interest, and responses have been streaming in.'

'Yes, I've been reading them. The one from Malcolm 81 says it all for me. 'Let sleeping dogs lie.' And remember, that's what we agreed to do.'

'I know we did, and I feel guilty for feeling this way. There's also the issue of Marcus. I don't want to enter our married life concealing information from him. If it came out in the future, he would be hurt and upset that I didn't trust him enough to tell him.'

'But there's no reason why it should come out in the future. That is your choice, Jess. Joe can't be hurt by the truth coming out. But so many people living in the here and now would, including this little one.' She emphasised by touching my stomach. 'The truth might make you feel better but imagine what it will do to everyone else.'

'You must think I'm being selfish. But it's important to me. I need to know the truth. If Ted killed Jane, then he got everything he deserved. But if he didn't kill her, then an innocent man got unjustly sent to an early grave. Margaret, the only way to know for certain what happened is to go back and experience the entire accident as it unfolded.'

'I'm not sure that's a good idea. I stopped you experiencing the death before because I considered it would be too traumatic. And besides, does it matter? Ted was responsible; you saw what he did.'

'I also saw him walk away. If he killed her, then he must have come back. Please, Margaret, I need to know.'

Margaret was looking annoyed. 'You aren't considering the consequences, are you?' She stood up and turned her back on me.

'I do understand the consequences and I don't want to lose you or this family. But that doesn't stop me wanting to know the truth. Margaret, I promise you, regardless of the truth, I will take Joe's secret to the grave.'

I was feeling very emotional and couldn't stop myself from crying.

'Please, don't upset yourself, you have so much to look forward to. A wedding, a new baby and a life surrounded by people who think the world of you.' She hugged me until my sobs subsided. 'If I agree to this, then you definitely promise that it will be the end of it, regardless of the outcome?'

'Yes, I promise.'

'Then I'll do it. But not while you're pregnant. I wouldn't want to traumatise the baby.' Margaret threw her head back and laughed, 'I can't help but feel I'm being blackmailed,' she said teasingly. 'Come on, let's get some lunch inside us. Cook is making fish and chips, and she makes the best chips in Yorkshire.'

The warmth of the kitchen and the smell of food were inviting, but I still had a knot in my stomach following the conversation with Margaret. Cook placed generous portions on our plates and everyone tucked in, but I could only push mine around. David and Madelaine were there along with Molly, Daniel, and Sheila. Madelaine dominated the conversation with food ideas for the wedding. Everyone else appeared a little solemn. There was an atmosphere in the room, and I couldn't put my finger on what the problem was. Maybe it was my overactive imagination. I still had Margaret's veiled threats running through my head. If I didn't do as I was told, I would be cast out of this family for good. It hurt; I thought I was part of this family, but now I felt disposable.

Madelaine was hard work to say the least, but she did have some great ideas for the decorations. I had to say no to a couple of suggestions, like having a llama bring the rings to the altar, and all the guests dressing in the same colour. But other than that, everything else sounded dignified with a touch of glamour thrown in. Cook would make us a cake like the one she made for Elspeth's birthday, except it would be all in white filigree decoration with a bride and groom placed on top. Madelaine said she would hire the same caterers they always use, so the only thing left was to choose the music. I said I would like a harpist for the dinner, followed by a small band that would play something modern so we could have a dance. Madelaine leaned into me, like she was my best buddy. 'Have you decided on your matron of honour yet?' I no longer had a desire to ask Margaret, so I said I was going to ask my friend Vanda who had worked with me at the salon. Madelaine looked hurt for a moment. Then composed herself before saying, she'd be happy to step in if Vanda couldn't do it.

Over dinner that evening, Margaret was pleasant, but I couldn't help but feel there was a coldness in her voice. I have come to know her well, and she has three voices. The schoolteacher - in charge voice. The best friend voice she uses with family, and the low melodic voice she uses during therapy. Now I was getting a mixture of schoolteacher and therapist. On the surface, she appeared friendly, smiling at me a lot and asking me my opinion, but her smile never reached her eyes.

It had been an exhausting day, so I was glad when it was time to retire. I lay on my bed in Jane's old room and closed my eyes.

'Jane, you said 'it wasn't his fault.' Were you referring to Ted or to Joe?' I waited in hope that she might connect with me from beyond the grave, but the room was eerily silent.

The next morning, I was about to leave my room, but on opening the door, I bumped straight into Daniel.

'Oops, sorry, I didn't mean to startle you; I wondered if you fancied a game of golf this morning.'

'That sounds lovely,' I said, my tone lacking conviction. 'I haven't played in a while, so I'll be a bit rusty.'

'No problem. After breakfast, spend twenty minutes on the putting lawn and twenty minutes in the driving range. That will soon get you back to par. I'll meet you at the driving range at 10.30 am,' he said, rushing off and not waiting for an answer.

After breakfast, I grabbed some clubs from the clubhouse and made my way to the putting lawn. It was cold, but the sun was shining. The welcome sunshine had brought lots of golfers to the club, eager to get back on form before the competition season starts. A couple of people were on the putting lawn, but they didn't hang around for long. I practised a few putts, and like Daniel predicted, I was getting better with each one. I bent down to retrieve my ball from the hole, and felt a woosh blow past my head, followed by the sound of breaking glass. I stood looking at the broken clubhouse window and froze. The window had shattered into tiny beads of glass. Malcolm, the general manager, was staring back at me in disbelief. 'How on earth did you manage that?'

'It wasn't me! I felt the ball woosh past my head and...' A few more committee members and golfers came to see what the commotion was. All I could do was keep proclaiming my innocence. A discussion took place suggesting that some kids had got through the edge and were messing about. Malcolm joked, 'Well whichever kid took that shot, get him signed up.' Malcolm organised everyone without delay. Some took buggies out to see if they could find the culprits. Sally from behind the bar got out an industrial cleaner and started vacuuming up the glass. Someone was trying to get Daniel on the phone and one of the lady golfers made me a cup of tea. I gulped down the tea and was sipping on a large gin and tonic when Daniel arrived. He was out of breath.

'Jess, are you okay? I was waiting for you at the driving range when I got a call to say there had been an accident. I got here as soon as I could.' I didn't get a chance to reply. Malcolm cut in, 'She's had a lucky escape. If that ball had hit her, we would have needed an ambulance. Either some kids have been messing around or one of the golfers has been extremely reckless. I've sent Robert and James out to have a look around.'

'What a bloody mess,' exclaimed Daniel. 'Sally, get onto the glaziers and tell them we need this fixing asap. Malcolm, I'm going to take Jess back to the house. Let me know if you find out who did this.' Daniel took my arm and led me back to the house. We went into the drawing room, and he poured me a large brandy. 'Drink that; it will make you feel better.'

'Honestly, Daniel, I'm fine. I'm more concerned about the damage to the window.'

'Don't worry about that; the glaziers will board it up and it will soon get fixed. I just can't understand why anyone would be striking a ball in that direction. I'm sorry, this should never have happened.'

'Hey, it's fine, I'm okay, but I don't think I'll be playing any more golf today,' I said with a faint smile.

Over dinner that evening, the conversation revolved around the incident this morning. I was bored of hearing about it and couldn't wait to go to my room. I excused myself early, saying I had some letters to write. Molly said she would have cook make me some hot chocolate and have it sent up to me. It was nice that everyone cared, but their fussing was a bit over the top for comfort. As I got to my room, I breathed a sigh of relief. Before turning in for the night, I checked my blog and replied to a few comments. I knew I would need to post something new soon to change the subject. I switched off the computer and climbed into bed. The electric blanket felt warm and soothing on my back. Cook had sent up my hot chocolate, so I plumped up my pillows and prepared to savour it. As I was about to take my first sip, a bright light caught my eye. It was a bright white orb whizzing around the room. It moved erratically, bouncing off the walls and circling my bed.

'Joe, is that you?' I whispered.

There was no reply, but the orb stopped and then it flew at me. I jumped so much that I spilled the hot chocolate all over the quilt. Next, it hovered by the window and then it was gone. I jumped out of bed and looked out of the window to see if the orb was outside, but it had vanished. Below my window, I could see Margaret, Daniel, and David. They were heading towards the lake. The thought of going for an evening stroll on such a cold night made me shiver. I stripped the duvet cover off the bed and sponged the hot chocolate stain. I turned the stain to the bottom of the bed. I hoped it would dry overnight, and I could remake the bed tomorrow. I was annoyed with Joe. Why had he been so aggressive? What had I done wrong? Could he be warning me to keep my mouth shut.

'Okay, Joe, I promise your secret is safe with me,' I said out loud.

The room was quiet, but it felt cold. I turned up the heat on the electric blanket and left the bedside lamp switched on. For the very first time, I was feeling nervous in this room.

The next morning, I rose early to fetch fresh bed linen from the laundry. I would feel guilty if I left this mess for the housekeeper. When I returned to the bedroom, lying on the bed was the Pinocchio puppet. Its trousers had fallen down so I started to adjust them. I noticed a scratch. It was two initials, GD.

'What are you trying to tell me Joe? I wish you would just speak to me instead of leaving me cryptic messages.'

Chapter 44 Caroline (Margaret) 2003

June 2003. The wedding day came in a whirlwind of preparation and a sickening feeling I couldn't fully ignore. I found myself drifting through the early hours, fingers busy with flowers, linens, and seating cards, each tiny detail giving me something tangible to focus on. But despite all this, a thought clung to me, my mind wondering 'where was Jess's head at?'

Everything looked perfect, Madalaine had transformed the old house with candles bathing every surface in soft lights and muted elegance. I watched as Jess descended the sweeping staircase like a vision. Her makeup was flawless, her silk dress draped across her still slim figure. She looked every bit like a fairy-tale princess. But still, I couldn't shake the questions spinning in my mind. Why was Jess here? Was she here to proclaim herself as one of the family or was she just here for the grand affair? A picture perfect, magical wedding in a setting fit for Royalty. Was she just using the family? I couldn't imagine she still regarded us highly now that she knows what kind of family we are. A family who will protect a murderer just for the sake of the family name. And my own harsh words of reality bullying her into submission increasing the feeling of nausea. Jess had glimpsed our shadowy side, and despite her promises, I couldn't help feeling she was not being honest with me.

I took my seat as the music started. The soft, ethereal notes of the harp filled the air, creating a dreamlike ambiance. Sunlight poured through the mullioned windows, casting golden patches across the altar, turning it into a stage waiting for its actors. As the ceremony began, I willed myself to focus on the moment, to let the doubts fall away if only for a little while.

Jess joined Marcus at the altar, her face radiant, a joyous smile spread wide as the registrar began the vows. Her voice was soft, steady, filled with emotion as she promised to love, honour, and support him, and to stand by him through good times and bad. But even as I listened, a prickling sense of uncertainty lingered. Would she stand by us, by the family, if times grew difficult? Or would she ultimately betray us, choosing truth over loyalty?

The vows continued, Jess's voice now clearer, making promises of love, respect, and honesty. I winced at the words. Little did Marcus know that Jess wasn't being honest with him. She has secrets about which he will never know. Secrets so deadly that it could tear the whole family apart. Then came their first kiss as husband and wife. A roar of applause erupted from the guests. I watched as the couple skipped down the aisle, confetti showering around them. I looked at my beautiful young niece, a pang of love came over me. This young woman who had spirited into my life. This Yorkshire lass I had taken to my heart. All I wanted to do was to love her and protect her. She was my niece, my family. Perhaps I could trust her? let go of the doubts that were coming between us. She has everything to look forward to. A doting husband, a beautiful house to live in and a baby on the way. Life was full of positives for Jess so why would she risk throwing it all away? She wouldn't! Not for a low life like Ted Malinson. After the baby is born, I know Jess will still want to know the truth about Jane's death. But she promised me no matter what the outcome, it would be the end of it. So why am I worrying? I made my mind up to shake off my concerns and put them behind me. I would dance and laugh and join in the fun. Today was a day for celebrating and tomorrow is unpredictable.

Chapter 45 Jess 2007

2007. After the wedding we moved into Marcus's family estate in Scotland. The MacAulay Lodge isn't as big as Bradbury Hall, but it is far more impressive from the outside. The Lodge is a secluded, traditional Scottish house. Situated on the northern shores of Loch Rannoch in the Scottish Highlands. It is surrounded by rugged landscapes and the rolling hills of Perthshire. The front of the lodge overlooks the majestic Loch Rannoch. It is typically Scottish, with thick stone walls and a slate roof. The inside is cozy with stone fireplaces in every room and window seats in the mullioned windows. The furnishings are plush with soft settees that you melt into, with plaid throws and deerskin rugs in front of the cosy fires. Every room has been designed with comfort and practicality in mind. The family always enter the property through the boot-room. This is an untidy area with a stone floor and hooks overloaded with coats. From there you go through into the warm cosy kitchen which is dominated by the largest Aga I have ever seen. This is where the family dine unless they have guests and then they use the formal dining room. The lodge has 6 bedrooms, all tastefully decorated with modern pine furniture, plaid curtains and soft bed throws. The whole atmosphere is one of relaxation and informality. This is in sharp contrast to Bradbury Hall which is rigidly stuck in its Jacobean formality. When I'm at the Hall I feel I need to be on my best behaviour, and I never truly relax; but here at the lodge, it's easy to feel at home. Marcus's parents, Morag and Billy are so laid back. Billy is a self-made millionaire. Making his money through distilling and exporting his own brand of whisky, and Morag is an ex-Infant School teacher. They are both down to earth and never stand on ceremony for anyone. Since my arrival at the lodge, they have educated me in the country pleasures of walking in the hills and woodlands, clay pigeon shooting, and deer stalking. Quite a transformation from my usual sedentary life.

Jack and Elspeth also live at the Lodge with their two children, so there's always plenty of chatter and games. Both Jack and David are less hands on than they used to be. They have found reliable tradespeople that they delegate to, which allows then more time to spend with their families. Katie has turned twenty-one and is engaged to a lovely Scottish boy called Callum. So, I can hear future wedding bells and the patter of tiny feet. Jack's son Matthew has followed in David and his father's footsteps and spends most of his time living at Bradbury Hall. He says he does all the hard work so David and Jack can put their feet up. He's very much a Metcalf through and through.

Our baby, Toby William MacAulay was born on the 18th of November 2003. It was the coldest winter I had ever experienced and because of the distance to the nearest hospital, I ended up having a home birth. From the moment he was born I could tell he was an old soul. The way he looked around inquisitively at everything, like he was evaluating his surroundings. Sometimes I wish I knew nothing about reincarnation because knowing makes me question his every movement or sound. One day, when Toby was two years old, we were making buns in the kitchen. I stuck my finger in the mixture and licked it. Toby smacked my hand and said, 'Naughty Jane.' Once, while visiting the Hall, we were in Jane's bedroom. He asked me to read 'Grim.' He meant Grimms' Fairy Tales. Toby had no way of knowing the book was on the shelf. As I read the stories to him, he seemed to know what would happen, even before we got to it. Toby is now four years old, and he refuses to call Molly grandma, he always calls her by her first name. There are so many instances that make me belief that Toby is the reincarnation of Joe. You should see the way he snuggles up to Ivy and won't let her go. He doesn't do that with anyone else. Yes, he's an affectionate kid, but the way he is with Ivy is bordering on obsessive. Marcus is aware of Toby's little idiosyncrasies, but we don't talk about it to the Metcalf family. As much as I would love to, I dare not blog about it. I don't think another reincarnated family member would go down well with the Metcalf's.

    Marcus, Toby, and I are going to stay at the Hall next weekend. I have made a formal booking with Margaret for past life regression. It was the only way I could get past the excuses she has kept making to put off facing the truth about Jane's death. I'm booked in for 1pm on the Saturday, so we will have to leave here early for the 326-mile journey. I want it to be the first thing I do. Whatever the outcome, I want it over and done with before the weekend festivities. It's Molly's ninety-second birthday and all the family will be there.

    It's a bitterly cold day and dark clouds are looming overhead. Bradbury Hall looks so neat with its manicured lawns and gravel drive. I can't help but compare it with our home in Scotland that blends perfectly into the rugged landscape. This looks more like a museum than a home. I feel sorry for future generations. They will never be able to change it or put their own mark on it. The dated Jacobean dark interior must be maintained. Not only because of Mr Stevenson's will, but because it's listed status also carries a myriad of conditions.

Marcus drives round to the Golfing Centre and drops me there, before him and Toby go and park at the Hall. I walk into the therapy centre and take a seat in the waiting area. Margaret must have heard me come in. She bounces out and hugs me and motions for me to follow her through to the treatment room. Malgo is sat in the corner with a notebook on her lap.

'I hope you don't mind Malgo sitting in. But as you know, I shouldn't be working with a family member.'

'That's fine, I don't mind at all. It's nice to see you Malgo. Are you coming to the party tomorrow?'

'Oh, most definitely, I wouldn't miss it for the world. Molly is serving lobster for the dinner. You know Molly, no expense will be spared.' We all laugh. Molly loves to splash the money around for special occasions. Now in her nineties, she considers all her birthdays special. We chat about the weather and the drive down, and I'm glad we do because I was feeling a little nervous. The casual chatter has helped me to relax.

'Okay, let's do this.' Says Margaret indicating for me to sit in her reclining therapy chair. She places a blanket over my knees. 'I don't want you to feel cold,' she says. The blanket is soft and warm. I pull it up over my shoulders and tuck it under my chin. Margaret changes her voice to her lower, more hypnotic tone.

'I would like to invite you now to relax.... Scanning your body for any tension... And letting go... Now take a deep breath in and let it go... Once more holding your breath for the count of five and then letting go.... Now focus your attention on your tongue and the soft tissue of the mouth.... and as you do this; saliva starts to build.... and you can swallow it down letting your awareness follow it down.... to a quiet place deep inside.... deep inside.... And now that you are fully relaxed you can become more aware of your body inside.... and outside.... Now float above your body.... and notice how relaxed you are, sitting in this chair.... know that here in this space you are perfectly safe. Now float even higher and notice your timeline set out before you.... Turn and place the past....'

Margaret takes me back through my youth, through my birth and to the place of my past life. I'm back at Stevenson's and I can see both Jane and Joe sitting eating lunch on the blanket. Margaret instructs me to go over and stand before Jane. I take Jane's hand and merge inside her body. Now I am experiencing everything that Jane is. I feel the sun on her skin and the coarse fabric of the picnic blanket. I hear Ted's voice, and I tense. I instinctively know that he is a spiteful man, and I wish he would go away. Ted takes my new puppet, the one Jojo has made me, and he won't give it back. My stomach is in knots, I try to grab my puppet, but Ted is so tall, and he holds it out of my reach. I see a young boy watching, he is laughing at me. I'm angry now and I'm screaming at Ted to give me it back. He slides down the embankment and I follow him, shouting at him as I go. 'You are a mean; horrible person and I shall tell my father over you. He will sack you, just you wait and see.' Ted is calling me a spoilt brat as he runs further along the side of the railway. I hear the sound of the train in the distance. Ted hears it too, and as the train appears around the bend, he throws my puppet onto the track and runs away. I stare at it; I'm glued to the spot, unable to move. I put both my arms over my eyes, I can't look. I hear a sound behind me, it makes me jump. I turn around and he pushes me. 'Ge...or...ge...' And then nothing at first, until I can see again. I'm floating through the air, and I can hear voices calling my name, but I can't stay, I have to go…. I have to go home….

Suddenly I'm back on the blanket and Jane is there once again with Joe. I hear Margaret's voice directing me back to my timeline, but I don't want to go, not yet. There is something I must ask Joe. I take his hand and we both float up onto a timeline, I'm confused, I'm not sure if this is mine or Joe's. I take my chance and ask Joe to take me to the women whose blood he was covered in. He leads me forward without making a sound, and then he stops. When I look down, we are above a lake. There're small rowing boats moored up in a line. It's dark but I can see Joe at the side of the lake. He is sat in his wheelchair. He waves me away with his hand. I can feel myself tumbling through the air, falling, and falling for what seems like an eternity. And then I'm awake and I'm gasping for breath.

Margaret pours me a brandy. 'Take this, you look like you need it.' I sip the spirit, allowing the liquid to warm my body and awaken my senses. When Margaret asks me to recount my experience, I deliberately don't tell her about Joe or about George. I tell her what I think she wants to hear, that Ted pushed Jane onto the track. I know it seems wrong to lie to your therapist, but Margaret is more than that, she is my auntie. The auntie that made it quite clear that I would lose this family if I didn't agree that Joe's actions were justified. If she knew it wasn't Ted that pushed Jane, then she would know that I was still torn between family loyalty and the truth.

'You said a name and it sounded like George. Who is George?' Margaret isn't looking at me, she is scribbling down notes. The lack of eye contact is unnerving.

I falter at first, unsure what to say. I pretend to have trouble remembering. But I know how insincere this sounds, so I make it up.

'Oh yes, there was a small boy. He was standing at the top of the embankment. He must have seen everything that happened. When Ted pushed Jane, she saw the boy and screamed his name.'

'That's interesting. I wonder why he didn't come forward and tell the police what he had seen. If he had, then Ted would have been convicted for sure.'
'He was only young, six or eight, so it's possible he felt scared. Maybe he shouldn't have been there and was anxious about getting into trouble.' I hoped I sounded convincing.

'Yes, that sounds a logical explanation. Back then children were more fearful of the police and their parents.'

I saw her give a sideways glance at Malgo before returning to her notes.

'Near the end, I was having trouble bringing you back. It was like you had gone somewhere else. Tell me about that? What was happening in that moment?

I can feel myself sweating now, the tension in the room is palpable.

'I guess I had what you call 'an out of body experience.' I found myself floating above the scene. I was still Jane, and I could see people running about and voices frantically shouting my name. I remember thinking, I must go home. A bit like Dorothy in the 'Wizard of Oz' I was praying to go home. I felt like I was spinning out of control and then, all of a sudden, I was back on the picnic blanket. The sun was shining, Joe was there, and I was happy again. It made me wonder if Jane was stuck in a loop, constantly reliving that day. What do you think? Do you think Jane could be stuck?'

'No, I don't think so, I think Jane's spirit has moved on. Remember you have only been regressed to the time immediately before Jane dies. So it is that memory that is being replayed, over and over again. If we were to go back even further, you would have more memories, and her life would feel less circular and more linear.'

'Is that something we could do?' I felt excited at the possibility of learning more about Jane's life.

Margaret looked at Malgo and raised her eyebrows. Malgo stepped in.

'It's highly irregular for a therapist to be working with a relative. There's always a chance that Margaret's own experience could influence what you experience. I wouldn't recommend it.'

'So, what about you Malgo, could you take me back? I was still hopeful of finding out more about my past life. Malgo stood up laughing. 'Oh no, I leave the past life stuff to Margaret; that's not my field of expertise.' Margaret followed suit, closing her folder, and walking over to retrieve my coat. She handed me my coat suggesting that I head over to the kitchen and get some warm soup inside me. I couldn't help but feel that I was being ushered out of the room.

Chapter 46 Caroline (Margaret) 2007

Malgo turned to me with a puzzled expression and asked, 'What did you think to all that?'

'She wasn't telling the whole truth, was she?'

'No, I got the feeling there was a lot being left out. How do you English say, 'shifty'?

'Yes, definitely shifty! When she was speaking about George, I could tell by the way she was moving her eyes to access the information that some of what she was saying was being constructed. Also, she was very matter of fact about him being there. Seeing someone who witnessed your last moment on this earth should have brought more emotion. But she didn't access her feelings once; she was totally in her head.'

'And what about her out-of-body experience? Malgo gave a frown of disbelief.

'Some of that was true. She was rapidly moving her eyes between memory and construction. Like she was deciding what to tell me and what to leave out.'

'Has something happened between the two of you? I could feel a distance between you and that wasn't only coming from her.'

Malgo doesn't know about Joe killing Ted. The fewer people that knew, the better. Both Jess and I had been careful not to mention anything about it during our session. Which could account for her leaving some information out and choosing her words more carefully. But it didn't explain everything. The way she described Ted pushing Jane onto the line didn't come across as true, and neither did her sighting of George. There wasn't enough emotion. I knew Jess well enough to know that she is a highly emotional person. But people don't get emotional telling a made-up story; they only get emotional when it is true.

'To be truthful, Malgo, I felt cornered by Jess. She knew I didn't want to continue working with her. She knows that it is against our code of practice. But she has kept pushing. I'm glad you said what you did at the end. If she wants any more past-life regression, she will have to find someone else.'

'I'm glad to hear you say that my angel; reputations can so easily be lost.'

I found Mother sitting in the drawing room reading a book.

'Hi sweetheart, how did your session with Jess go? She gestured for me to sit down and tell her all about it.

'One new piece of information came to light. Jess said she saw a little boy called George. She thinks he saw what Ted did to Jane on the day she died.'

Mum scratched her head, pondering. 'George... Let me think... Younger than Jane, you say? And at the workshop! Do me a favour and pour me a brandy while I think.'

I could see she was deep in thought, so I took my time fetching the brandy. I passed her the drink and sat opposite her, patiently waiting for her to continue.

'There was a little boy who came to the workshop. A sullen, plump little thing. Was he there the day Jane died?' She was looking at the ceiling, asking the question to herself. 'I don't remember him being there, but it's possible.'

'Who was he? Was he related to one of the workers?'

'No, no. During the war, some children came to Bradford from London to escape the bombing. Mr and Mrs Stevenson took in a brother and sister. You know, you are right; I think his name was George, but don't ask me what they called his sister, I can't remember. They were swiftly bundled back to London after Jane died. They didn't want the poor little mites around all that grief. How strange his name should come up. He'll probably be knocking on seventy now if he's still alive. I can't imagine him making much of his life; he was too pig-headed and refused to learn anything.'

'Do you remember his surname, by any chance?'

Mum laughed, 'I have difficulty remembering my own name, let alone anyone else's. Have a word with Sheila. There's a large archive in the cellar somewhere with all the records kept by Mr and Mrs Stevenson. There must be a paper record relating to their time here. Sheila can help you find it if you want. But you know my feelings on what happened in the past; the past should stay in the past. And on that subject, is Jess now content? Can we rely on her to keep Joe's secret?'

'I'm not 100% certain. She was holding information back from me. I could tell by her eye accessing cues that everything she related back to me wasn't exactly as she had seen it. It mystifies me why she would feel the need to lie or hold back information. It could have been because Malgo was in the room. I'll speak to her later and try to clear it up. Do you know where she is now?'

'Her, Marcus, and Toby have gone for a drive. They are picking Ivy up. They said something about wanting to see the house where Ivy lived as a child. They will be back for dinner so you will be able to catch her then.' Mum looked over her glasses at me and held my gaze. 'Make sure you nip this in the bud.' I nodded and left her to her book.

I went through to the study and found Sheila busily typing a letter. She never stops working. I would love to get her on my couch one day and get her to relax. This job has become her life. I don't remember her having a boyfriend. She didn't make room for love, except for her love of numbers. When it comes to talking about the accounts, she can be as passionate as any lover.

'Sheila, are you busy? I need your help with something.' She stopped typing and, with a big smile on her face, she said, 'Anything for you, darling.'

I told her I was trying to find any paperwork relating to the refugees who stayed at the Hall during the war. Sheila looked surprised.

'I didn't know any refugees had stayed here but then it was before our time, so I guess it's possible. Come with me, I'll show you where all the Stevenson records are kept. There are a lot of boxes, but they are all in date order.' I followed her down to the cellars. There's a catacomb of interlinking tunnels running under the house. If you weren't familiar with them, you could easily get lost down there. Sheila grabbed a paraffin heater from the entrance. '

'We keep the dehumidifiers on all the time, but it's mighty cold down here. 'So why are you interested?' she asked, her gaze fixed on me with curiosity.

'It was something Jess said during the regression. One of the children was called George and he might have witnessed Jane's death. If he's still alive, I was thinking I could track him down and see if he remembers. Jess said she saw Ted push Jane onto the line, and if this man can confirm that, then maybe Jane can rest in peace.'

'I hope you're not thinking of chasing after this man on your own; you're not an investigator; it could be dangerous.'

I laughed. 'Why would it be dangerous? I'm only going to ask him what he remembers. That is if I can find him.'

'I don't think it's a job for a wom... you.' She was going to say woman but thought better of it. 'We have used a private investigator in the past when we have had concerns about tenants. I'll give you, his details. Let him do the legwork. We can put the cost through the books because it is, after all, research into the Hall's history.'

'That would be good; he'll be better at it than me. There's one more thing: don't mention this to Jess.' I could see she had lots of questions, so I waved them away. 'Look, she will start fussing and wanting to know more. This is our family history, not hers.'

Sheila gasped, 'Really? Surely, it's as much hers, if not more.'

'Aren't you tired of this Jess/Jane thing? She has come into our lives and behaves like this place belongs to her. Reincarnation doesn't work that way. We don't have a right to anything belonging to a past life. We leave this world with nothing, and we come back with nothing. It's time she moved on and concentrated on the here and now, on Toby and Marcus and anything else she chooses to do with her life.'

'Wow, I've never heard you talk like this before. I thought you and Jess had a good relationship.'

'We do have a good relationship. But I want to be her auntie, not her therapist, constantly at her beck and call.'

'Okay then,' she threw her arms into the air, 'whatever you say.'

She placed the heater in the third tunnel from the left and lit it for me. Then she moved her finger over all the boxes until she found the one for 1939. 'Here, this is where you will need to start. I'll leave you to it have fun.' The sarcasm was evident in her voice as she walked away.

I finally found what I was looking for in the box for 1942. Their names and dates of birth were on the form, along with their mother's name and address. They had stayed at the Hall until the 16th of June 1946. The day after Jane had died.

Sheila gave me the name of the private investigator. An Ivan Pushkin, ex-military, or so he told me. I passed over the details I had for George and retained his services to find out what he knew. Three weeks later, Mr Pushkin called me back.

'This guy you want me to speak to is a dodgy character. George Davis has connections to the gangland underworld. As such he's not the kind of man I could easily approach. It could put me in danger.'

'I'm so sorry, Mr Pushkin. I wouldn't have asked you if I had realised. I guess you had better leave it.' I was disappointed, but I wasn't about to get my family mixed up with criminals.

'I'm not saying I won't talk to him; I'm saying it could be dangerous. If I do this, you will have to pay me more. Call it danger money.'

'The thing is, Mr Pushkin. If you ask George about Jane, he will know the enquiry is from the Stevensons. I don't want a gangster following up on that name, as it would inevitably lead to the Metcalf family. Paying you extra is not an issue. The issue is what the possible fallout could be. I appreciate you offering to put yourself at risk, but there's no guarantee that George would tell the truth. And if he does have information, a man like that might decide to use it to blackmail the family. Let me think about it, but I'm sure the answer will be no.'

Chapter 47 Jess 2007

2007. I was so glad to get away from the Hall and back to the peaceful surroundings of Scotland. Margaret had cornered me when I was putting Toby to bed. She as much as accused me of not telling her the truth about what I had seen during the regression. I was feeling more and more uncomfortable with what I knew. Margaret needed Joe's actions to be justified, and I got an eerie feeling that telling her otherwise could be dangerous. I had to keep up the façade of a collaborator to keep her off my back.

I called Harold and asked him for his advice on where to start my research. I had tried Google and that took me to the National Archives. I didn't have enough information to use this, so my only option was Harold.

'No, the National Archives are vast; it will be like trying to find a needle in a haystack. Luckily for you, young lady, I know exactly where to look.' Harold sounded pleased with himself. 'When I was younger, I used to work at the Bradford Archives. Any children who came to the Bradford area during the war were catalogued. It will be much quicker to start there. These catalogues can be searched by a child's name, but they can also be searched by the family they went to. Finding the children who went to the Stevensons at Bradbury Hall will be a piece of cake.'

'I could come down next month and stay with my mum for a few days. Would you come with me and show me where to look?'

'Look, Jess, I'm an old man with lots of spare time on my hands. Let me find the information for you.

You will be doing me a favour; I haven't been to the Archives for years now. It will be nice to smell the old place.'

'Well, if you really do have time on your hands, you could do me another favour.' I hesitated; I knew I was being cheeky. 'Remember the Calder Road bodies and them finding Ted Mallinson? 'Um, yes,' 'Well, his sister is called Joad Turner. I don't suppose you can find out if she is still alive and where she is living?' I cringed at my own audacity. Harold is a famous historian and I'm using him like my research assistant.'

Harold laughed. 'So, you're not asking much of me then? 'Ouch,' I said meekly. 'Okay, leave it with me. It shouldn't take me more than a day or two. I'll call you when I've finished.'

I thanked him warmly and promised to send him a bottle of the MacAulay whisky as a gesture of gratitude.

Three days later, Harold phoned me back. 'Well, young Jess, I have a lot to tell you; I hope you're sitting comfortably.'

'Wait, let me get a pen and some paper.'
'No need, I'll scan it all and send it to you.'
'Oh great, thanks, then I'm listening.'

'Young George turned out to be something of a career criminal with a liking for prison food. He has a string of convictions including aggravated burglary, arson, and drugs. Certainly not the sort of man a young lady like yourself should be going to speak to. So, I hope you don't mind, but I've taken the liberty of asking one of my contacts in the East End Historical Society to do some digging. I don't know if you know anything about the East End, but it's not for the faint-hearted. It can be a hotspot for villains of all nature. My associate Arthur grew up in that area, so he knows his way around and he speaks their language. He'll call me when he has some information.'

'Goodness, is it safe for him? I wouldn't want to put anyone at risk.'

'He'll be fine. After all, he is a historian, and he is doing his job, researching family history. Nothing suspicious about that. It's not like he knows why you want this information, is it?' The question mark was loud and clear; Harold wanted to know more. I hesitated, not sure how much to tell him.

'I've had some another past-life regression. During the session, I saw George. George may have seen everything that happened. He could prove Ted's guilt or innocence.'

'So, this is why you want to know about Sheila Turner, I suspect?'

'Yes, as you know, Ted worked at Stevenson's and he was suspected of killing Jane, not that they could ever prove it. If George is willing to tell us what happened that day, then he could prove either his innocence or his guilt. If innocent, then that is something Joan Turner should know.

'Well, hang on to the seat of your pants, I have some interesting information regarding his sister. Joan Turner was reported missing in 1970. A friend of mine in the police force pulled her report for me. He wouldn't give me a copy, but I have written down what he told me. He said that after she had been reported missing, the police searched her house. She had brochures relating to cruises and had made some notes on costs and sailing dates. They followed this up with the cruise lines she had highlighted, but there was no record of her ever having sailed with them. Of course, she could have gone with another line or chosen to travel some other way. But they couldn't find any proof to suggest she had left the country. Also, after 1970 she never accessed her bank account, so if she was alive then someone else was financing her. From what neighbours had said about her, Joan was a normal woman, liked by everyone who knew her. She had one son, who lives in Australia. In 1977 she was legally presumed dead, so he sold her house. But the police have kept a box of her personal papers in their archive, in case a body emerges in the future.'

'Let me get this straight, the same year Ted's body was found, she goes missing? Don't you think that is highly suspicious?' A cold shiver ran down my spine. This surely could not be a coincidence.

'I do indeed. Whoever killed Ted might also have wanted his sister out of the way. It could be that she knew too much.'

Later that day, Harold's email arrived. It had the records he found and his notes from the conversation with Inspector Gray of the York Constabulary. Harold had no idea, but I knew that Joe had killed Ted. Could Joe also have killed his sister? According to Grandma Ivy and Margaret, Joe wouldn't have been in any fit state to do away with her. During the regression, I had seen Joe by a lake, and he was in his wheelchair. If that was the same lake where I had the vision of a woman's body floating on top, then he would have needed help. Who would help Joe get rid of someone? I guess he could have paid someone, or it would have to be someone he could trust. Possibly someone who worked for him? Or someone in the family? I was starting to shake. Three deaths, one murder and two under suspicious circumstances. And all linked to the Stevensons and the Metcalfs. The veiled threats from Margaret to keep my mouth shut. I was starting to feel like I had opened a can of worms, and I was struggling to get the lid back on.

Another three weeks passed before I heard from Harold again. I was worried about his friend and desperately wanted to know if he was okay.

'It's not good news, Jess, I'm afraid. It looks like George Davis messed with the wrong person. His body was fished out of the River Thames two days ago. He had been shot. The police are putting it down to a gangland falling-out. Apparently, he was well-known as a drug dealer by the local police.'

I gasped. 'That's awful. I don't understand; if the police knew he was a drug dealer, why hadn't they arrested him?'

'They use surveillance, follow the dealers to get to the suppliers, but in this case, they were too late. I'm sorry, lass, but I guess you will now never know for certain who killed Jane or if she fell.'

I felt in shock. That's now two murders and two suspicious deaths. The thought crossed my mind: was George killed because Arthur was asking questions? Has someone stepped in to stop me from learning the truth? I was having palpitations, and my head was spinning. What on earth have I got myself into?

Grandma was right; I should never have contacted that family. I should have stayed well clear.

Chapter 48 Marcus 2007

2007. I walked into the bedroom to find Jess crying on the bed.

'What's wrong?' I said, is it your mother? Toby's okay, isn't he? I felt at a loss as to what to do. Here was my beautiful wife sobbing her eyes out, and I had no idea what was wrong with her. I sat on the bed and pulled her into my arms. Her hot tears trickled down the back of my neck. All I could say was, 'It's okay, I'm here.' I rubbed her back to try to comfort her. But I knew a cry like this would take more than a back rub. What does a computer programmer know about emotions? Dealing with numbers, statistics and formulars all day long doesn't exactly equip me for this.

'Oh Marcus, I have been so stupid. I should never have got involved with that family.' She blew her nose and wiped her eyes, but she was wriggling about like she didn't know what to do. 'I'm scared, I'm scared our family could be in danger. I've drawn you and Toby into a wretched situation, and I don't know what to do.'

'Danger! What's happened, what have you done? Jess, whatever it is, we can deal with it. Look, I'm Scottish, anyone threatening our family will get a 'Glasgow kiss.' I said trying to lighten the mood.

'I have kept a secret from you. I'm sorry I know I shouldn't have, but Margaret made me promise not to say anything.' Oh my god, I thought, has she had an affair with a shady man, and Margaret knows about it?

'Please, Jess, you are worrying me. I need you to pull yourself together and tell me all about it. Whatever it is you have done, we can work through this.'

'I found out that my grandad Joe had killed a man called Edward Mallinson, Ted for short. He thought he was responsible for Jane's death. In a fit of rage, he killed him.'

I was dumbstruck, not knowing where this was leading, so I stayed quiet to allow her to continue.

'He buried his body under the floor of a house in Low Dean. In 1970, When the houses were pulled down, his body was found. Nobody knew it was Joe, well not until he told my grandma, and she convinced him to keep it quiet. From what I can gather, everyone at that time thought Ted had killed Jane. The consensus was that whoever killed him did everyone a favour. He had got what he deserved.'

'How on earth did you learn all this? Was it Ivy who told you?'

'Not exactly. I mean, yes, she did tell me, but not until after I knew, anyway.'

I was still confused; none of this was making sense. I still didn't know why Jess was so upset.

'It was during the regression. Joe told me he had killed him. But that's not all. I've just found out that in 1970, the same time Ted's body was found, Ted's sister Joan also went missing. She's never been found. Which means she is probably also dead.'

I was about to butt in, but Jess raised her hand to stop me.

'I haven't finished yet; there's more. Joe also showed me the body of a woman floating on the water; he said he was covered in blood. Later, during another session, I saw him sitting in his wheelchair at the side of a lake. I'm sure he was trying to tell me that he was responsible for the woman's body in the lake.'

'And is this what Margaret told you to keep quiet about?' I whispered.

'Yes, she didn't want it to be known that Joe was a murderer. It would bring shame on the family. She said Ted deserved it. That Joe was protecting Jane, like a father protecting their child. She said if someone hurt one of her children, she would want to kill them.'

'I see her point. Imagine if anyone hurt Toby. I don't think I would be able to stop myself.'

'But what about Joan, Ted's sister? If Joe killed her as well, then that can't have been to protect Jane? And there's more.' Jess stood up and tied her hair back from her face. She was standing, looking at the floor with her hands on her hips.

'During the last session I had with Margaret, I saw a child. I saw the child push Jane onto the track. It wasn't Ted; it was this boy, a boy called George. He and his sister had stayed with the family during the war; they were refugees from London.'

'Are you sure the boy pushed her?'
'Oh, I'm sure all right. Everything I have seen during these sessions has been accurate, so I have no reason not to believe my own eyes. And wait, there's more. I asked Harold to help me trace George. I wasn't expecting him to confess, but I thought he might be able to exonerate Ted. I was foolishly thinking about his poor sister not knowing he was innocent. His poor sister living with the guilt that her own brother was a murderer.'

'But he was never convicted, so you would expect that she would believe he was innocent anyway.'

'Maybe, but Ted wasn't, especially a nice person. He drank a lot, and he gambled, so Joan could easily think the worst. Anyway, like I said, there's more. Harold investigated George and found out that he was a career criminal, mixed up with all sorts. He was going to get one of his Historical Society mates to talk to him, but when he made enquiries, he found out he was dead. Shot and thrown into the River Thames. This happened a few days ago. Don't you think it's suspicious that he gets killed just as I start looking for him?'

'Um, maybe, maybe not. If you mix with dodgy characters, then a shortened life is to be expected. Jess, you have told me quite a story. But I need you to string it together and tell me why you are so scared.' I took her hands and pulled her into a sitting position next to me on the bed.

'I'll try. Okay, Number 1, Joe kills Ted. Number 2, Joan also goes missing because she knows too much. Number 3, George is killed before he gets a chance to prove Ted's innocence.'

'But Joe can't be responsible for all of this. After all, he's been dead for years.'

'That's what makes it so frightening. Joe couldn't have disposed of Joan. He had COPD and he was in a wheelchair. If he were responsible for her death, then someone he knew had done it for him. Then there's George. The only person who knew about George was Margaret. I didn't tell her I saw George push Jane. I was scared to tell her. She wanted it to be Ted, and she was putting pressure on me to go along with that. So, when I saw George push her, I lied; I said it was Ted. But Margaret knew I was lying to her. She could tell. I tried my best to convince her I was telling the truth, but I know she didn't believe me.'

Jess was starting to ramble again, her anxiety rising. I held her close to try to quell her fears. I couldn't understand why she would be scared of Margaret.

'You say Margaret was putting pressure on you. What exactly was she saying?'

'She said that if I told anyone that Joe had killed Ted, not only would it bring shame on the family, but she made it clear I would no longer be welcome in the family. I didn't want to rock the boat. We had our wedding planned and Toby on the way. I wanted to smooth things over by going along with her. I said I needed to tell you. That I didn't want to start our marriage on a lie, but she convinced me that the fewer people that knew, the better. I started to believe that she was right. That it would have been unfair to involve you.'

She was looking into my eyes, seeking reassurance from me.

'Jess, just because you know these things, doesn't mean you have to be afraid. No one is going to hurt you.'

I hugged her close once more, but I could still feel her body shaking.

'I'm not so sure, Marcus. I think Margaret might have had George killed to stop me from learning the truth. That family will do anything to protect themselves. Maybe it was one of the family who killed Joan. And even if they didn't do it with their own hands, that still makes them murderers. I no longer know who to trust, and I'm worried that I could be next.'

This all sounded ridiculous. Margaret a murderer? No, that couldn't be. She was always quiet and caring. Therapists do not go around murdering people. If what Jess suspected was true, then I had got this family well wrong all these years.

'Look, let's say, hypothetically, that Margaret had George killed to stop you from learning the truth. If Margaret were worried about you, wouldn't she have killed you instead? That would have been the most logical thing to do. Eliminate the person who knows the most, and that is you. So, if she did kill George, then that means she has no intention of eliminating you.'

Jess jumped up and looked angrily at me.

'I'm not dismissing your concerns, but I don't think you are in any immediate danger.' I got the feeling I wasn't using the right words to reassure her. Jess needed me to be 100% on her side. Not hedging my bets.

'For *now*. I might not be in danger *now*. But what about the future? And Toby. We already think he might be Joe's reincarnation; what would happen if they found out? Would they see him as a threat too?'

Jess was almost screaming at me. Like I wasn't getting it, and she needed to drum it into me.

'Who do you think '*they*' are? Is it all the Metcalfs?'

'I don't know. I don't trust Margaret and I don't trust Molly. I'm not sure if I even trust David. He used to take Joe to see Ivy, behind his mum's back. Joe could have had a hold over him. I can't bring myself to trust any of them. They're always having their little meetings,' Jess said, pursing her lips. 'Anything that crops up, someone will say, 'we must have a meeting to discuss.' I get the impression that family do nothing on their own. They are like a secret society.'

Jess is throwing her arms about like a wild animal trying to escape its captors. I had to smile at her exaggeration, but I suppressed it swiftly to avoid angering her.

'What about Jack? I would trust him with my life,' I said.

'I like Jack; I like them all as individual people, but as a collective, I fear them.'

'Jess, darling, I'm not going to dismiss your fears, so the best thing to do is to make a plan. A plan of how to eliminate any danger that you are feeling. What do you think? Is that a good idea? Breaking it down on paper might help.'

I'm nudging her, trying to get her out of this hole she's in. There are things I want to say, like I'll protect you, but that's just words. Jess needs me to be on her side and making a logical plan seems to be the best way to move forward. She stops shaking and presses her hands into her knees, like she is trying to push some strength into her legs. She pushes herself up off the bed and turns to me. Her voice has softened, and her tears have subsided.

'Yes please, I'll get pen and paper. Writing it down might help. Thanks,' Marcus, and I'm sorry I lied to you. I promise I will never keep anything from you again.'

I stood up and joined her, allowing us to fall into a supportive cocoon. At last, I felt I was saying and doing the right thing. As I held her close, I could feel that all-consuming love I have for her. She and Toby are my everything, and I will do whatever it takes to make her happy.

We write our plan. Jess tells me her fears, and I produce a solution. Her first fear is that she should give up her blog, but I'm concerned that it would raise suspicion. So, our first plan is – keep the blog but never use it to talk about family.

Her second fear is Toby, and the things he says, that make us think he could be a reincarnation of Joe. I write – don't encourage Toby and don't tell anyone what we suspect.

Jess says she no longer feels comfortable with the Metcalfs. She would prefer if we kept our distance from them. – Tell them she wants to put Jane behind her and focus on the future. – When invited to the hall, we make excuses not to go.

As much as Jess loves Elspeth and my parents, she's uncertain if she can trust Jack; after all, he is a Metcalf. This is easy and it's something I have been thinking about for a while now, but we have never discussed it. – Buy our own home and make our own history. We have done what the Metcalfs and the MacAulay's have always done. Live with family and continue their legacy. Now was the right time to branch out.

Jess is concerned about the contact we have now with the family. Margaret phones her once a week, and David and his family regularly come up to stay with us in Scotland. – Keep the conversation present; don't talk about the family's history.

The colour has returned to Jess's cheeks, and her breathing is steadier. I can see that the process of planning has calmed her.

'Can we really get our own place? It will be so exciting! Looking for properties and choosing furniture and décor.'

I'm relieved to see that Jess is beaming with excitement.

'Yes, of course we can, and we should. And you can choose anywhere you like. The world is our oyster.'

'Oh, it must be Scotland, and not too far from your parents. I love it here and I'm not about to run away. It would be great if we could find one with an annex for Mum.' She's smiling and laughing now. The fear of earlier has gone. We look at our list.

- keep the blog but never talk about family.
- Don't encourage Toby, and don't tell anyone what we suspect.
- Tell them she wants to put Jane behind her and focus on the future.
- When invited to the hall, we make excuses not to go.
- Buy our own home and make our own history.
- Keep the conversation present; don't talk about the family's history.

We re-read our list and nod at each other. It seems like a good list, a list that will move us forward rather than being stuck in the past. I feel a deep sense of pride and, to be truthful, a little smug. Having an analytical mind isn't a bad thing after all.

'The Metcalfs are stuck in their museum, never being able to move forward. We can make our own choices. We can choose to move forward and look to the future. The past is in the past and that's where it will stay from now on.'

'I love you Marcus, you are my rock.'

I breathe a sigh of relief and take her hand. I lead her through to the nursery where Toby is happily playing. I ruffle his blonde hair making it stand up in spikes. Jess smooths it down again and lifts him onto her knee for a hug. Toby is much better at the emotional stuff than me.

Chapter 49 Ivy and Molly 2013

2013. Molly lay in her bed, her breath raspy and shallow, her body too frail to keep fighting the cancer that had ravaged her body. Discovered too late to do anything about it. A knock on her bedroom door made her jump. Sheila put her head around the door.

'Mum, Ivy has come to see you. Do you feel well enough to speak to her? I can ask her to come back if you don't.

'No, it's okay, let her in,' Molly stuttered as she pressed the button on the bed to raise her into a sitting position.

Ivy sat beside her, not knowing how she felt about this woman. Was she now a friend or was she still her rival? All she knew was that she felt a deep sadness that soon she wouldn't be here. She would miss the animosity, the sentences with an imbedded meaning that only she recognised.

'I wondered when you would show your face,' Molly said in a barely audible whisper.

'What made you think I would come?' said Ivy, pulling her chair closer so she could hear her.

'I knew you wouldn't be able to stay away. Have you come to gloat? You could have waited for the funeral to do that.' Molly broke off, her chest hurting. The cough came in deep chesty heaves that rendered her breathless.

To Molly's surprise, Ivy took her hand gently in hers. 'We have a shared history, you, and I. That's precious to me. Losing you will be like losing my life story. So, no, I haven't come to gloat. I've come to offer you, my friendship. The friendship that should have been there all those years. We could have supported each other. Shared the burden of loving a man like Joe. A complicated, twisted but brilliant man.

A tear ran down Molly's face, and Ivy wiped it away with tenderness. They stared at each other. The rivalry dispersed of.

'It doesn't seem that long ago that I sat on the edge of this bed and listened to Joe's final confessions. And here you are, the person who knew him better than most. Maybe even better than me.' Molly coughed, a red blood spot on the handkerchief.

'There's... there's something I need to tell you. Maybe you already know, but unless I tell you, I will never know. I don't want to take Joe's secret to my grave. It was wrong of him to burden me with it in the first place.'

'Does it really matter now. 'You should be conserving your energy.'

Ivy stroked Molly's hair out of her eyes. She wiped a dribble from her chin. Then, she sat back down and softly patted her hand.

'It matters to me.'

Ivy looked into Molly's fading brown eyes. 'You don't have to say anything, Molly. I know about what Joe did to Ted. It's past us now.'

Molly shook her head, her breath catching painfully. 'No, Ivy, you don't understand. There was more. Another death... another murder.'

Ivy's face drained of blood. 'What do you mean? There can't have been another. Not Joe. He wouldn't...'

'It was Ted's sister.'

Ivy became haunted by what Jess had told her. The things she had seen during her regression. The women in the lake. She sat there, her thoughts in her head, wondering if this was going to be the revelation she had dismissed as a dream.

'Molly swallowed hard, her voice cracking. 'She tried to blackmail Joe. She knew he had killed Ted. She approached him, and she demanded money for her silence.'

Ivy's head was spinning; she had to hold it and take some deep breaths to steady herself. Once again, Jess had seen the truth, but it was too fanciful for her to believe. Molly's voice wavered, but her words were coming faster, as if she feared she might run out of time.

'He agreed to pay her, Molly continued. He had an account no one knew about. He was afraid she'd go to the police, or worse, the papers. He couldn't risk the family reputation.'

Ivy knew what was coming, but she didn't know how. How could Joe kill a woman?

'He killed her,' Molly whispered, the finality of it hanging heavily between them. 'Joe took her life, and afterwards he put the money back. He told me that he had hidden the account and that it would be safe. But I think he wanted to make sure no one could trace it back to him. So, after he died, I also kept it hidden. I will have to tell Sheila because the account will come to light after I've gone.'

Ivy was stunned; she had no words to express her disgust. Joe had always been a powerful man. His reputation afforded him the respect of many powerful people. Joe always got whatever he wanted, including her, Christine, and his fame. The realisation that he'd killed two people, not one, left her horrified.

'Why did you keep it a secret? Why didn't you tell the police?'

'The same reason you kept his secret, love. And not only love, but I also feared him,' she murmured. 'He had a way of making you believe you were just as guilty, by knowing what he'd done – guilty by association.'

'But how, when, where…?'

'He never told me the details and I dare not ask. He would have needed help to carry it out. I knew Joe too well. He would have to trust the person who helped him completely. The only people Joe ever trusted were family.'

The implication hung in the air. Ivy knew this revelation was opening a can of worms. The door opened, and Sheila entered quietly. She could sense something was wrong. She looked at her mother, then at Ivy, worry flashing on her face.

'Mother… is everything all right?'

Molly motioned for her daughter to come closer. Sheila pulled up a chair and sat on the other side of the bed from Ivy. Her eyes darted between the two of them, wondering who would speak first.

Molly looked at Ivy pleadingly. Ivy nodded.

'I'm not sure how much you know about what your father did. So, I'll tell you everything from the beginning.'

Ivy started with Jane's death and the conviction Joe held that Ted was to blame. She told her about him burying Ted under the cellar floor and him buying the house to hide his secret forever. She told her the compulsory purchase order had frightened Joe. He was terrified that someone would discover the body, and he would become the chief suspect.

'After they discovered the body, Joe wanted to turn himself in, but I convinced him not to. We all needed him,' she said, looking at Molly, 'and I believed that Ted got what he deserved. Joe would have torn apart two families if he had gone to the police. At the time, it seemed the right thing to do. To keep the secret buried.'

Ivy told Sheila about Joan's blackmail attempt and her disappearance.

'Joe, on his deathbed, confessed to the murder of Joan to your mother.'

Sheila looked shocked. She turned to Molly with tears in her eyes. Why have you never told me this?

'I didn't want to burden you with it, love. Joe was my responsibility. I wasn't about to let his lies ruin your life.'

'And what's this about this hidden account? Does it still exist?

'Yes,' Molly's voice was growing faint. It's full of blood money. Money, he used to buy her silence. But he never paid her. He killed her and put the money back. After your dad died, I changed the account into my name. The papers are with Franclin Solicitors. Sheila, love, I need you to hide it. You are a better accountant than I ever was. You will find a way to make it disappear.'

Ivy watched Sheila's face as she absorbed her mother's request. A steely resolve settling on her face. Sheila had always known her father was a complicated man, but she had never suspected he could sink so low. With unexpected anger in her voice, Sheila said, 'I'll do this for you, but I hate that man for what he's put you through.'

Her voice softened as she looked at her frail mother with deep affection. 'I will take care of it, Mum.'

Sheila leaned and held a lingering kiss on her mother's forehead. 'I promise you; no one will ever know.'

Molly closed her eyes and relaxed. A weight had been lifted from her frail shoulders. The burden of her husband's sins was finally off her hands. Ivy and Sheila watched her breathe, the life slowly draining out of her. The two women looked at each other, both now left to carry the terrible truth. A quiet knowing passed between them, creating a silent vow that Joe's secret would remain safe and be buried forever.

Ivy quietly left the room, leaving mother and daughter to share their last moments together. As Ivy returned to the drawing room, David, Jack, and the rest of the family were there. They looked at her expectantly.

'I think you should all go up. I don't think she has long.'

Chapter 50 Christine 2014

2014. Christine visited Ivy daily. Her health was deteriorating, and she was struggling to look after herself. The stubborn woman refused to go into a home, saying it was full of smelly old people. Christine felt torn. A love-born sense of responsibility clashed with a feeling of burden. The heavy rain beat against the windows. Christine closed the curtains, hoping to ease the tension in the room. In her favourite armchair sat her mother, Ivy. Once vibrant, she was now worn by years of secrets and lies.

Ivy motioned for Christine to sit down.

'I need to tell you something.' Her voice was hardly audible above the rain.

There was only one subject that would make Ivy so forlorn. Christine knew it would be something to do with her father. Joe the man of mystery, the keeper of secrets, a dark past layered underneath his brilliance. A man she loved but had barely known.

'Mum, you don't have to tell me anything you don't want to. The past is in the past.'

But Ivy shook her head. 'No. I have to. I don't want to carry it to my grave.'

She paused, taking a deep breath. 'It's about Jess and your father. There's something she needs to know. You have to tell her that she was right. Everything she saw was real. The body in the lake was real.'

Christine felt her heart sink. She thought that this was all in the past. Jess had moved on with her life.

Raking this up again wasn't something she wanted to do.

'Molly told me, on her death bed, that Joe had confessed to her. The body in the lake was Ted's sister Joan. Joan had tried to blackmail Joe over Ted's murder. He promised to pay her to keep quiet but instead he killed her. He had a secret account where the blood money was held. Molly asked Sheila to bury this account to hide a paper trail. The most disturbing aspect of this second murder is that Joe couldn't have done it. He was too weak due to his COPD. Which means that he got someone to do it for him. Joe was not the most trusting man in the world. He wouldn't have risked hiring a stranger. Whoever helped him was most likely one of the family.'

Christine's face turned ashen. She paced the room for a brief time, letting the cogs turn quickly in her brain.

'So, there's still a murderer out there. Potentially one of the family? I don't think Jess knows about this. I think if she did, she would've told me.'

Christine continued to pace the room before dropping onto her knees and staring up at Ivy. The rain seemed to fall harder, as if nature itself were battering the truth into her. Christine felt a strange surge of anger.

'Why tell me this now, Mum? Why not leave it buried?

'One day you will come to understand, when your maker comes knocking at your door. It's hard to take a secret, so evil, to your grave. But don't wait that long. That family could be dangerous, and Jess knows too much.'

Ivy looked down, her hands shaking. She reached for Christine's hand, her grip surprisingly strong.

'She needs to know that her visions were real.'

For a long time, they sat in silence, Christine's mind racing with the consequences. She could feel the weight of it all crashing down on her. It was her burden now. Would she tell Jess? She wasn't sure. What would happen if she did tell her? Would Jess try to unravel the truth? Would she be putting herself in danger? She had a beautiful home, an adorable little boy, and a doting husband.

Jess was due to visit this weekend. Leaving Christine with only three days to mull over her dilemma. As she climbed into bed that evening with a heavy heart, she wept. Her tears were filled with sorrow and anger. Christine felt responsible. She had been enthusiastic and had encouraged Jess in the early days of her journey. Now she wished she had been stronger and had told her to leave it alone. But Jess wasn't like Christine. Christine had always followed her mother's wishes and hadn't tried to contact her half-siblings. She told herself she wasn't interested, that they were nothing to do with her. Did she really believe that or had there always been a desire to meet them? Secretly she had been excited by Jess's discovery. She finally got to learn who she was and where she belonged. The power of knowing filled her with a feeling of control. For the first time, it was her decision whether to bond with the family or to keep them at arm's length. She chose the latter, but she still revelled in knowing that she was the daughter of the famous Joseph Metcalf.

Jess was curled up on the settee with her little dog Milo asleep next to her. Christine took out her phone and snapped a photograph. She wanted to capture the serenity of the moment, the setting natural, not posed. The moment should have felt surreal in its quietness. Her grandson Toby asleep upstairs, Jess with her little dog and the fire crackling in the hearth. But, for Christine, her burden would not lift.

Christine paced the length of the living room, her hands twisting together as she wrestled with her conscience. She knew that keeping the secret buried was probably the safest choice for her daughter. But how could she not tell her? A voice screamed in her head that Jess had a right to know.

'Mum.' Jess's voice interrupted her thoughts. 'Are you okay? You look worried?'

'I have something to tell you, something your grandma said. I know I have to tell you, but I want you to understand that I do so reluctantly.

Jess looked concerned. This could only involve Joe. The thought of raking up this subject again made Jess uneasy.

'I guess it's something to do with Joe, am I right?'

Christine caught the sound of nervousness in Jess's voice. But she couldn't backtrack now. She would have to continue and tell her the horrible truth.

Christine's chest tightened. She sat down and poured herself a large glass of wine. The hit of the alcohol giving her the courage to continue.

'When Molly was dying, your grandma went to see her. Molly told her that Joe had revealed a secret to her on his deathbed. He told her he had killed Ted's sister, Joan.'

Jess gasped. 'So, I was right.' She lifted Milo into her arms and started rocking him vigorously. Her nerves seeking comfort from his soft warm fur.

'Yes love, everything you saw was real. 'Joe had Joan killed and put her body in the lake.' She paused, waiting for Jess to speak. But her daughter could only look at her with fear in her eyes.

'He must have had help. Your grandma thinks it would have been someone in the family that helped him. Joan had tried to blackmail him. Somehow, she knew he was responsible for Ted's murder. He had money in a secret account which he drew out, but he never paid her. Molly was fearful that this account provided evidence of Joe's actions. She must have told Sheila the whole story because she asked her to bury the account.'

'Mum, I always knew that what Joe was showing me was true and that he wanted me to know. So please don't alarm yourself. I'm glad Grandma told you. At least now I know I wasn't imagining it.'

'I'm worried about what you will do with this information. I don't want you chasing this up or worse still blogging about it. That family could be dangerous.'

'I know, Mum, I have already come to that conclusion. I hardly see any of them anymore, and when I do, I'm careful not to discuss Jane or Joe. I've moved on from Joe's ghost. I don't want to know what he's done or who could have helped him. I agree that family are dangerous. They would do anything to protect Joe's reputation and the family name. You don't have to worry, Mum. I won't be telling anyone this.'

Jess's rocking of Milo was now slow and steady. She looked at her mum and then at the ceiling to where Toby was sleeping above.

'I have all the family I need right here. You, Marcus, and Toby. There's a saying 'keep your enemies close' and that's how I feel about the Metcalfs. I'll keep them sweet, but I'll always be wary of them.'

Chapter 51 Caroline (Margaret) 2020

2020. It's been two decades since I first met Jess, and in that time, so much has changed. Mum passed away in 2013, and Ivy followed in 2015. When they both left, it felt like a part of Joe went with them. The two people who knew him best took his essence, leaving only his legacy behind. His presence no longer lingers, and his secrets no longer weigh on me. Now, the things Dad left behind, his children, his work, and his reputation, reflect his memory. Talking about his private life now almost feels like it would diminish the dignity of his memory. Bradbury Hall never really belonged to him; he was only its steward. Today, it's the next generation that has made it their own: David and his family, Sheila, and now my children and me.

My son, Simon is a renowned golf pro, with many major titles under his belt. When he's not on the competitive circuit, he's at Bradbury Hall giving golf lessons. His fame has brought us a wealthy, prestigious clientele. He is very much a product of his grandfather, proud and successful. He married in 2010 and has given me two lovely grandchildren, Polly and Brian, whom I see often and adore. Gail, meanwhile, lives with her wife Susan in my old cottage. Susan, it turned out, was more than a friend! I see Gail almost every day. She manages Bradbury Hall with precision. Always a clipboard in hand, directing the workmen in preserving our historic estate. Maintaining a Grade I-listed building is a full-time endeavour. I couldn't be prouder of her achievements.

As Mr Stevenson intended, our family wealth is transitioning to the next generation. David's two sons have taken up the mantle. Overseeing property maintenance and new projects across our growing estate portfolio. David has finally retired, and rightfully so; at 82, he deserves a break. Jack, too, has retired, relocating to Portugal with his wife Elspeth. They love the sunshine and have no plans to return to rainy Yorkshire. Their children have gone into accountancy, allowing Sheila to oversee Bradbury Hall. With her new title of 'Lady of the Manor,' Sheila embodies the strength of her mother's legacy. She is now the matriarch of the family and rules over us as strictly as Mum did.

Jess, Marcus, and their children live near Loch Rannoch in a lovely home close to Marcus's parents. Their seventeen-year-old son, Toby, has unruly blonde hair. He is the spitting image of his father. Their three-year-old daughter, Felicity Jane, whom we call 'Sissy,' brings endless joy. Jess and Marcus have a hectic schedule that prevents them from visiting, but Jess and I speak regularly. She has found peace in focusing on her new life. She's moving on from her past obsession with Jane, which I always found somewhat concerning.

Jess's blog and her two books on past lives are popular. I often direct my clients to her blog to connect with others on similar journeys. Her blog gave me the visibility I needed early in my career. It let me build a name for myself in regression therapy. My early books were autobiographical, but I've since moved on to writing novels with a fictional twist on past lives. After a challenging journey, I'm finally enjoying the recognition and success I dreamed of.

Christine moved to Scotland to be closer to Jess and her family after Ivy's passing. She never sought anything from the estate. She was content with her own means. Christine agreed to sell Joe's drawing back to the family. She said it was where they belonged. They're now proudly displayed in Bradbury Hall's Long Gallery, honouring Joe's artistic legacy.

Sometimes, it feels like a dream. I'm surrounded by breath-taking beauty, family nearby, and the fame and fortune I once only hoped for. The only missing piece has been finding a 'special person.' I always believed love would come in time, but while I've had fleeting romances, they never lasted. Yet, I've found love in my work and in the presence of my family. Each morning, as I take my coffee to the window and look out on the world, I'm filled with gratitude. Life is good, and I am content.

Chapter 52 Jess 2020

2020. Toby has just turned seventeen. He's tall like his father, with the same broad shoulders and confident stance. But his personality is all mine, far too inquisitive for his own good. Since he was eight, he's been keeping a journal, pouring his thoughts onto its pages. He meticulously records his strange dreams, moments of déjà vu, and fleeting feelings he can't quite explain. At first, I thought it was a harmless outlet for a curious mind but over time, I have come to fear it.

Toby reads my blog obsessively. He's fascinated by the stories. There are thousands of accounts from people who believe they've lived before. He hangs onto every word, every shared experience that resonates with his own. Now, he's determined to share his story. He's been pestering me to feature it on my blog, to let the world know that he too has lived before. It hasn't been easy steering him away from sharing too much. How do you tell a child to suppress what makes them unique, to keep their most personal and puzzling experiences to themselves? He doesn't understand why I ask him to stay quiet. Time is running out. Next year, he'll be eighteen. He'll no longer need my permission to speak his truth, whether I agree with it or not.

Toby knows part of my story. He knows about Jane and Joseph Metcalf. But he doesn't know everything. He doesn't know about Ted, or his sister, or the other dark revelations I've uncovered. I told myself that Jane and Joe were part of the past, that I would focus on the future and leave their shadows behind. But for Toby these dreams of his present a problem for him to solve. And the truth is, I haven't left them behind either. Not entirely. The knowing still haunts me, it still brings a pang of fear when I think about the secrets.

I occasionally read his journal. I know it's a betrayal of trust, but it's the only way I can make sure he's safe. His words are raw, unfiltered, and sometimes frightening. Today, as I leaf through the pages, I'm scanning for anything alarming, anything that might hint at danger. Even after all these years, I can't shake my unease about the Metcalf family. Some part of me will never fully trust them.

March 12th, 2013 – Had a bad dream last night. I woke up with painful chills down my spine and covered in sweat. I dreamt I was digging a hole. It was dark. I pushed something heavy into the hole.

March 19th, 2013 – I've been having the same recurring dream all week. Each time, I wake up feeling terrified. The dream doesn't get any clearer, but I can't shake the feeling that I've done something terrible.

This entry repeats over the next three months. My heart breaks as I reread the words. My little boy was shouldering so much fear and guilt over something he couldn't possibly have done. What troubles me most is the way he writes, as if it truly were him committing these acts. But it wasn't him. It was Joe.

I flip through more pages. There's a mixture of clarity and confusion, fragmented memories, dotted with question marks.

- Memories of woodworking—the scrape of a chisel, the pride in carving intricate designs.

- Déjà vu at Bradbury Hall—the sense of knowing every corner of that place.
- Dreams of Jane—visions of her that feel happy, despite the knowledge that her life ended in tragedy.

June 20th, 2015 – I keep looking for a silver cigarette case. I know I have one somewhere, but I can't find it. Mum says I must have dreamt it??

September 10th, 2015 – We went to a fair in Rowntree Park in York. I had the strangest feeling I'd been there before. After the fair, we fed the ducks by the pond. Suddenly, I felt dizzy and threw up. Dad said I'd eaten too many sweets, but I don't think that's why?? Just before I got sick, I was overwhelmed by fear.

I skip ahead, past entries that feel repetitive, skimming over fleeting impressions and fragmented thoughts:

- Holidays by the seaside.
- Dreams of carving wood in a noisy workshop, the air thick with the scent of raw wood.
- Moments with Jane - sitting together on a blanket, laughter, happiness.

Over time, the entries grow sparser. His recollections of his past life are fading, the memories slipping away like sand through his fingers.

August 23rd, 2017 – I seem to have inherited Mum's fear of trains. The school booked us a trip on the Settle to Carlisle railway, but when I got to the station, I couldn't step onto the train. Luckily, Dad was there to wave us off, so he took me home. I'll get some stick from my mates at school tomorrow. I know about Jane being killed by a train. Mum thinks she's, her reincarnation. She won't talk about it, but I've read her blog.

September 10th, 2019 – Had a bad dream last night. I saw a woman's body floating on the water. I feel like it's my fault she's there. What did I do??

That was his last entry.

I cry, my hands trembling as I close the journal. One day, Toby will share all of this with the world, I know he will. He's fearless, driven, and determined to make sense of his experiences. But he doesn't understand the weight of his revelations, the consequences they could bring. Am I being paranoid? Maybe the danger has passed. But someone put Joan in that lake, and it wasn't Joe. So, who was it? I keep circling back to Joe's boys. I've ruled out the girls, they wouldn't have had the strength to push a body into the lake. Or would they? I don't know anymore. My head aches, I don't want to think about it. Why won't it stay in the past? It's all my fault. If it weren't for my stupid blog, Toby would be able to put all this down to a vivid imagination.

Chapter 53 Detective Superintendent John Smith 2024 - The Beginning of the End

2024. DSI John Smith stood silently in the corner of the briefing room, his hands clasped behind his back, observing the room with a quiet authority. Though his face was impassive, his mind was already churning with the details of the cases under discussion. There had been no fast-track route for John, he'd earned his authority, rising steadily through the ranks from a young constable. This sat well with his team, they could relate to him, they knew he understood every aspect of the job. He was both a listener and a problem solver. He had worked many high-profile cases in his career bringing him the recognition he deserved from those below and above him. Now, he watched his officers. Some fresh recruits clustered at the back, trying to blend into the shadows, others ambitious for advancement sat up front, eager to be noticed.

Beside him stood Detective Chief Inspector Trevor Ward, his trusted second-in-command, a capable and relentless investigator. Ward was built for the kind of police work that required both brains and brawn. There wasn't an ounce of hesitation in him, and when he got the scent of a lead, he was known to pursue it like a dog with a bone. John trusted Trevor implicitly, knowing he'd go to any length to close a case. And yet, despite his trust in Ward's abilities, John still liked to be present, to hear the threads of information directly. The force had a saying: the devil was in the details, and John had lived long enough to know how true that was. Some things simply couldn't be left to second-hand accounts.

As the briefing began to wind down, John's sharp eye noticed the faint, familiar shuffle of impatience rippling through the room. A silent cue that the formalities were about to conclude. But just as he turned his thoughts to the afternoon ahead, a voice from the back cut through the room, as it so often did. 'Just one more thing,' Sergeant Will Thomas announced, raising his hand with an expectant look on his face. Thomas cleared his throat, glancing at the notes in his hand before continuing.

'I've received a request from York Constabulary, sir. They're asking if we have the files relating to the murder of Edward Mallinson.'

John's ears pricked up at the mention of the name. He leaned forward slightly, the flicker of interest visible in his otherwise steady gaze.

'What information do you have, Sergeant?' he asked, his voice controlled but pointed.

Thomas straightened, reading aloud from his notes with a meticulous air, as though he, too, understood the gravity of the case.

'They drained the old boating lake in Rowntree Park York, as part of the future development project there. The construction team stumbled across a body, partially embedded in the mud. Forensics have done a preliminary analysis, and from the skeletal structure, they estimate the remains belonged to a woman of a certain age and height. When they ran a cross-check with missing persons records, a potential match came up. It's believed to be Joan Turner, reported missing in 1970 by her son.'

The tension in the room thickened. John felt his pulse quicken, though his face betrayed nothing. It was as if the air itself had grown heavy, drawing the attention of everyone in the room. Sergeant Thomas continued; his voice steady but laced with a nervous unease.

'Further DNA analysis of the bones matched with an existing profile in our database. That of Edward Mallinson. As you may recall, Mallinson was a suspect in the death of a young girl decades ago, so his DNA was still on file. They're certain the remains match Joan Turner.'

A murmur rippled through the room. Edward Mallinson had long been the stuff of quiet whispers and shadowed discussions. A name rarely mentioned except in hushed tones. His guilt, by rumour, had lasted to this day. John's father had worked this case at the time of the little girl's death. He had only picked it up after Ted's body had been discovered. The decaying body had haunted John's mind. Someone believed that Edward Mallinson was guilty of Jane Stevenson's death and had exacted their revenge. But this was the first time John had heard about Joan's fate,

His fists clenched, and a prickling sense of frustration crept over him. Joan Turner was reported missing in 1970. Yet, the details had slipped through the cracks of an era burdened by poor records and scattered protocols. He had known nothing about her disappearance until now. The realisation hit him like a blow. It reminded him of a flawed system that had failed too many times, both then and now.

Stepping forward, John's voice cut through the silence, authoritative and charged.

'Sergeant Thomas, I want you to make copies of all the relevant files and send them over immediately. When that's done, I want the full file on my desk. Also, include the name and contact number of the York sergeant making this request. And check off the evidence file numbers and retrieve them from the archives. Send those off to forensics and request new DNA tests.'

'Yes, Gov,' came Thomas's immediate reply.

John's mind spun, his thoughts drifting back to the last time he'd laid eyes on Edward Mallinson's file. It was a case he'd reluctantly closed, years ago. A letter from Joan Turner had arrived at his desk, a letter that suggested her own mother might have had a hand in Mallinson's fate. Joan had insinuated that her mother knew far more than she let on. At the time, John had weighed the evidence carefully but ultimately decided there was too little to pursue. Also, it seemed cruel to drag a family's name through the mud without enough evidence. So, he'd let it lie. Yet here was Joan Turner again, or what was left of her, dredged up from the murky water, the ghost of a woman still seeking justice.

He had long wondered if he had made a mistake in leaving it be if he'd ignored a vital clue. The choices of his younger self now seemed clouded with a sense of missed opportunities. A fear that he had once failed a woman who had reached out for help, and he had turned away. Why hadn't he contacted her after he received her letter? He should have realised it was suspicious, that it wasn't in character with her earlier enquiries.

Trevor glanced over at John. He saw the steely look in his eyes. He knew he had the bit between his teeth. This case had touched a raw nerve, and Trevor was eager to find out why. He nodded at his boss a silent message that he was there for him, and he would help him follow the case wherever it led. This time, John wouldn't allow the system to bury the truth. He'd seen too many cold cases brushed aside; too many voices drowned out by the noise of the next investigation. He wouldn't let Joan's case fall into the same void. Technically, this case belonged to the York team, but he would use the weight of his rank and reputation to take it over. He would put his own best man on the job. He whispered in Trevor's ear, 'How do you fancy a secondment to York?'

Trevor nodded. This was a juicy case, the type of case he relished, and they didn't come along too often. This is the type of case that leads to fast promotion. That is as long as you he could solve it. Failure would not go down well with his boss.

The meeting ended but the work now begun. John would be relentless this time, no longer a silent bystander held back by rules and protocols. He would dig into every corner and interrogate every detail. He would pursue every lead, no matter how inconvenient or uncomfortable it made those around him. He couldn't shake the feeling that he owed it to Joan, that he was somehow in her debt. In a swift but deliberate movement, he turned and marched to his office. The file on Mallinson was already weighing heavily on his mind. He would reopen every record and revisit every statement, going all the way back to the death of Jane Stevenson. He would put his men on the job, re-interviewing anyone still living who had known Joan, known Ted, and had known Jane. He would look into every loose end that had been left to fray in the case's abandoned file.

John's heart pounded as he closed the door behind him, a new intensity burning within him. This time, he wouldn't rest until he uncovered every dark secret. They were buried, and someone wanted them to stay that way. Trevor knocked on his door and entered, looking at John expectantly. John rubbed his hands.

'There's a lot of footwork to do; I hope both you and the team are up for it. I don't want any stone left unturned.'
'Yes, Gov.' came the reply.

Thank you for reading my book. If you want to know what happens next, then watch out for the sequel, 'Revealed in Time' which will be out later this year.

Jan French

Printed in Great Britain
by Amazon